Readers love *Bridging Hope*
by GREYSON MCCOY

"Essentially, it's a charming, romantic biography of Pierce and Dalton, and... reading it will remind us of the best of love and family."

—Rainbow Book Reviews

"I truly enjoyed this short, poignant story of overcoming what life has thrown at you and rising above to succeed and live."

—Love Bytes

"For a shorter-length story, this one packs a punch. The world- and character-building are clear and concise, giving plenty of details about the farm, the children, and the MCs."

—Archaeolibrarian

"Greyson McCoy's beginning short story introduces us to what he intends for this series, and sigh, I am all in."

—Paranormal Romance Guild

"This was a low angst, short story with a lot of heart."

—OMG Reads

By Greyson McCoy

BRIDGING HEARTS
Bridging Hope
Bridging Love

Published by DREAMSPINNER PRESS
www.dreamspinnerpress.com

Bridging Lives

GREYSON McCOY

DREAMSPINNER PRESS

Published by

DREAMSPINNER PRESS

8219 Woodville Hwy #1245
Woodville, FL 32362 USA
www.dreamspinnerpress.com

Bridging Lives
© 2024 Greyson McCoy

Cover Art
© 2024 Reece Notley
reece@vitaenoir.com
Cover content is for illustrative purposes only and any person depicted on the cover is a model.

Trade Paperback ISBN: 9781641087841
Digital ISBN: 9781641087834
Trade Paperback published October 2024
v. 1.0

Acknowledgments

A SPECIAL thanks to Jo Bird and Renee Mizar for helping me pound out a decent draft. Your support means the world to me!

Cliff

"I'M NOT evacuating, Walt," I shouted, refusing to look my elderly neighbor in the face. "I just got these plants in the ground, and I'm not going to let a stupid wildfire destroy them all."

"Cliff," he said pointedly, "your father wouldn't have stayed."

His mention of my dad brought me up short, but I didn't have time for this. Not when everything my family had worked for was at stake.

"Walt, if I leave, if I miss watering for even a day, the crop will die," I said, not hiding my exasperation. "Two hundred tomato plants, three hundred seventy-five squash and zucchini plants. Not to mention the corn, the beans, the—"

Walt put his hand up. "Son, I know. I totally understand, but your life is worth more. Think about what your parents would've done."

I shook my head in desperation. I'd have to go eventually, but I was conflicted about abandoning my farm. "If the fire reaches Mayfield, I'll evacuate."

"You're a man of your word, so that's good enough for me," Walt said. He turned to go, then quickly disappeared into the smoke.

Spring in this part of California was usually wet, but not this year. The drought had stretched through the winter, and now a heat wave baked us drier than a popcorn fart, as my dad used to say.

I pulled on his old respirator mask as I entered the greenhouse, because the smoke was even more concentrated inside. Typically, I didn't plant anything until May, but the warm winter and spring had prompted me to get a head start.

That was good because it opened up the greenhouse for herbs. In recent years we'd made almost as much on those as the other crops. With the crops in the field, I now had all my tender herb plants growing in here.

I glanced around at the plants I'd spent the past several months cultivating. Even if the fire destroyed the fields, if I could save these plants, I'd still have a farm and enough income to at least pay the taxes on the place. My crops might burn, but I'd be damned if I let my family's legacy go up in smoke too.

The old refrigerated truck Dad had used to transport produce to the farmers' markets sat beside the house. I rushed over and hurriedly slid the plant shelves inside it.

"You need to go." I could hear my father's voice in my head, but his authoritative tone didn't slow me down. Both my parents died a year ago, but I still sometimes heard them. Most days, I found their presence more comforting than concerning. It helped me pretend that they were still around. I had even taken to responding to them out loud, but only when alone, lest anyone think I'd gone off my rocker.

"Dad, I can't lose these plants. You know what that'd mean for the farm."

There was no response, but I could feel him. He wasn't happy with me staying.

"All I need is an hour to pack the truck," I said, as if negotiating with my father's ghost would keep the fire at bay.

I pulled my phone out of my pocket and clicked on the local news app while I made a quick dash inside the house. The forecaster reported the rapidly spreading wildfire was thirty miles outside Mayfield and the wind had picked up. The worst was going to happen. I could feel it deep in my bones.

Mom had long ago developed an evacuation plan, and when fire broke out within a hundred-mile radius of our farm, she began to pack. She'd ingrained disaster preparedness in me over the years, and it had practically become family tradition. Most everything my mom considered valuable was packed in a chest near the front door during the last evacuation and still sat there.

I raced to my bedroom to pack some clothes and other incidentals, like my phone charger, that I might need. This wasn't my first fire-fleeing rodeo. We'd fled from wildfire several times over the years, but this one was hitting different. For the first time, I had all my parents' belongings to consider.

I hadn't entered their bedroom since the accident. It had been frozen in time since that awful day. It hurt too much to see their things. They'd driven to the city for a party and were simply in the wrong place at the wrong time. A drunk driver had gone down a ramp the wrong way and hit them head-on at over seventy miles per hour. "It was fast. They didn't even know what hit them," a police officer told me. That was good, I guessed. I took some comfort in knowing they hadn't suffered, though the pain I felt at losing them would never go away.

I ignored the knot in my stomach as I rifled through their things. I found the only tie Dad ever wore. It was ugly as homemade sin, but I gave it to him when I was five or six, and he'd worn it as proudly as if it were a designer brand.

Next, I found Mom's scarf, the only thing she ever knitted. The stitching was off, and I remember her mumbling curses to herself while she struggled through it. It was so unlike her, but that's why I cherished the memory. Dad's ugly tie and Mom's pitiful scarf—the two things that would always make me think of them.

Mom's jewelry was already packed in the evacuation chest, although she had never worn any of it. "Farmers don't have much use for jewelry," she said in my mind. Still, some of it had been passed down from her mother, so it had sentimental value.

Mom had also packed away some memorabilia, including my college diploma. She was ridiculously proud when I was accepted to university and prouder still when I graduated. "My baby is the first of the Baker crew to earn a college degree," she said, beaming. Baker was Mom's maiden name. I never brought up that my cousin Levi was a year older and got his degree before I did.

Dad's brother had college degrees, not that he needed them. My uncle was wealthy and snooty—not worth looking up to, not worth my time. He hadn't even come to my parents' funeral. His absence was confirmation enough that we might be related but he wasn't family.

I pulled my respirator mask back on as I rushed outside with my irreplaceable family treasures and tossed them all into the old trailer that I could pull behind the refrigerator truck.

By the time I finished hitching them together, the news app was reporting that the fire had reached Mayfield. Despite my promise to Walt to clear out once it hit town, I couldn't leave yet. I still needed to rescue the plants, and I didn't have much time left. I drove the truck out to the greenhouse and began loading plants onto trays. Even in my hurry, I had to be careful and methodical. If I damaged the plants or they slid around in the truck, they'd be no good to me in the end.

I'd been at it for a while when Walt pulled his ancient pickup in front of mine. The minute he got out, he yelled, "You need to get out of here, time's up. The fire's ripping through town."

A sense of dread suddenly came over me. It was as if I could feel my dad pushing me to leave.

I shoved my respirator mask off. "I just need thirty more minutes."

"You don't have thirty minutes," Walt said. Walt grabbed a half-filled tray and slid it onto a shelf in the truck before I could load what was left.

"You're as stubborn as your daddy ever was," Walt said.

"Where's Martha?" I asked, and he said his better half had already evacuated.

"I knew you'd still be out here acting like a fool. I'm not willing to let you die for some plants, boy," he yelled. "I'll drag you out of here kicking and screaming if I have to. Don't think I won't."

Hearing the old man's voice break snapped me out of my tunnel vision. The smoke had grown thick, and I could feel the increased heat around us. The fire was close. I was leaving good plants behind, but I closed the greenhouse door on them, climbed into the truck, and followed Walt off the farm and onto Bigford Road. We'd only gone a few miles when I saw the red glow. Until that moment, I hadn't really believed the wildfire would destroy my family's farm, Walt's farm, and all the homes in the area. Now it seemed more like a certainty.

Tears flowed when I drove past Rhonda Greene's farm, already ablaze. I wiped them away as we then went through an area burning on both sides of the road. At least the road remained passable. I had to focus on that, on the literal road ahead, rather than the destruction all around us.

Thirty minutes later we pulled into the Chevron station in Weaverville and filled up with gas. "The evacuation center is at the school," Walt told me. "Martha called and said it's a crowded mess, but our neighbors are all there and safe."

"I can't keep the plants in the truck for long, and they won't have anywhere to store them at the center. What should I do?" I asked Walt.

"I don't know, son. All the surrounding counties are under states of emergency too."

Adrenaline was still pumping through me, so I hadn't thought about the full ramifications of what all this meant until that moment. But seeing the weariness on Walt's face, it hit me hard. "It's gone, isn't it?" I said. "The whole town, all our farms, everything."

He glanced away, and I knew his emotions were getting the better of him. He took a moment to get himself under control and then said, "Let's go on over to the evacuation center and let everyone know we made it out okay. We'll figure the rest out then."

I found a shady space to park on the outskirts of the center's nearly full parking lot. The truck's refrigeration only worked sporadically and almost always broke down when the truck was parked. The temperature was already too hot for the plants, and if experience proved true, it would only get worse by noon.

I followed Walt inside and was overwhelmed by the number of people I recognized from the community. Since I knew most of them, I figured the faces I didn't recognize must've been people from the surrounding areas. A desk was set up with a volunteer who wrote down my name and phone number.

After we located Martha, who greeted us with hugs and a relieved smile, I found a quiet corner of the gym and called my aunt and uncle. Between the local news coverage and the chatter circulating in the center, I knew the wildfire had become national news.

My mom's sister answered on the first ring. "Hello, Cliff?" she asked, sounding stressed.

"Hi, Aunt Sue. I wanted to let y'all know I'm safe. I made it out, and I'm at the evacuation center in Weaverville."

"Oh, thank the Lord. We were so worried."

My uncle interrupted her. "Does it look like the fire is headed toward the farm?" he asked.

It took me a moment to get my emotions under control enough to answer. "It was headed that way when I left. The farm is probably gone."

I didn't know for sure, and wouldn't be a hundred percent convinced until I could lay my own eyes on the land, but I could feel it. The home where I'd grown up, the greenhouse Dad and I had built together, the fertile fields we'd spent years cultivating—all destroyed by nature. It was almost like I'd been connected to the farm on a soul level and felt the life drain out of it.

"Come here, Cliff, to Wilcox," my aunt said. "We've got the space now Levi has moved out. You can have his old room."

"I don't know, Aunt Sue. I'm still trying to figure things out."

Aunt Sue had struggled when I came out as gay a few years back. She'd told me she loved me, but I could still feel a subtle strain in our relationship. That could've been me projecting my own fear of rejection, but I still wasn't entirely sure where things stood with her.

My cousin Levi, on the other hand, had been cool about it, even saying he had a friend he could fix me up with. When I acted interested, he laughed his butt off. He'd married his high school sweetheart, Keya, last year and moved down the road from his parents. Levi had grown up on his parents' large traditional dairy farm and still helped his dad with some of the day-to-day operations.

"Uncle Chris, is that okay with you? If I come to Oregon?"

"Of course," he said, sounding surprised. "Why would you even ask?"

I didn't have the nerve to admit it was because I was afraid he wouldn't be okay with me being gay. Aunt Sue and Levi were the only two I'd discussed that with. Uncle Chris wasn't there when we talked, and although I figured Aunt Sue had informed him at some point, I didn't know how he felt about it.

"I am what I am, Uncle Chris."

"What you are is family, and we want you to come here," he said without hesitation.

Tears ran down my face. "I'm gonna talk to some people here. Then I'll let you know what my plans are. Thank you for being there for me."

When we hung up, I had to take a moment to get myself together.

Walt found me with my forehead resting against the wall, and he placed a hand on my shoulder. "They're setting up cots and bringing in food and supplies," he said as he gave my shoulder a comforting squeeze. "They said we could stay here as long as we need."

"I think I'm gonna head to Oregon to be with my mom's sister and her family. They just invited me to stay with them."

"That's probably best. It'll be a while before they let us get back out there anyway."

"Will you let me know when they do?" I asked, embarrassed by my childlike tone. I sounded small, even to my own ears, but couldn't help it. I felt utterly defeated.

"Of course. You gonna wait till tomorrow to leave?"

"No, I'm worried about the seedlings. I won't have time to restart them, and if I can salvage any harvest this year—"

"I know, son, I know," Walt said, patting my back.

"Okay, I'm gonna head out as soon as possible. My uncle has a greenhouse. Hopefully I can use it to store the plants until I figure out the next steps."

Walt nodded and accompanied me back to the check-in desk. I let the volunteer know I'd be in Oregon and Walt and Martha would handle any immediate issues regarding my land.

I had to fill out paperwork, and the sheriff wanted to see me before I left, so I couldn't get away until much later than I wanted.

I gave Walt and Martha hugs goodbye. Then I finally climbed into the truck and called my aunt and uncle to tell them I was on my way. "I need your greenhouse, if it's available. I'm bringing several hundred plants with me that I saved."

"That'll be fine," Uncle Chris said. "We'll empty the shelves so it'll be ready when you arrive."

When I hung up, I gave in to my emotions and let myself weep. I couldn't fully digest that my family's farm was gone. I had the insurance papers in the trailer, thanks to Mom's previous evacuation packing, but I hadn't looked at the policy's value. It had cost an arm and a leg to keep the insurance paid, so I assumed it had to be significant, but I doubted I'd ever rebuild unless it was in the millions. Money had always been tight, but I had never known any different. My parents had chosen farming, and I couldn't imagine my life without it.

Despite inheriting the land from them, most of Dad's family were city dwellers from San Francisco. They hated everything about our lifestyle and ostracized us for it. But Mom and her sister had come from farm life and embraced it for their own families. That's why I was bound for tiny Wilcox, Oregon. Farming was all I knew, and a truckload of plants was all I had left of it.

I PULLED into my aunt and uncle's around eleven that evening. Despite the fatigue, I smiled when I saw the sign for Owens Century Farm that stood high over their driveway. I'd driven straight through without stopping for anything other than gas and restroom visits. I had never been one to eat when stressed, even though I could still hear one of my mom's recurring lectures regarding how important it was to keep my strength up. But I'd been too focused on getting to Oregon and hopefully saving the seedlings to worry about food.

Uncle Chris had to get up before dawn to milk the cows, so I wasn't surprised the lights were out in the house. Instead of waking them up, I lay across the bench seat in my truck and let myself fall asleep. I was startled awake by a knock on the driver's side window.

"Cliff, honey, get up and come on in for some breakfast."

I sat up and rubbed the sleep from my eyes. My aunt Sue was the spitting image of my mom, and in the morning sunlight, it took me a moment to realize who it was. I blinked back the tears and shook my head to get rid of the cobwebs.

My stomach rumbled loudly when I entered the house and smelled bacon and eggs. Aunt Sue pulled me into a hug before I could sit down at the table. "I'm glad you came, Cliff. I was so worried." She turned quickly and rushed to dish me up a plate. I didn't let myself ponder the sadness in her voice. I couldn't let myself get into that kind of emotional state, not right now anyway.

I sat beside Uncle Chris at the table, and he put his hand on my shoulder and squeezed it tight. The gesture was his way of letting me know I was welcome.

When Aunt Sue reappeared, she placed a mound of steaming hot food in front of me. "You want coffee?" she asked.

"Yes, please, ma'am."

She returned a moment later with a half-empty pot. I must've looked confused since neither she nor Uncle Chris drank coffee. Aunt Sue smiled. "Levi's been here," she said, and I had to laugh.

I dug into the homemade biscuits and gravy and the bacon and fresh eggs. My mother was attacked by a rooster when she was little, so she was afraid of chickens, and we'd never raised any. But the rest of the spread mirrored the huge breakfasts Mom used to make, and her sister's cooking tasted just as delicious.

Aunt Sue and Uncle Chris were strangely quiet as we ate. "Everything okay?" I asked.

"Are *you* okay?" Uncle Chris asked. "You've been through a lot in the past day."

I shook my head. I didn't feel okay, but I also didn't feel like breaking down again. I had my hands full with saving the plants, operating on minimal sleep, and combating the stress of losing my parents and our family farm in the span of a year.

Fortunately they didn't push. When I took my dishes to the sink, my aunt shooed me out of the kitchen. "You go with Chris. Those seedlings won't live long in the back of that truck," she said.

Uncle Chris was a stoic man. Salt of the earth, as my dad always said. That was what I needed right now—someone who could help me get the work done first and worry about emotions later.

The greenhouse sat next to a large historic dairy barn. Chris's grandparents built the barn when they started the dairy, but Uncle Chris installed a more modern system when he took over operations. The old barn now housed equipment instead of animals, and the old milking shed had been converted into a greenhouse so they could extend their growing season. But it'd been vacant for as long as I could remember.

I unhooked the trailer where Uncle Chris said it would be safe and out of the way. Then I pulled the old truck around to the greenhouse, inspected the space, and began to unload the trays.

Luckily, most of the plants had made the trip safely. One tray, the partial one I'd run out of time filling, had a few damaged plants, but it looked like I'd be able to save most of them. Uncle Chris connected a hose while I finished unloading. I watered the plants immediately and hoped it wouldn't be too much of a shock.

I knew it was ridiculous that I wanted to save the plants, but it felt important. My gut told me I wouldn't be returning to my farm this year, if ever. Those plants were the only *living* thing I had left of my life in California, and I couldn't just let that go.

With the plants tended to, Uncle Chris headed out to do some farm chores. He waved me off when I offered to help. "Today is for rest, but I'll gladly put you to work tomorrow. Just remember, the girls don't tolerate tardiness," he said. He'd made that same joke about his cows before, and I found his humor comforting.

Confident my seedlings would be okay, I drove back to the house and parked the truck next to the trailer.

Then I gave Walt a call.

"Hello?" he answered.

"Hi, Walt. I'm in Oregon. How are you and Martha? Have you heard any updates?"

"We're okay, son. Still holed up in the evacuation center. Word is the fire continues to rage, and they haven't told us which properties, if any, made it through. It's all still just wait and see."

"I figured that'd be the case. Just wanted to check in on you both."

"That's mighty appreciated. This won't come as a surprise, but my Martha has taken it upon herself to ensure everyone in this place gets fed on the regular. Truth be told, I think her keeping busy helps keep her mind off everything else. Anyway, how was the drive to your aunt's place?" he asked.

"Thankfully uneventful. I drove straight through, so I'm gonna go crash now."

"The plants?" he asked.

"Nearly every single one made it. My uncle helped me get them into his greenhouse. They're watered and looking fine."

"Good, son. I'm really glad."

I sighed. "Thanks, Walt. I don't think I'd have gotten out in time if it weren't for you."

"That's what neighbors are for," he said, and I had to hold my breath to keep from completely losing it. That's not the way everyone's neighbors were. Just the ones I'd grown up with, the ones whose homes had likely burned to the ground along with mine. My parents and I regarded them as lifelong friends.

"Okay, well, let me know if you hear anything," I said.

When I returned to the house, my aunt took one look at me and sent me to Levi's old room. I loved that she didn't dote on me, since I didn't have the emotional capacity to deal with it. What I needed was matter-of-fact support and more sleep, and luckily it appeared that's exactly what I would get.

Brandon

"SURE, I can come. Want me to bring Xander?" I asked Levi.

He laughed. "No, he'll just spend the entire time distracting the workers. We need to get the milking done and whatever else Dad has up his sleeve."

I chuckled, knowing Levi's dad would have plenty of other chores for us. The old dairy farmer was nothing if not gifted at finding work to foist on us.

I'd helped on the farm off and on for years, and when our buddy Xander was in town, we pulled him into the fray as well. But Xander drove poor Chris insane, hence Levi's recommendation to leave him out this time.

Our graduations from high school and college had done nothing to slow Chris Owens down. In fact he thought my teaching job, which temporarily ended at the close of each semester, made me his go-to for grunt work. Truth be told, I was glad to have some semblance of a job while I figured the rest of my life out.

I never minded manual labor. I liked physical work. I'd grown up in Medford, but we moved to Wilcox when I started high school. That's when I met Levi and began learning my way around the farm.

Xander's and Levi's families had owned land in the area for generations. Xander's family had mostly sold up, except for a small farm across from Levi's parents. Xander had inherited it from his dad's aunt. It would eventually be mine, provided Xander kept his promise to sell it to me.

I climbed into my car and wondered, not for the first time, why I hadn't bought a truck. Of course I hadn't planned to work on the farm. At least not more than simply helping out Levi and his dad on long weekends and summer breaks. And my parents, who'd helped buy the car, were convinced I'd go into medicine like them. God help me, I'd rather have plucked out an eye.

My parents almost had a conniption when I majored in English and then pursued a master's at the University of Oregon in Eugene.

I remember when I informed them I was taking a job as an English professor there. Mom actually cried. My parents hadn't batted an eye when I came out at thirteen, but when I told them I wouldn't be a doctor liked they'd hoped, Mom sobbed.

I'd taken to teaching well enough, but my real passion was writing—unfortunately not the kind of writing that leads to grants and tenure. I'd churned out two fantasy novels and was actively working on more.

I knew I'd leave teaching eventually, so when the opportunity came to gracefully bow out of the spring term, I took it. But I remained on the faculty roster with the expectation that I'd return for the fall term. Unofficially I was still on the fence. I hoped to make it as a full-time writer, but few did. I intended to pursue it as a creative outlet, but I needed something to fall back on—something like running my own farm.

Because I wasn't tenured, my university teaching job didn't pay all that well, and my books didn't bring in a whole lot, so it was a blessing to be able to pick up odd jobs on the farm. I saved every extra penny I could toward purchasing Xander's farm someday.

I pulled up near the barn, wandered inside, waved at the full-time crew, and began to clean the cows and hook up the milking machines. Chris's hired hands could joke around to beat the band, but they were all business this early in the morning—not a bad quality when dealing with animals that weighed over a thousand pounds each.

I hadn't caught sight of Levi, but I figured he was refilling the feed bunks while the cows were being milked. He had always been a hard worker—hell, the man had a full-time job but dedicated every spare minute to helping on the farm—but he'd never struck me as someone who genuinely enjoyed farm life. I'd never say it out loud, but I often thought he remained so involved out of a sense of duty and obligation to his parents and the family legacy. I would've swapped places with him in a minute.

As I managed the cows, I relived the dream of owning my own farmstead. My first project would be to convert the old barn on Xander's property into a rustic cabin. Then I'd build fences and outbuildings to house goats, chickens, and maybe one of those cute little miniature cows—all to keep as pets.

Yeah, I had the farming bug bad. I'd fallen in love with Levi's family farm when I was growing up, and it's where my imagination seemed to take flight. I'd discovered years ago that my best writing came after a hard day's farmwork.

When I followed the last cows out of the milking barn, I found Levi's dad, Chris, repairing an old tractor. "What's your plan for the next few days?" he asked.

"Not much. Why? You need help?" I asked, though I knew the answer.

He nodded. "The cows are calving, and I need an extra pair of hands to help prep the silage."

"Sure, I'm game," I said. I'd planned to travel to Portland to visit friends, but if Chris needed me, I'd be more than happy to change my plans.

I knew things were bad right then. The drought had hit all the farmers in the area hard. But one of the best parts of helping out on the farm was that I was treated to a huge home-cooked meal every evening, and I got to listen as Chris and Sue talked candidly about the challenges in keeping their farm going.

"Want me to call Xander for reinforcements?" I asked as I glanced at the tractor Chris was inspecting.

"No, I ran into his mama in town last Saturday, and she said he's up to his eyeballs with work in Portland. We'll just have to make do," Chris said.

I nodded, although that news bummed me out. Next to Levi, Xander was my best friend. He and I had fooled around a little in high school, but it went nowhere. We just weren't attracted to one another. Turned out we liked the same kind of guys. So instead of becoming boyfriends, we became buddies. My favorite memories were when Levi, Xander, and I worked together on the farm. Then we'd escape to the swimming hole under one of the covered bridges that spanned the Compass River, or we'd hide out in Xander's aunt's barn and while away our afternoons.

Toward the end of high school, Xander's aunt passed away and he inherited the farm and a property in town. The summer following graduation, Levi and I helped him renovate the little bungalow in town, and he sold it for a pretty penny. That set him off on his trajectory. Now he worked for a huge construction firm in Portland.

Levi and I had gone in totally different directions. We went to college together and even got the same degree... mostly. He went into English education, but I had absolutely no desire to teach kids. I could handle a classroom full of college students, but that's where I drew the line. Unlike me, Levi loved being a schoolteacher, and I sometimes wondered if Chris ever worried because his son didn't want to take over the farm someday.

Chris bumped me with his shoulder, snapping me out of my thoughts. "You're always daydreaming, boy. It's like you've got an overactive imagination or something."

I chuckled. "Or something. What was it you said?" I asked.

"I was just saying I need you and Levi to begin mowing the oat and pea fields tomorrow for the silage. Don't wanna wait much longer with this heat," he said, looking irritably up toward the sun.

The rest of the day sped by as I helped Chris work on the tractor for several hours, did a few other random chores, and milked the cows again. We headed for the house just as Levi and his wife, Keya, drove up. "Well, look what the cat dragged in," I said, which earned me an eye roll from Levi.

"Don't you start. Need I remind you this is supposed to be my spring break? I've been out there since the sun came up, working on a sunburn, same as you," Levi teased. "Fed the cows, repaired fencing out in the south field, fed the cows again, and capped off my day by slipping on a cow pie and then landing in it. Thought it best I run home to shower before supper rather than risk stinking up the house."

"And thank goodness for that or you'd be eating out on the porch and sleeping there too," Keya said. She grinned as she elbowed her husband. "I made him strip in the backyard, then hosed him down before he crossed the threshold." I was still laughing when Keya hugged me, and I gently tugged on her pigtails like I'd done since we were all in high school together.

"Hey, are you gonna help in the fields tomorrow?" I asked.

Levi shrugged but then looked at his dad and smiled. "Do you think my father would let me not work when I'm available?"

"No, never," I said, and Chris snorted as he went into the house.

I followed them all in and immediately washed my hands in the lower bathroom. No need to get Sue after me again. She'd all but flogged me last week when I sat down at the table without "washing proper," as she called it.

I took a seat in the dining room as Sue yelled up the stairs, "Cliff, we're sitting down to supper. Come on down."

I looked at Levi with my eyebrow raised in question. "My cousin," he said quietly. "His farm was swept up in the California wildfires. Only just arrived in the wee hours."

I cringed. I'd been watching the news about the horrendous wildfire currently scorching through California. It seemed fires were eating up the forested parts of California and Oregon more and more every year. "That's awful," I whispered. "He must be devastated."

Levi nodded, and a somber mood fell over the table. As talk shifted to fences that still needed repair, I popped into the kitchen to help Sue. I was bringing out a bowl of mashed potatoes when I came around the corner and looked right into the eyes of one of the most handsome men I'd ever seen.

When his eyes locked on mine, I stumbled. In one swift move, he caught me, put me right, and then took the bowl from my hands and placed it on the table.

I was still feeling flustered when he shook my hand and introduced himself as Cliff Anderson—chiseled jawline, lean build, and kind-but-sad eyes.

"I'm Brandon Forest, a friend of Levi's. Nice to meet you."

Despite his weary expression, his genuine smile caused my heart to flutter.

Sue brushed past us carrying a platter of pork chops and took her customary seat opposite Chris at the end of the table. Only then did I notice Levi had switched seats. Instead of sitting across from Keya, like usual, he was seated next to her. That left two empty chairs side by side, which meant I'd be sitting beside the handsome stranger all through supper.

"Let's say grace," Sue began, and as was the custom, Chris said his blessedly short prayer over the meal.

The conversation took its normal turns—which fields had to be mowed, which cows were calving, and whatever else needed doing around the farm. Then Sue shared a little gossip about the neighbors—Mrs. Horace needed a knee replacement. Mr. Frost had gone into hospice.

Chatter buzzed around the table, but Cliff sat silently. I glanced his way a few times, asked him to pass me the potatoes and to fork me up a pork chop, which he did without a word.

A whiff of smoke wafted off him, which must've permeated his clothes, and it reminded me of all he'd just gone through. My heart went out to the poor guy. I couldn't imagine what he was feeling.

I'd seen videos of the fires that had consumed California and Oregon in years past, and pictures of destroyed homes and burnt-out vehicles. The devastation was overwhelming. Experiencing that firsthand would be a real-life nightmare. I suspected Cliff was relieved no one asked him any questions about it.

"When is your next book gonna be out?" Levi asked me, though he already knew the answer. He had a mischievous grin on his face, so I knew this was for his cousin's benefit.

I played along. "I should get my manuscript back for revisions any day now," I said. I couldn't even say that without feeling a bit of dread. I'd soon be faced with a document that my editors had completely ripped apart.

"You're an author?" Cliff asked, and I smiled.

"Well, I'm trying to be. I have two books out, and now I'm working on my first series."

"What do you write?" he asked, looking around the table shyly.

"Mostly science fiction and fantasy. My new series will be young adult fiction, though. I wrote it in honor of my buddy Levi, the middle school English teacher."

Everyone chuckled except Cliff, who must not have gotten the joke.

"Your cousin over there challenged me to write a book he could use to motivate his students to read more. So I bragged about that being easy. Just so you know, writing a book for teens is not easy."

Cliff smiled warmly at me, and my heartbeat did the same pitter-patter flutter in my chest as it had when I first saw him.

"I remember being that age. I hated everything."

"Yes, you did. You were a pill back then," Sue said.

Cliff's smile brightened. "Levi was always a bigger pill, so I felt like I could get away with being a little surly."

"Hey, don't pull me into this," Levi complained.

Cliff winked at his cousin, and with just that bit of humor, it's like he came out of his protective shell.

"Do you write under a pseudonym?" he asked me.

"I use my own name. Brandon Forest."

"Oh, shoot. I should've realized that. I've read your books. I got them last year for my birthday."

Just like that, the shutters went down again. Something bad must've happened on or around his birthday. I didn't pry but said, "I'd be happy to sign your books."

He shook his head. "I doubt they survived," he replied quietly.

A sadness permeated the room, and he must've noticed because he quickly forced a smile and said, "But I loved them. I can't wait to read your young adult fiction."

I smiled at him but wasn't quite sure what else to say. So I went back to harassing Levi, which seemed to put everyone in a better mood.

After supper, Cliff helped Sue clear the table. When everything was put away, he excused himself to call a friend for news about the wildfires. He shook my hand and told me it was a pleasure meeting me. Then Sue waved him off.

A thrill, almost like an electric jolt, zapped my heart when he took my hand in his, and I was certain something sparked in his eyes. Whatever this was, and despite the awful timing in Cliff's life, I wanted to explore it. I'd never had such an immediate, visceral reaction to someone, and there'd been plenty of opportunities. I wouldn't consider myself a man-slut, but I wasn't far off.

I decided to pull Levi and Keya aside and get the story on Levi's ridiculously handsome cousin.

Cliff

DEPRESSION. WHEN I experienced it after my parents died, I thought it would swallow me whole, but the never-ending work of farm life had kept it at bay. I didn't have the benefit of busy distraction now.

Although it wasn't as intense, I felt its familiar tug when I woke up that afternoon. Aunt Sue had knocked on my door around three, telling me I shouldn't sleep any more if I hoped to get any shut-eye that night. "It'll be suppertime soon and you need to eat, so come on downstairs. Besides, Levi's friend Brandon will be joining us. He usually does after he's spent the day working with them."

"Thanks, Aunt Sue." I resisted the urge to groan. I didn't want to meet new people, but I also didn't want to seem ungrateful. I knew my aunt and uncle had folks coming in and out often, working at the dairy, and it made sense they'd invite people to supper. I could fake my way through one meal for their sake.

I began to put my clothes away but stuffed them all back into my bag. Everything reeked of smoke, like it'd been hung to dry over a campfire. I would need to run every stitch of clothing I owned through the washer tomorrow. Until then a shower would have to suffice.

In the meantime, I flipped open my laptop and searched for the latest news about the fires. I found footage of homes and vehicles, all burned, but no coverage about my area specifically. But my home was in the middle of the burned-out area on the wildfire map. It wasn't confirmation that I had nothing left to return to, but it felt just as disheartening.

I closed the laptop and went to the bathroom to shower, hoping to at least wash a layer of soot off. When I collapsed onto the bed earlier, I hadn't realized how filthy I was. I would need to wash Aunt Sue's bedding along with all my clothes.

Feeling somewhat refreshed, I descended the stairs and caught sight of a guy I didn't know just as he tripped and nearly fell. The stranger was tall, and as my arms circled his body to steady him, I could feel how muscular he was under his clothes. Even in my depressed state, my body took notice.

He looked a little embarrassed, but he smiled at me in appreciation and we made our introductions. He introduced himself as Levi's friend Brandon as we found our seats at the table.

Then I noticed we'd be sitting beside each other. When I glanced at Levi, he was smirking. I gave him a stern look, which just resulted in his typical ornery smile.

The conversation flowed steadily throughout supper, but thankfully no one asked me to participate. For most of the meal, my mind kept drifting to my farm.

Levi caught my attention when he asked Brandon when his next book would be out. I loved to read and preferred sci-fi and urban fantasy, so I was blown away when I realized Brandon was *the* Brandon Forest, author of the two books Mom had bought me for my birthday. Forest, as I'd always referred to him, had quickly become popular with the fantasy crowd I followed online. I knew several of them would be jealous if they knew I was sharing a meal with the author of *Graceful Awakenings*.

I was pleasantly distracted until Brandon offered to sign my copies of his books. I hadn't brought them with me. Like so many other things I cherished, the last gifts I'd ever receive from my mom were probably ash.

Everyone got quiet when I mentioned the books likely burned, so I quickly told Brandon how much I enjoyed his stories, hoping that would take away the somberness of my statement.

Once we finished eating, I helped Aunt Sue clear the table. Then I told everyone good night and rushed back to my room. I was still so tired that I collapsed into bed as soon as I closed the door.

I had planned on calling Walt and Martha but thought better of it. If they had news, they'd tell me. I only wished no news meant good news.

I SLEPT the entire night and woke well before sunrise. Clearly, my body clock was still set to farm life, so I decided to get on with my day. Hopefully I could contribute something to pay my aunt and uncle back for letting me stay with them.

I used the flashlight on my phone to light the way as I walked to the greenhouse. My uncle had outfitted the building with lights, so I could see my way around once I got inside. All the seedlings seemed to have made it through the night, so I watered everything again. It was still chilly outside, but the greenhouse was warm. I guessed a lot of that had to do with the ancient composting manure on the barn's lower level.

When I returned to the house, I wasn't surprised to see my uncle sitting at the dining table, eating a bowl of oatmeal.

"Morning, son," Uncle Chris said. "How did the seedlings fare overnight?"

"Pretty well, sir," I told him. "I got lucky. They're still so young and fragile. I didn't know how the transport would affect them."

"Well, plants are designed to be rugged."

"Is there coffee on?" I asked, and he shrugged. "Don't touch the stuff myself," he said, "but Sue might have some brewing."

I walked into the kitchen and laughed when I saw my aunt wearing a salmon-colored head wrap with hair curlers peeking out of it. "That's some hairdo you got there, Aunt Sue," I said.

"You hush up, young man. Just 'cause your mom kept her hair short doesn't mean all the girls do. If I didn't keep my hair curled, it'd be flat as a pancake."

I kissed her cheek as I walked past. "Gotta do what you gotta do." I grabbed a coffee mug out of the cupboard and poured myself a cup. Then I leaned against the counter as I took a sip and hummed as the piping-hot caffeine hit my system.

"This is good."

Aunt Sue smiled. "Your uncle has to eat oatmeal most days 'cause of his cholesterol, but I can cook you up some eggs and bacon if you like."

"No need to go to all that trouble. Oatmeal will be fine for me. I've gotten out of practice with eating a big breakfast since…." My voice trailed off when a lump formed in my throat, and I couldn't look her in the eye for fear I'd start crying. I knew it hurt for her to remember too. I swallowed thickly and added, "Well, since it's just been me."

She patted my back and sent me out of the kitchen. "I'll bring it out. You go sit with your uncle for a bit."

After breakfast I followed Uncle Chris to the barn. "If you're willin', I'm gonna put you to work, 'cause with calving season in high gear and me short-handed, we can use all the help we can get."

"Levi is coming around today to help too, right?" I asked.

"Yeah, but probably not until the milking is done. Boy grew up on a farm and still fights being an early riser."

I smiled. "He never was much into farming."

"No, he wasn't. Don't guess he ever will be. My boy works hard, but his heart never was set on being a farmer. Took me a long time to accept that. Farm life ain't for everyone."

I nodded but didn't reply. It was the curse of modern farmers that their kids didn't usually follow in their parents' footsteps. Frankly, there wasn't much money in farming any longer, and the work was hard and unforgiving. Either you loved it and did it for that reason, or you didn't do it at all.

Brandon showed up about half an hour later. "Morning," he said cheerfully as he climbed out of his car.

"Morning, son," Chris said, clapping his shoulder, and I smiled a greeting at him.

Seeing Brandon in the full light of day, decked out in ass-hugging jeans, worn boots, and a flannel shirt with rolled-up sleeves that showed off strong forearms, there was no denying he was an absolute hunk. The hard labor that went into this business meant a lot of young farm guys were. Unfortunately for me, they were usually straight or so deep in the closet it wasn't worth crushing on them. I'd made the mistake of getting carried away once before, only to end up with my heart crushed under the bootheel of a closet case. Despite my instant attraction to Brandon, I decided I'd be better off keeping my nose to the grindstone, as my dad used to say.

I followed Uncle Chris and Brandon into the milking barn, where Uncle Chris said Brandon and the other dairy workers could train me. Then he climbed into an ancient four-wheeler and drove off.

"It's not complicated," Brandon said as he showed me how he washed a cow's udder and attached the milking machine.

I chuckled at the irony—I'd been a farmer my whole life, but I'd never milked a cow. And as I quickly learned, it wasn't that easy. It also didn't help that Brandon's constant touches, innocent as they may have been, kept leading me to distraction. At one point he wrapped his body around my back as he helped me attach the machine to the cow's teats.

Electrical pulses danced across my skin. His body heat reached me even through my clothes, and I had to resist the urge to lean back into his warmth. If I were straight, I wouldn't have thought anything of our close proximity because he was genuinely trying to teach me. But damn, the only reason I didn't end up embarrassing myself was because the other farmhands were laughing at us when the machine kept falling off.

Finally, with a little disappointment at losing Brandon's nearness, I got the hang of it and was able to help milk the cows.

I didn't have much time to talk to him or the other workers. The pace was fast as the cows lined up for their morning milking. I'd heard my dad say time and again how he didn't understand why any farmer would want to tromp around in cow shit when they could spend their days plowing fields instead. I was enjoying myself nonetheless.

When Brandon and I finished the milking, we headed outside and met up with Uncle Chris and Levi.

"You boys are gonna work the fields on the west side of the road, and I'm doing the ones over here," Uncle Chris told us. "But before that we need to let the girls out into the pasture. It's gonna be another scorcher today, and I don't want them stuck in the barns."

When he walked away, Levi shook his head. "Milk production is down almost fifty percent. Cows are getting sick too. It's just too hot for these old girls. This has been the hottest spring in years."

"Really?" I asked, feeling concerned and forcing myself not to think about how the dry, hot spring had led to the fires back home. Like all farming enterprises, I knew margins were tight at the best of times. I couldn't imagine what losing over 50 percent of overall productivity would do to their bottom line.

I let the cows out into the pasture, which boasted a nice grove of oak trees near the top of the ridge, and Levi started talking to Brandon about the fieldwork. "If we're lucky, we'll get most of it mowed today and finish the rest tomorrow."

I looked at my cousin, surprised. "Isn't it too early to harvest oats and peas?"

He nodded. "Yes, but if we don't do it now, we won't get any in at all because the heat will kill it."

"Hottest spring on record," I repeated sadly, thinking again of the baked soil around my farm.

"Yep, and there's no end in sight," Uncle Chris said as he came up behind Levi.

"Then we better get to it." I followed my cousin and Brandon over to the tractors.

Just as I was about to climb into the tractor cab with Levi, he smiled ruefully and said, "No, you ride with Brandon. He's going to mow the larger field, so you'll get more experience with him."

I gave Levi the side-eye but did as I was told. Brandon said nothing as I settled in beside him and he started the old tractor and drove toward the field. "Have you driven a tractor before?" he asked.

I couldn't help but laugh as I yelled my answer over the engine noise. "I've been driving tractors longer than I can remember. There's a rumor that I might even have been born on one."

"Cool," Brandon said, and he pulled up to a stop when we reached the fence line. "Why don't you take the controls and I'll talk you through the process."

I bit my tongue and let Brandon give me instructions, even though I already knew how to use a brush hog. Hell, my dad's old tractor was the same model as this one, only newer. But I did enjoy the sound of Brandon's voice and his obvious enthusiasm about farming.

Once Brandon saw I had the hang of it, he sat quietly and watched as I mowed the field. It was too loud to talk much, but he occasionally told me quirks about the tractor and showed me how to use the GPS that kept us from veering off course.

I enjoyed being with him. He showed me the process without being a jerk, and he genuinely seemed to like working on the farm.

When we were halfway done, Uncle Chris called us in for lunch. "Bit different from the farming you're used to, huh?" Brandon clapped me on the back. I didn't have the heart to tell him running a tractor was something I'd done literally most days since childhood.

The moment I walked inside the house, my stomach began to growl from the smells coming out of the kitchen. Levi was already eating at the table, and Brandon and I made a beeline to the bathroom to clean up.

When we came back, two plates were waiting for us. Steam rolled off the open roast beef sandwiches, homemade mashed potatoes, and green beans.

I dug in without a second thought. I'd always been too busy to bother much with cooking when I was on my own, but Aunt Sue was one of the best cooks I'd ever met, so I planned on fully enjoying every single one of her meals while I was here.

"So, Cliff, my buddy was showing you the ropes, huh?" Levi winked at Brandon and then looked at me.

"Yeah," I said hesitantly.

"Did you *learn* a lot?" he asked.

I cocked my eyebrow, and Brandon shook his head. "Your cousin is trying to out me."

"Really?" I asked, surprised.

"Yeah, but it's no secret," he said, smiling. "It just so happens that I'm gay."

I flashed back to the feeling of his body lined up perfectly with mine, his chest plastered to my back while he showed me how to use the milking machine. A wave of heat coursed through me at the memory, and I hoped it wasn't noticeable.

"Cool," I said nonchalantly. "Since Levi apparently thinks that sharing is caring, I'll let you in on a non-secret of my own. I'm gay too."

"Yeah, your very nosy cousin already filled me in on that."

I smiled and shook my head. "He's always been that way."

"What way?" Levi asked. "I just thought you two should know you bat for the same team."

"Did you just quote a rom-com?" I asked.

Levi cringed. "Yeah, Keya makes me watch them all the time."

I laughed. "I love your wife."

We were still chuckling when Uncle Chris joined us for lunch. He didn't say much, just ate quietly and then leaned back in his seat. I figured he must be stewing on something. My dad had been that way when farm issues worried him.

"Uncle Chris," I said, drawing his attention, "you said we'd only be halfway done today, but we're on pace to finish the fields on the other side of the road."

"Yep, we'll finish this area today, then start on the land we bought last year, over by Levi's place."

"Oh, I'd forgotten about that. You've expanded the farm."

"Yep, had to if I wanted to compete. Levi and Keya bought the house, and I manage the land."

"Do you plant peas and oats there as well?" I asked, intrigued by his whole operation.

"No, we just use it for hay. With the summers getting hotter, I have to use most of my land for grazing. I can't justify making the poor girls miserable by keeping them inside, so they get their fields back."

After lunch I followed Brandon back to what I'd embarrassingly come to think of as *our* tractor.

I enjoyed the man's company and was happy Uncle Chris hadn't pulled him away for other farm chores. I wanted more time with him, especially now I knew he was openly gay. That made the little moments we shared, like when our hands accidentally brushed against one another, feel like more.

At one point we pulled up to a run-down house with a little barn behind it. Brandon motioned for me to turn the tractor off. "Is this Uncle Chris's property?" I asked, and Brandon smiled and shook his head.

"Nah, this belongs to my friend Xander. It's a nice place to get out of the sun for a moment, though. Come on." He led me up an overgrown path to the barn.

We collapsed on a couple of shaded hay bales. "This is cool," I said, glancing up at the barn. "Too bad these old farmsteads seem to be disappearing. Folks don't farm the way they did when this was built."

"It'd make a cute home, though, don't you think?" Brandon asked.

I chuckled. "Yeah, I used to tell my mom I was going to convert our barn into a house someday," I said, feeling a stab of sadness at the memory. "Looks like I missed my chance to ever do that."

Brandon reached over and took my hand. "I'm sorry, Cliff. I know this must be hard."

I smiled and enjoyed the feel of my hand in his. I'd expected his hands to be soft, but they were callused—the hands of a working man. I'm not sure why that pleased me, but it did.

After a moment he gave my hand a gentle squeeze, then let go and leaned back against the barn wall. "I love this place, have since I first discovered it. I don't know what it feels like to have lost something you've always known, but if something happened to this old barn, my heart would break."

That was all he said, but it was enough to make me feel marginally better. Brandon showed he understood what it meant to be attached to a place. If things had been different, even slightly less depressing, I'd have leaned over and kissed his handsome face. As it was, I just sat back and appreciated his support.

Brandon

As Chris predicted, we got the fields around his house and across the road mowed on the first day. After Levi's bumbling attempt at playing gay matchmaker, I ended up having a pleasant time hanging with Cliff. He was clearly competent on a tractor. After just a few times back and forth to adjust to Chris's way of doing things, he took over the entire process.

That gave me the freedom to watch him as he worked. Cliff was smaller than me but farmer strong. Instead of my bulky build, he had a wiry frame that'd been honed solid by work. His light brown hair, cut short, complemented his tanned face.

I was determined not to put pressure on him, particularly since he was in such a vulnerable spot, but he was definitely my type. Cliff proving himself highly skilled and capable around the farm only turned me on more. I had to force myself not to imagine what it'd feel like to have that lean and strong body under me in bed.

Instead I thought of peas and oats and the work we had to finish tomorrow. Heck, any subject was safer than dwelling on the gorgeous man in front of me.

Driving a tractor all day wasn't hard work, but it *was* exhausting. Maybe it's the unforgiving jostling and bouncing around for hours on end or merely that I was more used to working with my mind than my hands.

Regardless, when we pulled up to Xander's farm, I was ready for a break. I also wanted to show Cliff around the old place. I figured, since he was a farmer, maybe he could look past the dilapidated buildings and see the same possibilities that I saw in the property. I almost told him about my dream of buying it and fixing up the barn, but it wasn't the right time, not when he'd just lost his own property.

When our conversation shifted to that immense loss, I took his hand and held it, trying to offer support. For one brief moment

I thought Cliff was going to kiss me, but the moment passed and we just sat in companionable silence for a while.

The sun was setting by the time we finished our work and parked the tractor next to Chris's barn for the night. I was tired, and I could tell Cliff was too.

Despite that, as soon as I turned off the tractor, he jumped out of the cab and said he had to check on the greenhouse. I wasn't sure why, and he didn't wait to explain.

So I walked up to the house alone and found Keya and Levi sitting on the front porch.

"Where's Cliff?" Levi asked.

"Had to do something in the greenhouse," I said.

"Probably watering his seedlings. It was a scorcher today. I'm sure he's concerned they got dried out."

"He brought seedlings with him?" I asked, perplexed.

Levi nodded sadly. "His planted crop was probably destroyed in the fire. Dad thinks he rescued the seedlings in hopes of yielding at least one harvest this year."

"Do you think that's possible?" I asked.

Levi shrugged. "No idea, but at least it's hope."

"Seems strange," I said.

Keya, ever the wisest among us, sighed and looked toward the greenhouse. "When you've lost everything, you need at least a little hope to get through."

Even after spending all day with the man, I hadn't fully appreciated what he was going through. The tractor was too loud for much talk, but he seemed content. Only after we stopped for a break, when he and I hung out in the old barn, did I get a glimpse of his pain. It took an incredibly strong man to spend the day working on someone else's farm while his own likely lay in ruin. Keya and Levi must be right; he was holding on to hope.

Sue had prepared another big meal for supper. This time it was chicken-fried steak, potatoes, green beans, and broccoli. I had eaten at the Owens home enough to know what you had for lunch, you often had again at supper in one form or another. I loved that about being on the farm.

I didn't believe women should be confined to a kitchen—quite the opposite—but there was something special about coming in from the fields to find a home-cooked meal waiting. As I often did, I wondered what it'd be like if I were to find the right guy to settle down with on our *own* farm. I loved cooking and farming, and if I could somehow couple that with finding love and being a full-time writer, it would be a perfect life.

With my plate full, I glanced at the man sitting next to me, completely engrossed in his food. Cliff was a thinker. He seemed to be able to disappear into himself, the exact opposite of his cousin. For a long time in high school, I thought I was in love with Levi. But after he and Keya started going together and I saw how much they adored each other, I realized it'd been puppy love on my part.

I seemed to pick my dates based on personality—loud, gregarious, and maybe a little annoying. The other common denominator was that none of them worked out. Those relationships usually only lasted a few weeks before I became fed up and ready for peace and quiet.

I wondered if I would do better with a quiet, reserved man. *Stop creeping on Levi's cousin*, I scolded myself. *Just because he's gay doesn't mean you've got to date him.*

Chris pulled me out of my thoughts, and I chuckled inwardly since I'd almost missed what he said. "When do you think you'll be here tomorrow morning?" he asked.

"I can be here same as today. Sixish?"

Chris nodded. "Sounds good. Cliff, do you think you could run the larger tractor tomorrow?"

"Sure, I think so. Got a plan in mind?" he asked.

"I figure if you take that one and Brandon runs the other, Levi and I can pair up on the hay fields. There's a chance of rain, thank heavens, and I'd like to have this all done in case it pans out."

"I can be here earlier if need be."

"Okay, let's get started around five, then. Everyone else okay with that?"

Cliff smiled. "You met my father, Uncle Chris. You know I was never allowed to sleep past five anyway. I'm not even sure I can unless I'm sick or something."

"Good, then we have a plan." Chris looked positively pleased.

I'd been around long enough to know that few things were more stressful than managing a farm around the weather. Even though the rain would be welcome amid the drought, it could still pose a problem if we didn't finish our work before the sky opened up.

I'd miss having the handsome man in the tractor with me. Working alongside Cliff had been awesome. I just wished he was in a better place emotionally so I could feel less restrained. I'd love to test the waters with him and see if he was as interested in me as I was in him.

Cliff

BEING BUSY was great, particularly when your world was falling apart. As long as I was working and worn out by the end of the day, my mind didn't wander back to everything I'd potentially lost. Working with a guy as hot as Brandon also didn't hurt.

I woke around four the next morning and wandered down to the greenhouse to check my seedlings. They were still damp from the night before, so out of fear of rotting their roots, I decided not to water them again.

"We're gonna get through all this, little plants. I'll have you tucked nicely in the soil by June." I'm not sure if speaking the declaration aloud was more for the plants or me, but either way it felt good.

I returned to the house and found Aunt Sue cooking bacon and eggs. "I'm sorry about the store-bought biscuits," she said, "but these frozen ones are almost as good as mine and make a whole lot less of a mess."

I chuckled. "Aunt Sue, you don't have to cook for me. I'm good with the oatmeal."

"Son," Uncle Chris said behind me, "don't lie to your aunt. There ain't nobody wanting oatmeal over a home-cooked breakfast. You'll be getting old soon enough and having to eat oatmeal, same as me. You should enjoy the good life while it lasts."

I nodded, grateful my aunt and uncle were trying to take care of me in their own ways. I didn't care what I ate as long as I had coffee in the mornings. But if Aunt Sue genuinely wanted to cook for me before the crack of dawn each morning, I'd eat every bite with pure enthusiasm.

The day went fast. I helped with milking before we headed out to the fields to begin the tedding process. I admit it was a part of haymaking I knew little about. Mowing? Yeah, I had plenty of experience with that, but making silage was different.

Levi pulled me aside and explained a bit about what needed doing and why. Mostly, our goal involved piling the silage up and covering it so it fermented properly.

We skipped lunch because dark clouds loomed overhead and blessed rain seemed inevitable. With all of us working nonstop, we finished in midafternoon just as the first raindrops fell.

The suppertime conversation that evening revolved around whether the rain would prevent the right moisture content for optimum silage fermentation. "It's been dry for over a month, no indication of rain. Then I decide to mow, and boom! Rain," Uncle Chris lamented while we ate.

"Not calling for much more than sprinkles," Aunt Sue said, concern etched on her face.

"I know we need this, but I hope you're right, Sue," he said.

Even though I felt worn out, it was a good sort of tired. We all shared in Uncle Chris's worry about the silage crop, but I also felt content simply being with my family, especially given everything that had happened. I loved my aunt and uncle and even my nosy cousin. I didn't know Keya well, but I hoped to remedy that soon. And I was enjoying Brandon's company, even though that posed a potential can of worms. If things were different, I would happily open that can and dive in. But I wasn't ready.

After supper I excused myself and then showered before bed. The dust in the fields was overwhelming. I knew I was covered, and the mud that flowed off me in the shower confirmed it. That wasn't new for me. It was just part of the life I'd chosen.

Only when I slipped on fresh pajamas did I realize Aunt Sue had moved more of my belongings in from the truck, and the pile of smoke-scented clothes in the corner was gone. I'd have to thank her. As always, Aunt Sue reminded me so much of my mom, quietly taking care of her family in a thousand unspoken ways.

That night I dreamed of hay fields, of milking cows and soft kisses with Brandon. We were standing in the doorway of that barn he took me to, looking out over the property, when he leaned in for a gentle kiss. The dream got more intense after that, and I woke up aching all over, hungry for him.

The early-morning phone call from Walt and Martha quickly cooled me off. I had just returned to my room after brushing my teeth when Walt's number popped up. I put them on speakerphone and had barely managed a greeting before Walt got straight to the point.

"I'm sorry, son, but they told us yesterday that our farms are a total loss. The fire burned all our buildings and everything else in its path."

"Nothing survived?" I asked, hoping maybe Walt was exaggerating.

"No," Martha said. "The firefighters struggled to save the town, which they mostly did, but the fire rampaged through the rural areas. I'm afraid there's nothing left."

I choked back a sob. It was expected, but to have it confirmed was a gut punch. "What are you gonna do?" I asked them.

"Our son and his wife rented a short-term apartment in their building for us. We're gonna go stay there until we can rebuild. The crews are still dealing with hotspots and aren't allowing anyone to set foot on their properties until next week."

I quietly wiped my tears away. "Okay," I said in a whisper. "Keep me up to date on how you are."

"Sure thing, and son?"

"Yes?" I asked.

"It'll be okay. It always is. We'll survive. I promise we *will* survive, and so will you."

"Yes, sir," I said and hung up. Then I lay back on the bed and let the tears flow. My whole life, everything I'd worked for and everything my parents had worked for, really had gone up in smoke.

I lay in bed until Aunt Sue knocked a while later and asked if I was all right.

"I'm okay," I croaked out through the closed door. "I'll be down for breakfast in a bit."

"Take your time, Cliff."

She must've overheard my conversation with Walt and Martha. Oh well, at least I wouldn't have to tell her and Uncle Chris myself. I'd probably start sobbing if I tried. It felt like my insides were going to spill out of my feet. I doubted I'd be much help on the farm today.

Eventually I washed my face, put myself together, and went downstairs. The only thing keeping me from falling apart was my stubborn determination not to make a scene about my losses.

"We're gonna head into town, if you wanna join us," Aunt Sue said over breakfast.

"Thanks, but I'm not really in the mood, to be honest. I'm gonna go through the insurance paperwork my mom had packed. I'm not sure what I need to do, but I should probably get that process started."

She squeezed my shoulder as she walked past on her way back into the kitchen.

"If you need to empty the rest of your trailer, you can store everything in the new barn. It's the driest, and you can back right in," my uncle said over his oatmeal.

I nodded. "Thanks, Uncle Chris."

"Sure thing, son." He hesitated for a moment. "Cliff, you're welcome here as long as you need, okay? Your aunt and I, well, we want you here. Times like this, you need family. So stay as long as you need to."

He left the table after that, not that he needed to say anything else. I was being pulled into the arms of the only family I had left, and I needed them. He was right. I decided then and there that I'd take my uncle and aunt up on their offer to stay.

Wilcox, Oregon, was my new home. For how long, I had no idea. But I understood how lucky I was. A lot of my neighbors might not have the same available to them.

After Aunt Sue and Uncle Chris left for town, I backed my trailer up to the big steel building and began to go through the few things I had left of my life and the life I'd had with my parents.

I silently thanked my mom for having the foresight to prepare us for this kind of emergency. If it hadn't been for that, all of these now-precious possessions and important documents would've been lost. I'd never been big on material things, but my heart clung to each item like a life raft.

When I finally found the fireproof box that held the paperwork, I rummaged until I found the insurance information and then gave the agent a call.

Thanks to my parents' estate attorney, the policy had been transferred to my name.

With that call done, I rifled through more papers and discovered what I already suspected about the farm vehicles. They only had liability policies, so they weren't covered.

Next, I found my birth certificate, Mom and Dad's marriage certificate, and the deed and proof the mortgage had been paid off.

I also found my school report cards and funny pictures I'd drawn when I was young. Mom had even tucked away a couple of Valentine's Day cards Dad had given her in which he'd written simple but sweet notes about how much he loved her and the life they'd made together. I was glad I was alone because that sent me into a long bout of tears.

I repacked some items with more care than I'd had time to do before, ensuring they would be safe until I returned to California. Then I stored the boxes in the barn. When I returned to the house early that afternoon, I brought the box of paperwork with me.

Uncle Chris and Aunt Sue weren't back from town, so I took a long shower and let the hot water relax my tense shoulders. When I got out, I dressed in jeans and a T-shirt, then gathered up the dusty, dirty clothes I'd worn the day before. I also stripped my bed and tossed the linens into the washing machine in the laundry room behind the kitchen.

I was just finishing the laundry when I heard a knock on the back door. Brandon stood there, smiling. "Hey, your aunt told me you were here by yourself, and I wanted to know if you'd like to join Levi, Keya, and me for a wild night of pizza and Netflix at their place."

I chuckled. "Come on in. I just pulled my clothes and sheets out of the dryer. Give me a second to bring them upstairs, and I'll take you up on that."

"Why don't you grab some clothes too, so you can stay over. We'll make a night of it."

"Really?" I asked.

"Sure, I'm staying with them too. I don't like staying with my parents if I can help it, and having a movie night is a good excuse to relocate."

"You don't get along with your parents?" I asked.

He chuckled. "I love them, but let's just say they're laced a bit tight."

"Oh, well, that's too bad. You seem to be easygoing."

"I suppose in some ways that's true. Unfortunately, in my parent's eyes, I'm a great disappointment," he said, but he continued to smile.

"A disappointment? I can't see how that's possible. Are they not a fan of your writing career?" I asked, feeling a little guilty for prying, but he'd opened that door.

"I'm not a full-time writer, not yet anyway. I make my living as a professor at the University of Oregon. I'm on a break from teaching until fall term."

"Wow, you're a professor. I would never have guessed that. What do you teach?"

He cocked an eyebrow, which I thought was beyond adorable, and said, "English."

"Ah, that makes sense at least. And your parents aren't happy about you being a university professor?"

He shook his head. "My dad's a doctor, my mom's a nurse practitioner, so they were sure I'd follow their lead into the medical field. The sight of blood turns my stomach, though, and biology bores me to tears. So I followed my passion. Hence their disappointment."

"I see, sorry about that. As you can tell, I've pretty much walked in my parents' footsteps. The only thing that disappointed my mom was that I wanted to raise chickens. She hated chickens." I laughed at the memory.

Brandon smiled. "That must've been nice. I'm sure you had fewer family meetings about your life choices than I did. Anyway, it's best for me to stay with Levi and Keya than to get in the middle of another lecture on the money I could've been making had I pursued science instead of the arts."

He helped me carry the clean laundry upstairs, then waited patiently as I rummaged through my clothes and laid some out to pack. I turned around too fast and ran into him as he was about to sit on my bed. He reached out to steady me, but we crashed onto the mattress, and I ended up sitting on his lap, wrapped in an embrace.

I'm not sure what came over me then—the need to feel something besides sadness, I guess. Before I could stop myself, I slid my arms around his back and rested my head on his shoulder. Without hesitation, he hugged me in return.

We stayed like that for a few minutes. When I finally pulled back, I started to apologize, but he pressed a finger to my lips. I had to resist the urge to stick my tongue out to lick it.

He must've sensed it, because he was grinning. "I like you, Cliff, a lot. But I don't want to push things too far too fast. I know—"

I didn't let him get the words out. I cupped his face, took his mouth with mine, and poured all of my emotions into a long, sensual kiss. At that moment I didn't want to think about wildfires, insurance companies, or parents I'd never see again. I didn't want his sympathy. I just wanted him.

When Brandon let out a moan, my brain snapped back to reality and I pulled back. "Shit, sorry, you were telling me you felt sorry for me, and—"

"No, no, I wasn't saying that. I was saying take your time," he said, still holding me tight. "But if you're ready, I sure would like to find out where this could go. I wasn't joking. I like you, Cliff."

"Same," I said, which earned me a quick peck on the lips.

Brandon ran his big hands down my back all the way to my ass and winked at me.

In short order I packed some clothes and my toothbrush, sent Aunt Sue a quick text that I'd be crashing at Levi's, and we were out the door. Brandon and I held hands on the short drive to Levi's place, but we both let go before we turned into the driveway. Neither of us needed my nosy cousin sniffing around this, whatever *this* was.

Brandon

THAT NIGHT, despite Levi's constant meddling, Cliff and I got to know each other better. We also came to an unspoken agreement not to let Levi know we'd passed first base.

Cliff didn't talk much about the fire or his parents, which was understandable. Sue had overheard Cliff talking to his old neighbor, who told him the farm was gone. She also told me Cliff had lost his parents in a car accident last year.

Given the emotional turmoil he must've been feeling, I hadn't expected him to accept my offer of dinner and a movie, let alone what happened in his room.

I'm not the kind of guy who swoons over a kiss, but that kiss with Cliff rocked me. His lips tasted like the most delicious wine I'd ever sipped, and I craved more. If we hadn't been standing in Chris and Sue's house, I probably would've pulled him onto the bed, ravaged every inch of that amazing body with my mouth, and worried about how fast we were going later.

Luckily, being in Levi's old room helped restrain me. Chris and Sue were supportive and always had been, but I didn't want to test their limits by getting caught dancing naked under the sheets in their home.

Although I wanted to be alone with Cliff, hanging out with Levi and Keya proved a great stress relief after hard days working the farm. We played video games—and Keya handed us our asses—then we ate pizza and sat around watching Netflix. We all had early mornings, so we turned in around nine.

"Thanks for inviting me," Cliff said as we stood in front of our respective bedrooms.

"My pleasure. It was fun."

"It's what I needed," he said, smiling. Then he glanced down the hallway, saw we were alone, and stole a chaste kiss.

Cliff made me feel a lot of things—desire, attraction, a kinship about farming, and deep sadness for all the pain and heartache he had to endure.

I lay awake that night staring at the ceiling and thinking about the sexy man asleep across the hall. I wanted to go to him, but the walls of this old farmhouse were as thin as paper. You could hear every movement. Levi would need to do something about that if he and Keya were to have kids one day.

The lack of soundproofing meant I didn't make a move on Cliff. Instead I let my imagination run wild with all the ways I could soothe him. Luckily I was tired enough that I wasn't too tormented and I fell asleep. Although I don't usually remember my dreams, I'm pretty sure they were filled with Cliff.

The next morning we arrived at Chris's farm before dawn to do the milking. Chris met us as we all congregated in the house afterward. He let us know the fields looked good and there hadn't been enough rain to ruin the silage. In fact he was confident the rain had helped bring the moisture levels up to where they needed to be.

We all dug in, determined to get the silage covered. Chris was worried about not having enough grass to feed the cows if the dry season persisted, and Levi had told me things were tight for his parents and the farm. Several things were working against them right now.

Unfortunately, the drought was the least of it. The large dairy buyers down in Roseburg had just sold to a family from out of state. The new owners announced that they would be moving the entire operation. That meant Chris's top buyer was leaving the area. There was also the fact that milk prices weren't going up at the same pace as the economy, which put additional pressure on Chris to make the process more efficient.

Chris wasn't the kind of person to let his animals suffer. As other farmers tightened their belts and forced their cattle into more restrictive environments, Chris opened up his fields to let his cows have more freedom.

I knew it was just a matter of time before he reached his limit, and I wondered what that would ultimately mean for the farm.

Over the next few days, we worked from morning to night to get the silage situated. Cliff and I only saw each other in passing, and

I wondered if maybe he'd gotten cold feet. But it was strange that he hadn't even eaten with us, so I asked Levi what was up. He shrugged and told me Cliff was working on some project in the old barn during his spare time.

Unfortunately, I didn't get a chance to say goodbye to Cliff before I had to head back to Eugene. My editor had returned my manuscript, and I had a tight turnaround to make revisions. My parents' house promoted anything but creativity, and I didn't want to overstay my welcome at Levi and Keya's place, so I rushed back to my home office to finish the work.

"We need your final rewrites back ASAP," my editor had said in her last email, pushing me to get done. "We're hoping to push up your pub date and release book one ahead of Black Friday."

"Message received," I wrote back. I wanted them to publish my series, and to get that, I'd have to finish all three books sooner rather than later. Hell, they'd barely given me a contract on book one.

I sighed as I stared at my computer. I'd only finished drafting book two and hadn't even started writing book three.

I was happy I'd managed to help Chris get his silage mowed and covered before I had to return to Eugene. However, if I was going to make writing my full-time career, I had to seize this opportunity and make it my top priority—even if that meant cooling things off with Cliff, though it seemed he'd already stepped back himself.

Cliff

"So YOU don't mind if I use the old barn to experiment?" I asked Uncle Chris.

He scratched his chin. "You know you shouldn't put a lot of money into it, but sure. No harm in trying."

When I was young, Dad had become obsessed with aquaponics—a process that combined raising fish with hydroponics. At the time California was dealing with another drought, and Dad had lost most of his crops due to water shortages. He'd been convinced aquaponics was the key to surviving climate change.

The following year was better, so he never pursued it for our farm. But he did keep up on the latest developments and would chat about it with me from time to time.

I had developed an interest in it as well and wrote a term paper on the subject in college. I'd even visited a couple of successful enterprises in Wisconsin and Washington. It was fascinating, but there never seemed enough time or budget to make it happen.

But things had changed. The farm had been destroyed, and everything had to be rebuilt from the ground up. It was the perfect time to pursue Dad's dream and set up a system that might enable us to thrive instead of just survive.

Of course, there was no longer an *us*, but I tried not to think about that. Bad stuff happened, and I'd certainly had a lot of bad things happen to me, but that didn't mean I could give up. Keep focused and keep going. That's the farmer's way. That's what Mom and Dad taught me.

I spent a lot of time in the greenhouse, planning things out before I sprung the idea on Uncle Chris. Then I pulled him aside and explained how I'd like to use the greenhouse and part of the barn to set up the aquaponics system. If I could start the fish process, I could expand next year when they were old enough to lay their eggs. I was grateful to have Uncle Chris's support—and the use of his buildings—for my big experiment.

The biggest expenses would be the equipment and the fry, as the baby fish were called.

I had the plants. I had a good barn to get started in. And I'd spoken to a guy who lived a few hours away and who was selling several large blue tanks. He said he'd happily deliver them for a nominal fee. And I need to buy some other supplies—like a shade cloth to cover the greenhouse windows—but I could fund those with my savings. There was no reason I couldn't make this work.

I deliberately focused solely on the task at hand because I could control it. I tried not to think about Brandon or my parents since, in both cases, I didn't know what to do with my swirling emotions.

I shouldn't have kissed Brandon. I had too much going on, and I felt like a mess. But damn, I really did want to kiss him again. Despite that, I needed to focus on getting my life back—a life rooted in California, not Wilcox, Oregon.

Before Uncle Chris agreed to my plan, I showed him how I wanted to set the tanks up inside the old barn and where I wanted to drill holes for the fish water to be plumbed and pumped up to the shelves we'd have to build for the plants.

He listened to me and probably thought I'd lost my mind. But he didn't argue. Instead he nodded, scratched his head, and asked a few questions here and there.

"Well, from what you've described, it looks like you're gonna need some help. Calving season is about over. I only have a few more heifers due to drop. After that I should have more time. Spring break is about over for Levi, but he's available when he's not teaching. Brandon might be around some too, not sure. The boy's run off to work on his books or something. No matter, between all of us, you'll have help getting it all set up."

As was my uncle's way, he nodded, clapped my shoulder, and headed back through the door.

I sat in the old, weathered barn a while longer, looking around the cavernous space and thinking about my uncle's words. That's when I realized, for the first time in a long while, that I didn't feel alone in the world.

Brandon

I SIGHED heavily as I plopped down at my writing desk. My editor had been impressed with my first novel, or at least that's what my agent told me. Despite that, I'd been reticent to send drafts of my other books. I just didn't feel confident they were ready.

Trying not to let my frustration run away with me, I opened my laptop and found the file with the edits of the first book. It didn't take me long to read through the comments and make the handful of revisions my editor suggested, then email the final manuscript to the editor. After that, I reluctantly opened the first draft of book two.

First drafts were known and expected to be shit. I'd lectured my creative writing class on that fact multiple times, but it still didn't make me feel better as I began to read my own work. "Well, if shit is the norm, I'm about as normal as they come," I said to myself.

I tended to be more of a pantser than a plotter. Sure, I wrote an outline like the good English professor I was, but then I tended to let my characters wander wherever they chose. As a result, my first few read-throughs always involved fixing scattered plot points and ensuring it all flowed smoothly.

Without realizing it, I became fully engrossed in the story. Only when my stomach growled did I notice hours had passed and I'd missed sunset.

By then I could feel the manuscript coming together, and that gave me hope. I threw together a ham-and-cheese sandwich—the easiest thing to make with the ingredients I had on hand—and sat back down to edit the draft again. I worked all through the night, and come sunrise, I sent a relatively decent draft of book two to my agent.

I GRABBED a shower in hopes of catching a second wind, and then I opened the outline document for book three and laughed at how far I'd veered from it. The story no longer resembled what I thought would happen to conclude the series.

I decided to start fresh rather than try to revise what I'd already written. I got a few hours of sleep and then played around with the outline before I finally started to write the first draft.

Sometimes the words just flowed. Those were my favorite moments as a writer. That's when my experience and education took over, and I wrote without worry about edits or corrections.

When my eyes refused to stay open any longer, I'd put down three thousand words. Then I crawled into bed, slept like a log for six hours, and woke up thinking about the story. *Yes*, I thought, *I'm finally in the zone.*

I rushed to get a cup of coffee and returned to my laptop.

I looked up as my phone rang, surprised it was already late morning. "Hello?" I answered.

"Hey, buddy, it's Levi. What's up?"

I chuckled. "Well, I'm running on caffeine and minimal sleep, book two is with my agent, and book three is flowing as fast as I can type."

"Dude, congrats!"

"Thanks. Keep your fingers crossed for me that the words keep coming."

"Will do," Levi said. "So, I'm calling because Cliff is setting up an aquaponics system in the old barn, and Dad wondered if you could come by next week and help us put it together."

My mind flashed to the memory of Cliff and me locked together, devouring each other's lips, and all thoughts of the books left my head. "Um, well, I've got this series hanging over me," I said, knowing if I let my mind linger on the man, my hope of writing more words today would vanish. "But if I can crank out this first draft, I'd be happy to come help."

"That's perfect," Levi said. "Just keep me posted. Good luck."

When he hung up, I looked at my calendar and sighed. I'd planned an excruciating timeline with likely unreasonable expectations for getting this series done. And I had taken the semester off to make this happen. There were long days and nights ahead of me to get the edits done and returned in a timely manner. It was a lot to commit to.

Not for the first time, I wondered if I'd overly romanticized being a full-time published author. The pressures of writing like clockwork and meeting constant deadlines didn't mesh well with the creative, passion-driven life I'd envisioned for myself. But then, farm life had its own rigid schedules and stressors, but I still loved it. I just needed to find that same balance in my writing. And meet my damn deadlines.

Cliff

THE TANKS I'd bought were crap. Two had gaping holes in the side, even though the seller had sworn they were all in pristine condition when he packed them for transport. "What happened?" I asked the truck driver.

He shrugged. "Had an idiot loading them. Rammed the sides with a forklift. Not my department, though. I just drive the truck."

I shook my head as Uncle Chris unpacked them. I immediately called the seller, who apologized for the damage. "They should be fine if you patch them, but I've already filed a claim with my insurance company. I can refund you a big chunk of your money if you want to keep them."

I ended up agreeing. I'd patched tanks before. It wasn't that difficult, but I was more than a little annoyed that my project was getting off to such a rocky start. Uncle Chris moved the tanks into the barn before he had to get back to managing his cattle.

I surveyed the damage and wrote a list of supplies I needed to make the repairs, then went into the house to ask Aunt Sue about suppliers in the area.

"Your best bet is Eugene," she said. "You could try the local hardware store, though. Want me to call the owner, Stewie?"

"No, this is a specialty, I'm afraid. They won't have what I need. And I'd rather gather it all myself if I can than order online again."

She gave me the name and number of where she and Uncle Chris went for farm supplies, and luckily, when I called, they said they had what I needed in stock.

I was feeling grumpy about the busted tanks, but the long drive to Eugene cooled me down a bit. Oregon was so pretty and inviting. The landscape in my part of California seemed harder, more rugged. Here lush hills rolled into beautiful valleys. It felt idyllic in some ways, like a painting come to life. I'd always liked this part of the world.

When my phone rang, I pulled into a rest area as I answered.

"Hey, Mom said you were headed up to Eugene." Levi sounded cheerful.

"Yeah, picking up supplies. Do you need me to bring something back?"

"No, but Brandon lives there. Why don't you go drag him away from his computer? He's been locked up there for over a week. The man needs to be reminded what outside looks like."

"Levi," I said heavily, "I barely know Brandon, and if he's busy, I doubt he'll want to see me. But thanks for thinking of me."

"Hey, wait. If he calls you, would you go out with him?"

I waited a moment before I answered. "Levi, why is this so important to you?"

He shocked me by laughing. "You know how it is with us married folks. We don't like to see our friends and family single."

"You jealous?" I asked, and he laughed again.

"I am a happily married man. That's all I have to say about that."

I couldn't help but laugh as well. I could imagine Keya standing beside him as he spoke.

"I planned on driving back tonight, but if he wants to grab a bite to eat, I'm game. But Levi, please don't push him. I don't need a babysitter or a matchmaker."

"Okay, I hear you. No playing Cupid," he said, but I swear I could hear him smiling. "Anyway, I'll call him now and give him your number." Levi hung up before I could respond.

There was a reason my cousin had a reputation for being nosy. I couldn't help but roll my eyes at his antics. Not that I would object to seeing Brandon again.

I'd felt a little unsettled a week ago, not knowing what I'd do about my farm and then diving in headfirst with the aquaponics idea. I knew I'd left Brandon hanging, not that we'd made any promises, but when he returned home, I figured that was the end of it. Now, thanks to Levi's meddling, maybe not.

Brandon

"HEY, MAN," my best friend said as I answered the phone, my mind still on the story I was writing. "Whatcha doing?"

"Working. What's up, Levi?" I asked, trying not to sound distracted.

"Guess who's in Eugene?"

I stopped typing to focus on what Levi was saying. "In town? Am I supposed to know?"

"My cousin, that's who," he said, making it sound like it was some fantastic event that Cliff was here. I had to bite my cheek to keep from laughing.

"That's nice, Levi, but I'm not exactly sure why I need to know."

"God, you make me work for everything. You like him, he likes you, and he's in your town. You could invite him over or take him on a date."

"Levi, seriously, I'm trying to get this draft finished enough that I won't cringe if anyone else reads it. I need to focus, not go chasing…." I almost said tail, then stopped myself because Cliff was his cousin. "I don't have time to chase after a guy," I said instead.

"I just wanted you to know he's in town, practically on your doorstep, for the next few hours. What you do with that information is up to you."

I could hear Keya in the background, and I immediately knew she was fussing at him about being too pushy. Keya tended to mellow my best friend out, and thank God for that, because Levi was like a dog with a bone when he got an idea in his head.

"Okay, send me his number. If I can wrap this up soon, I'll text him, but no promises. Don't go trying to set something up."

"No problem, dude," he said, trying to sound indifferent but failing.

"Levi, I'm hanging up now. Go bother your wife."

I hung up without waiting for a reply. The conversation could continue for hours if I let it.

I dug back into the story, but moments later, my phone pinged. Levi had texted me Cliff's number, and damn, the mere possibility of having the man here in my home, just the two of us, led me to distraction.

"Ugh!" I shouted at the blinking cursor on my laptop. "Levi is going to be the end of my career."

I picked up the phone and called Cliff's number. He answered on the third ring.

"Hello?" he answered, sounding distracted.

"Hey, Cliff? This is Brandon Forest."

"Oh no, Levi talked to you," he said, causing me to laugh.

"The one and only. Yeah, I hope you don't mind me calling, but Levi said you're in Eugene."

"I am, running some errands. I'm sorry about Levi. He's got in his head that we need to be coupled up."

"Yeah, I know. He'll never admit it, but the man's a hopeless romantic. He blames Keya on wanting to watch rom-coms all the time, but I guarantee you, she'd rather watch action flicks. Anyway, since you're in town, it *would* be nice to see you."

The phone went silent for a moment, and I thought we'd been disconnected until Cliff let out a breath. "I don't plan to be there long. I was gonna try to get back to Wilcox tonight, and I got a late start anyway."

"No problem, I'm busy too. What about we meet up for some Umpqua ice cream? I know a place that serves it, and then you can tell your uncle you helped make him a little money since he sells his milk to their dairy."

Cliff laughed, and the sound made me smile. "Okay, you have a deal. I'm going to get the supplies I need, and I don't know how long that'll take, but I'll text you afterward. Does that work?"

The instant thrill that shot through me told me it worked really well. "Yeah, it does. Meanwhile, I'm going to try to get some work done. If you don't hear back from me right away, try calling. I sometimes miss texts when I'm caught up in my writing."

When we hung up, I couldn't wipe the grin off my face. I knew reviewing my draft would go nowhere because now all I could think of was Cliff. So I got up, fixed myself a quick sandwich, and turned on some music. I never listened when writing or editing, but it was a good way to clear my head when I needed to refocus.

I plopped down on the oversized sofa I inherited from my parents when my mom decided she needed a new one. It was too big for my apartment, but I'd had my first kiss while sitting on its plush cushions, as well as some other firsts, so it had sentimental value. Despite trying not to think of him, I couldn't help but wonder what it'd be like cozying up to Cliff on this sofa. Unfortunately, my return to Eugene had put the skids on my getting to know him better. Maybe this was a good thing, but damn if I ever admitted that to Levi.

I only barely got restarted writing when my phone dinged with a text a couple hours later, it pulled me out of the draft. *Damn*, I thought, *I sailed through this*. I hoped that meant I had a decent story.

I grabbed my phone and couldn't help the cheesy smile that spread across my face.

Cliff: *I'm done chasing my tail all over Eugene. Giving up. You still up for ice cream?*

Me: *Sorry about that. Yeah, I'll text you the address for the ice cream shop. It's just a couple blocks from me, so text me when you get there and I'll walk over.*

I quickly sent him the address and returned to my computer to save my work and read through that last chapter. I had a couple things I wanted to fix before I forgot.

With the fixes done, I rushed into the bathroom to clean up a bit. We'd met on a dairy farm and had stunk to high heaven each day after working in the hot sun, but this was sort of like an actual date, so I needed to make an effort to put my best foot forward.

I'd just finished brushing my teeth when I heard my phone ring.

"Hey, you there already?" I asked.

"Yeah. Do you want me to order you something?"

I thought for a moment. "No, I'll be right there and we can order together. I happen to know what the specialties are on their secret menu."

Cliff chuckled. "Okay, I'm waiting."

I gave myself a quick look in the mirror and regretted it. I hadn't shaved in a while and my beard was a woolly mess. *Oh well, no time now.* I slipped my shoes on and headed out the door.

When I got to the ice cream shop, I saw Cliff outside, sitting under a table umbrella and talking to a young woman with two kids. He was smiling as the little girl asked him something, and then he leaned back and laughed.

The sight stopped me in my tracks. The man was downright gorgeous and seeing his face light up in amusement could stop a man's heart. When he looked over and saw me, his cheeks pinked ever so slightly. *Adorable.*

I took a seat beside him, and the woman with the two kids blushed. Apparently I wasn't the only one to think Cliff was an attractive man. But she quickly overcame it, and Cliff introduced me to her and her kids.

They continued making small talk until the woman's name was called. She rushed to get their order, then ushered her kids back to the car and tucked them in with their ice cream cones. I stifled a chuckle when she waved at us as she drove away.

"So, flirting with the locals," I said, and Cliff turned to me, surprised.

"No, she's… she's got kids."

"I hate to tell you this, but she looked at *you* like the little ones were looking at their ice cream."

Cliff barked out a laugh. "You're just jealous."

"Jealous of her or your ice cream cone?" I said with a wink and enjoyed watching Cliff's blush deepen. "So, know what you want?"

Cliff gazed at me for a long moment, his eyes flicking down to my mouth and back up. "Maybe I'm jealous of the ice cream."

His expression left no room for misinterpretation, and I swallowed hard. "Well, it's, um, it is good here," I said, my voice breaking on the last word. He laughed.

"I think I might prefer to eat a hamburger first. I basically skipped lunch."

"The burgers here are nice and greasy," I assured him as I tried to keep myself from getting embarrassed by the pressure building between my legs.

I was still full from my sandwich, so I just ordered some fries. I paid for his order without a word, which earned me a cocked eyebrow.

When we sat at the table to wait, I asked him about his day.

Cliff's face fell. "Not that good. I drove all the way up here just to find out the supplies they supposedly had in stock weren't."

He told me a little more about what he needed to fix some broken tanks, and I smiled. "Well, I might be able to help. A friend of my dad is a hydroponic pot grower."

Cliff cocked his eyebrow again, and I couldn't help but laugh. "I doubt he'll have supplies to fix a busted fiberglass tub. Why would he?" he asked.

"Oh, you don't know Tracy. The man's old-school, doesn't even own a cell phone, but he knows hydroponics inside and out. He'll either have what you need or know exactly where to find it within a hundred-mile radius."

When they called my name with our order, I said, "If you'll go get our food, I'll give him a call."

Tracy once told me he didn't answer the phone until at least the fifth ring, because if it was a salesperson, they never waited that long. When I called, it rang six times before he picked up.

"Hello!" Tracy answered.

"Hey, Trace, it's Brandon. How are you?"

"Oh, Brandon, I'm good. Nice to hear from you. You need some stuff?" he asked.

I cringed. Tracy's "stuff" was potent as hell. When I was in college, I accepted his offer once and went on one of the most intense trips of my life. "No, man," I responded. "You almost killed me last time."

Tracy laughed loud enough that Cliff, who was coming back to the table, overheard and cocked that sexy eyebrow at me again. I winked at him just to see that familiar blush return.

"Hey, my friend is starting an aquaponics operation and needs some supplies. He didn't have any luck finding them here in Eugene, and I figured you'd know where to direct him."

"Dude, don't get me started. They haven't got crap here in town," he said, and I could hear genuine frustration in his voice.

"Evidently," I said, looking at Cliff. "Do you have a moment to talk to him to see if you have anything he needs?"

"Oh, yeah, I'm happy to. What's his name?"

"Cliff," I said. Then I handed the phone over.

They chatted about what Cliff needed while I ate my fries. As I predicted, Tracy had Cliff smiling about a minute into their conversation. Tracy might be an old stoner, but he was a good guy through and through. I figured that was why he and my uptight medical-doctor dad were still best buddies after all these years.

Cliff handed me the phone back, and Tracy told me to bring him over when we were done.

"Do you really think he has all that stuff?" Cliff asked when I hung up.

"Oh yeah, I'd bet money on it. You'll see," I said and had to stifle a laugh. Tracy's place was unique, as Cliff would soon discover. "Can I ask why you're so set on this fish thing?"

That's how Chris described it when I spoke to him on the phone a few days ago. Not only had Levi called and pushed me to return to the farm, but his dad had as well, asking if I could spend the weekend helping out. Unfortunately, I had to decline due to the work I needed to do on my books. But, when I asked Chris about Cliff, he told me about him pursuing aquaponics. I could tell Chris was happy that Cliff had found something to interest him.

Cliff looked up from his burger. "Uncle Chris mentioned it, or was it Levi?"

I smiled. "Chris might've brought it up."

He sighed. "I know I'm getting caught up. I should stop and let things go, but I—" He stopped talking when his voice caught.

I hadn't anticipated such a shift in emotions, but the man seemed to deflate in front of me. "Hey, Cliff, I'm sorry. I didn't mean to discount what you're doing. I'm genuinely interested in learning more about it."

"I've been kicking myself all day for dragging everyone into this pipe dream, even you now. It's just, my dad and I were both interested in it, and he talked about doing it for years before he… well, before."

I nodded and reached over to put my hand atop his. "Hey, I'm guessing this is good for you right now, and that's great. You don't have to justify it to anybody, especially me. I'm just wondering why you're doing it at your aunt and uncle's place, why now?"

He shrugged. "Everything can be transported back when I go home, if I go home. It takes several years to get an aquaponics system set up and running properly. That's why we never did it. I'm probably being foolish, but I thought it might be a good idea to start here so I can move right into it when I return to California."

I patted his hand and then pulled mine back. "So, you're using the old barn, right? I'm sure Chris is pleased it's being used for something worthwhile. And if it makes you feel better, then why not?"

Cliff gave me a smile, and I thought it a good cue to end that conversation for now. "Do you like chocolate, strawberry, and banana?" I asked.

"Yeah, I guess. Why?"

"We're not leaving until you've had some Umpqua ice cream, as promised. Let's share a banana split. Does a caramel topping sound good?"

When he nodded, I dashed up to the counter and ordered while he finished his burger. I might not be able to fix the tragedies in his life, but I could make the here and now a little better with some sweet carbs.

Cliff

I WAS ready to throw the towel in by the time I arrived at the little ice cream shop to meet Brandon. Not only had my day started with the wreckage of the tanks, but as I drove up to Eugene, I had a lot of time to think about what I was doing and why.

I was restless. Even after long days helping my uncle with the dairy, I felt fidgety. I hadn't experienced that feeling since college, when I'd had to leave the farm. I functioned better with a daily routine, and I knew this aquaponics thing would help give my life the structure and purpose I'd been missing since I arrived in Oregon—something to work toward that provided hope for the future.

The seedlings represented what I hadn't wanted to give up, but I wasn't ignorant. I knew my life would never be the same, and even pursuing a pipe dream wouldn't make things okay again. Nothing would bring my parents back or restore what I'd lost in the fire.

I had all but talked myself out of the entire project by the time I got to Eugene. Then every store I visited was either out of the supplies they'd said they had, or what they had wasn't going to be adequate to fix the holes in my tanks.

It all seemed to confirm I was doing the wrong thing. I'd made a mistake, and the universe was trying to tell me so.

"Don't quit just 'cause it's hard," I heard my dad's voice in my head. It was so pervasive that I glanced over at the truck's passenger seat.

"So now you're following me all around Oregon," I said to Dad's ghost. Of course I didn't get a response, but the memory of his encouraging words made me smile for the first time that day. Not just because it felt like my dad confirmed that I should keep going, but because it felt like he was still here with me. My parents had always been staunch supporters of mine. It felt healing to believe they still were.

"I miss you and Mom so much," I said to myself before I picked up my phone and texted Brandon.

"We miss you too," I heard in response.

Even I had to admit that hearing my parents' ghosts might be considered woo-woo, but it was comforting to still have them around, even if only in my mind. And on days like this, I needed that comfort.

By the time Brandon arrived at the ice cream shop, I was in a much better mood.

I ended up venting to him about the day, not expecting more than a hopefully sympathetic ear, and he seemed to have an epiphany regarding my troubles. When he put me on the phone with his friend, I was pleasantly surprised the man knew exactly what I was talking about for patching the tubs. And then Brandon and I finished sharing a banana split, which was very romantic, and I followed him to his friend's place.

Being a farmer, you learn quickly not to judge another person's farm on first impressions alone, but damn, Tracy's place looked like it'd been vacant for years. It looked like it could even be condemned.

Rusted-out cars sat permanently parked in front of a sagging barn on its last legs. An overgrown driveway led to a big wooden fence that looked like its owner had started painting every year but with a different color each time. The old trailer home that sat on the other side of the fence was on the verge of being swallowed by blackberry bushes and appeared to have been vacant for decades.

"Where has Brandon brought me?" I said to myself.

"Don't judge a book by its cover." This time, the voice I heard was distinctly my mother's.

I laughed out loud. "Yeah, like you wouldn't be judging this," I said to the empty truck.

I could almost feel the playful slap to the back of my head like my mom had done when I was a snarky teenager. She never popped me hard, but she'd occasionally bop my head when I was being a jerk.

Just as I was about to get out of the truck, the gate began to open, and I followed Brandon as he drove through. If the derelict property I'd seen from outside the fence had shocked me, what I saw after I passed through the gate caused my mouth to drop open.

Following a bend in the road, just beyond the old trailer, the overgrown driveway changed to a paved path along a tree-lined valley. A small bridge crossed a little stream before the road wound up the other side.

It was picturesque and the opposite of what I expected.

I followed Brandon to the top of a hill, where I was in for another surprise. The area opened onto a set of greenhouses lined up behind a midcentury brick home—all immaculately maintained.

Brandon got out of his vehicle and waited for me to join him.

"What the hell?" I whispered when I got close.

He smiled but didn't have time to answer before a white-haired fiftyish guy with a pointed beard and handlebar mustache came out the front door, smiling from ear to ear.

"Brandon, you brought a guest. Does he like to smoke?"

Brandon huffed a laugh. "That, I don't know." When he turned to me, I shrugged.

"No, not often. I'll decline the offer, but thank you."

The older man laughed and then took my hand and shook it. "I'm Tracy Morris. You must be Cliff. Come on in, and I'll give you a tour of my operation."

I followed Brandon and Tracy around the greenhouses with my mouth agape. "We're a Tier II operation in here, where I do all my hydroponic production, as well as outside, where I grow in the soil."

It was remarkable. A hydroponic wet dream, pun intended. Not that I wanted to grow pot, but this operation was state of the art regardless.

"This is a competitive business, but I've been doing this a long time and have built up a reputation," Tracy said. "I'm known for my specialty plants, and people buy mine because of the quality of the product."

"What Tracy's not telling you is he had a following *before* it was technically legal for him to have one."

Tracy winked at Brandon and touched his nose.

I decided it was best to avoid that conversation. Besides, I could tell the old guy was doing pretty damned well if he could afford to run all this.

"So, you're having trouble with some old tanks, huh?" Tracy asked me as we came out of the last greenhouse.

"Yeah, I ordered some off the internet, but they were damaged upon delivery."

He nodded and led us around an old outbuilding that looked like it had been a lean-to for cows once upon a time. "You can have any of this, if you're interested. These were my old tanks before I switched them out for my new systems."

Once again, I stood with mouth agape. Hundreds of rubber cattle tanks were stacked around the back of the building. "Why do you have all this?" I asked.

"I was a novice when I started, so I was growing in what's called a deep water system. I mean, it worked well enough, but now I've advanced, and we have all these just sitting here disintegrating."

I knew there were tens of thousands of dollars in equipment sitting in front of me. Way more than I would need even after I got everything set up. "How much do you want?" I asked. My heart was beating a mile a minute, waiting for him to name his price.

Tracy looked at me for a moment before he said, "How about the same as you paid for the broken fiberglass tanks? Unless you want to just repair yours. If so, I'm sure I've got what you need for that around here too."

"What? No! I mean, if you're serious about the cost, I'll absolutely buy these from you."

I couldn't believe my good fortune, or Tracy's generosity. These were, like, premier tanks for my project. Each tank would've cost me over a hundred dollars new. He was practically giving them to me for pennies on the dollar.

Tracy held out his hand, and I quickly grabbed it for a shake. "Good, we've got ourselves a deal," he said. "Now, come look at my old plant equipment. I think that could be used for aquaponics as well."

By the time we looked at everything and agreed on a final price, I had nearly all of the essential parts I needed to begin my aquaponic system.

Tracy could have made three or four times what he was selling it all to me for, but as my dad had said repeatedly as I was growing up, "Don't kick a gift horse in the mouth."

I was definitely not going to do that. I was going to take the blessing for what it was.

I shook Tracy's hand again and thanked him profusely when he told me his guys would bring the stuff to Uncle Chris's farm sometime next week. "I'll call when they're free," he told me.

When we were headed to our vehicles, I couldn't hold back. I grabbed Brandon in a bear hug. "Thank you so much."

Brandon's expression when he drew back was pure lust. I almost went in for the kiss, but I heard Tracy coming up behind us. "Hey, boys, I just talked to my guy with the truck. He said he could come by tomorrow. Is that too soon?"

"Hell no," I yelled. "Man, I don't know how to thank you."

"Oh, no need to thank me. I need to get rid of this stuff, and I might have an ulterior motive."

I froze. Well, here it came. I should've known this was all too good to be true.

"You're doing something I've been thinking about for a while. I'd like to offer an organic marijuana product but haven't had the wherewithal to try it on my own. So, if you're successful and wouldn't mind an old guy following you around for a few days, I'd like to come learn how to do what you're doing."

I couldn't help but laugh. "Sir, you come visit anytime, and if you do get started and I have extra fish, I'd be happy to help you start your seed stock."

"That sounds like a great plan," Tracy said. "Now, you two can get back to kissing. I'll just go on in and pretend like I'm not watching out the window."

I almost choked on my tongue.

Brandon leaned his head back and laughed out loud. "You're a lecherous old man, Tracy."

"Hey, I resemble that remark," Tracy said as he waved, still smiling, and disappeared into his house.

"Um, I'm sorry," I said, embarrassed.

"No, Tracy was giving me what for. I once caught him kissing my uncle and accidentally told my dad about it. Since then, it's been free game between Tracy and me."

"Tracy is gay? Are he and your uncle together?"

He laughed again as we continued walking toward our vehicles. "Tracy is bisexual, but Uncle Joe is a total rake. Tracy dumped him years ago and now refuses to be anywhere near him. Currently, Tracy is dating a woman. He swears it's not long-term, but I think he's a bit stuck on this one."

"Cool," I said, still reeling from the embarrassment. "Regardless, the man is making my project a real possibility. I owe him big-time!"

Brandon clapped me on the back, which made it clear our moment was over. "Trust me when I say Tracy meant what he said. He'll want to see your operation and learn more about it. He's been a pot-smoking Gen X hippie his entire life, but he's also a serious businessman, which is why this operation is as successful as it is."

"Speaking of that, what the hell is going on with the entrance to this place? I seriously thought it should be condemned."

Brandon laughed again. "That's his way of deterring unwanted guests. He says a lot of the growers have had vandalism issues. People come up to his property and all they see is a junkyard. They can vandalize all they want, and no one would ever know what's farther up the road."

I chuckled at the truth of that. I'd certainly been fooled by it.

"Want to come back to my place?" Brandon asked, and I stopped at the door to my truck.

"Yes, but no. I need to get back and prep Uncle Chris for the arrival of all this stuff. Can I get a raincheck?"

Brandon looked disappointed but nodded. "Yeah, but I'll hold you to it. Next time you come to town, I'd like to take you on a proper date."

I couldn't help the giddy smile that crossed my face. "I'd like that very much."

"Good, then it's a date." Brandon leaned over and kissed me, which made me blush and want to jump him right here in front of his friend's house.

Instead I forced myself to climb into my truck. "I look forward to it," I said as I shut the door.

I didn't need to follow Brandon back, so I waved as I drove down the winding path, out the gate, and back through the junkyard.

It looked even worse coming from this direction. But I had to admit that Tracy was smart to use smoke and mirrors to deflect attention.

I'd been lucky as hell to meet him and was feeling good as I pulled onto the main road. I glanced at the empty seat next to me and sighed. "Thanks, Dad, for not letting me give up."

The hairs on the back of my neck stood up as I felt a hand on my shoulder, just like Dad used to do when I said something like that. For a moment, I let myself believe it was actually my dad, before the feeling dissipated and I set out for Wilcox alone.

Brandon

WHEN CLIFF drove off, I decided to hang back and chat with Tracy. Of course he opened the door for me as soon as I set foot on his stoop.

"You really were watching, weren't you?" I asked.

He smirked. "I plead the Fifth, Your Honor. So, wanna talk about it?" Tracy was my dad's best friend, but he'd been one of my confidants since I first realized I was gay. I could talk to my parents about a lot of things, but boys had never been one of them.

"Yeah, sorta."

"Well, good, come on in. I've made some cookies."

"Uncle Tracy, I'm not interested in getting high."

"Damn, boy, you wound me. Not everything I bake has weed in it." I cocked my eyebrow, and he laughed. "Okay, well, most things do. But I baked these for Lucinda's kid. Hell, they're even gluten free."

"Wow, you've become domestic. Maybe you're the one needing to talk." Tracy flipped me off as I followed him into his kitchen. "For real, tell me about you and Lucinda. It's sounding serious."

He settled onto the stool across from me, gestured for me to sit, and slid a plate of fresh cookies toward me. "You pry worse than your dad. It's almost like you two are genetically related." I chuckled but waited for him to respond. "I do like her, a lot. In fact, I haven't liked someone this much since your uncle. But once bitten, twice shy."

I reached over and squeezed Tracy's hand. "Uncle Joe did you bad, we all know that, but he shouldn't be the last person you let yourself love. If you like Lucinda, you should go for it."

We sat silently and ate our cookies. I knew Tracy was waiting for me to talk to him about what I'd stuck around for. So, when I finished my second cookie, I took a deep breath and let it out slowly.

"Well, you know Cliff, right?"

"Yep, just all but gave him a bunch of equipment, so yeah, I know him."

I ignored the comment and continued. "I like him, but he's a bit skittish. That and my best friend Levi, who happens to be his cousin, is pushing us together at every turn, which makes him even more skittish."

Tracy picked up another cookie and took a bite. I had seen this tactic before. He'd nibble on something, usually with weed, to give me time to get my thoughts out before he responded.

"I'm afraid if I push too much, he'll go running. But if I don't push at all, nothing's gonna happen."

"He sure didn't look unsure about you a moment ago out front."

I chuckled. "He's got a lot on his plate. His parents died recently, and then he lost his family farm in California to wildfires. That's why he's here, actually, because there's literally nothing left for him back home. I think he's grasping at straws, and I don't want to be something he goes after for fun."

Tracy leaned back in his seat, smiling like the cat that ate the canary. "So, you want him to grasp for your straw, but you don't want him to run away after he gets it."

I closed my eyes and shook my head. "Tracy, I swear you are the crudest man on the planet."

He laughed, then patted my hand. "Listen, I think you're overthinking this. If the boy has all that shit going on, maybe all he can think about right now is relieving the pressure. And if you go into this trying to start a relationship, you'll end up scaring him off for real. Just be his friend. Love up on him some, if that's what you both want, and don't try to make it more than it is."

I sighed. Tracy was right. "I'm just tired of the dating scene. Most guys are looking for a quick roll in the hay, and I've rolled in it a lot. It'd be nice to meet someone I could do that with more than once before they run off to roll with someone else."

"I'll repeat, you're overthinking it. I get that you're looking for something more, but let things move as they will." Tracy got up to fill glasses of water for us, and when he sat back down, I saw sadness cross his face. "Listen, Brandon, I made the mistake of pushing things with Joe. I had this vision of spending my life with him out in his cabin, looking over the river, smoking, and just loving life, but it wasn't what he wanted. It never was what he wanted. As a result, I ruined any chance of us being friends."

He took a drink of water and then sighed. "I miss him. Not just as a boyfriend. I miss his friendship. I wish now that's all I ever pursued. So my advice as an old guy who has experience with fucking up is let this happen if it's meant to happen. Don't push, pry, or try to make it anything but what it is. Just enjoy yourself and your time with him while he's in your life. You'll never regret it."

Tracy got up then, walked toward the back of his kitchen, picked up a battered old Scooby Doo cookie jar, and put it down beside me. "Now, if you want something to ease your mind, these are my cookies *not* baked for teenagers."

I laughed, stood up, and pulled Tracy into a hug. "I love you, man. But no on the weed cookies this time. Maybe next time, when I don't have a shit-ton of work to finish for my publisher."

Tracy shrugged and walked me toward the front door.

"Let's give the boy a couple of days to get the delivery. Then I'd like to go with you to his farm to see how he's going to set all this up. I wasn't pulling his chain. I want to see this whole aquaponics thing in action. I'll let him make all the mistakes figuring it out, and then I can avoid it when I set my system up."

I laughed. "Ever the businessman."

"Hey, man, gotta make the money."

I hugged him and headed to my car. Tracy was always the guy I turned to when I needed to talk things out. And as usual, Tracy was right. As difficult as it might be to do, I needed to give Cliff space and let things happen naturally. If that meant we'd only ever be friends, so be it.

Cliff

I CALLED my uncle to tell him my news before I hit the highway. "Do you think you and Levi can give me a hand preparing for the tanks?" I asked.

"Of course," Uncle Chris said, and sure enough, he and Levi were waiting for me as I drove up the driveway. Uncle Chris had put heat lamps in the barn. We didn't need heat in this weather, but they made good spotlights. Together we cleaned out the lean-to part of the barn that had a concrete floor strong enough to support the weight of the tanks. Luckily the greenhouse was attached to the edge of the lean-to, so it worked out perfectly. Otherwise the timber floor of the main barn wouldn't have been able to support the weight.

Aunt Sue came out to help sweep up just as we finished moving the last of the stuff out of the lean-to and into the main barn. "This is all very exciting," she said. "Your mom used to talk about how you and your dad were into this." She paused, and I could tell she was holding back emotions.

I looked away to give her a moment and to avoid letting my own sorrow get the better of me. I needed to stay focused on getting everything ready before my poor plants got too old to transition into the aquaponics system.

I worked late into the night, long after Levi and my aunt and uncle turned in. There was so much to do. Once the lean-to was cleaned, I rinsed the walls with the pressure washer. I didn't want to invite disease into the system because I neglected to start in a clean environment. It was a barn, after all.

I moved all the plants back into the lean-to and washed down the inside of the greenhouse. I still needed to order a shade cloth for the exterior before I washed off all the years of debris on that side, but for now I could have a nice clean interior space to start.

When I was done, I looked around the old greenhouse and sighed. I would need to add gravel to the floors. The dirt floor wouldn't be good once the systems were up and running. Gravel didn't cost much, and because Tracy had given me a heck of a deal on his old equipment, I could afford to throw a little money at it.

I'd assured Aunt Sue I'd be in to eat the supper she'd put aside for me. I just wanted to do a few more things before I turned in for the night.

When she disappeared out the barn's front door, it was almost as if I could hear my mom saying, "Just don't get carried away."

I smiled at the thought of my mother's advice still actively influencing me. She would tell me not to put all my eggs in this one basket just because I was in a bad place. I tended to go all in with a project, and it was a reminder that this wasn't my home, not my property. This was my uncle and aunt's place and I was simply a guest here.

"I won't, Mom," I whispered, then collapsed on the old milking stool in the corner of the lean-to. I'd brought it into the greenhouse when I first arrived because it was comfortable and gave me a place to just sit with my plants.

This outlandish idea wouldn't fix all my problems, but at least I now had a project to keep myself occupied while I figured out what to do with my own farm. Everything I'd purchased could be transported back to California when I was ready. I knew there were decisions to be made, and when it was time, I'd make them. But for the here and now, I could put my mind to something that made me happy, something my dad and I used to dream about doing together.

I CRAWLED into bed around two in the morning. The next morning my aunt woke me up shortly before ten saying a truck was out front.

"Already?" I asked, surprised. I didn't expect Tracy's delivery until later in the day.

As I came out, the driver was unloading the tanks next to the barn while Uncle Chris gave him directions. "Wow, that was fast," I said to the driver.

He chuckled. "Well, you can call Tracy Morris if you didn't expect this to be here first thing this morning. That guy never sleeps."

He used a crane to lift the tubs off the bed while he explained that he and Tracy had loaded the equipment early that morning so he could get the items delivered as soon as possible. "Tracy said he didn't want to delay you getting on with your project," the driver told me.

I couldn't stop myself from smiling. The driver had everything unloaded within an hour, and I was just about to call the gravel people Uncle Chris had recommended so we could move the tubs into place when I got a phone call from Walt.

"Hey, Walt," I said. "It's been a few days."

"Hey, buddy. So, they're gonna let us return to our properties to survey the damage. We just got word this morning. I'm on your contact list, so they called me about your land too."

"When can we go back?"

"Martha and I are going to drive up there next Monday. Do you wanna meet us there?" he asked.

I could feel the bile rising in my throat and barely had enough time to pull the phone away from my mouth before I puked.

"Cliff, you okay, buddy?" I heard the concern in Walt's voice through the phone.

"Let me call you back, but yeah, I'll meet you," I managed to say. Then I hurled again.

I hung up and bent over to try to stop the cold sweat that had broken out on my forehead. A moment later my aunt was by my side, pressing a cool washcloth to my head. "Hey, Cliff. Cliff, look at me."

I did as she asked, but I still felt like I could pass out. She hollered over to my uncle, and the two of them escorted me to the nearest chair on the front porch.

"What happened, son?" Uncle Chris asked.

"My old neighbor Walt just called. They're letting us back in."

Through the haze still clouding my vision, I saw their faces register understanding. "I'm sorry I overreact—"

"Don't you start," my aunt insisted. "You didn't overreact. You reacted like any normal person would. Now you sit here and I'll get you something to drink."

She disappeared into the house, and Uncle Chris sat on the glider beside me. I put my head in my hands and forced myself to calm down.

When Aunt Sue returned with a glass of water, we all sat silently on the porch. The only sound was the squeaking of the old glider.

My stomach was still pitching, but at least the cold, clammy sweat had subsided.

"I'm okay. It was just a shock." I finally leaned back in the chair.

Uncle Chris reached over and squeezed my shoulder. "Son, you're handling all this really well and I don't just mean about the farm."

I wiped away the tear that slipped out. I knew if I let loose, it might never end.

"Okay, I feel better. Let's go get to work. I don't want to sit around thinking about this. I just—"

"You just want to avoid it." Uncle Chris looked over at Aunt Sue and sighed. "Son, you can avoid it now if you wish, but take it from an old man who's seen his share of bad times—you can't avoid your emotions forever. Go work on your project, but when you're ready to talk, your aunt Sue and I are here, okay?"

I nodded. "Yeah, I will."

I had no intention of talking to them or anyone else about it. I just needed to work. Work solved most problems. Keep focused on the good, and the bad would slip away eventually.

As much as I might want it to be, I knew that wasn't true, but I was almost sure I wouldn't survive the breakdown if I let loose completely. I didn't think I had a choice but to keep it packed so deep it couldn't hurt me.

By that afternoon I had worked long and hard enough to call Walt back without falling apart. I arranged to meet him and Martha in Weaverville so we could drive together to see our farms. "Son," Martha said on speakerphone, "you should be with someone after that. Why don't you come on down to San Francisco to stay with Walt and me before going back to your aunt and uncle's?"

I'm sure Walt had told her I'd broken down on the phone earlier. I thanked Martha for the offer but explained I needed to return to Oregon as soon as possible. She wouldn't let me hang up until I gave my word that I would ask my cousin or someone else here to accompany me on the trip.

After that I threw myself into my project. I worked late, caught a few hours' sleep, and got up before my uncle. It was my new routine.

By the weekend, I'd nearly completed the last hookup to test whether the system worked.

At least I was doing something productive. If I ignored the concerned ghostly messages of my parents, who chastised me in my head for being stubborn and pushing myself too hard, so be it.

I had to focus on the future and let go of things I couldn't fix or change. That's what was important, and that's what would keep me going. At least, that's what I kept telling myself.

Brandon

WHILE REREADING my latest draft, I envisioned Cliff as the main character. A young, strong, and dashingly handsome man who pulled through the most challenging circumstances to defeat the demons in the story.

Was I ashamed of using my infatuation with Cliff to work through my writer's block? Maybe a little, but he'd said he liked my writing. I'd make sure to thank him in the acknowledgments.

I knew I'd rewrite a good portion of it, and there remained minor plot holes to fill, but I was set on the main character fighting an epic battle as a finish to the novel and a conclusion for the series. I just wasn't sure how that would look in the end.

Oh well, first draft, I thought as I sent the updated manuscript to my agent as well as my editor, with a note saying I might still rework the ending.

The moment I pressed Send on the email, I picked my phone up and dialed my best friend.

"Hey, it's Levi. Leave a message."

"Hey, buddy. I'm thinking about visiting this weekend. If you and Keya aren't busy, maybe I could come tonight. Give me a call back."

I hung up and went to shower. I'd been working nonstop for two days and barely remembered to brush my teeth, much less bathe and shave. My beard had grown thick, but unlike most guys who could get away with a full lumberjack beard, the look didn't suit me.

Hopeful and excited about spending time with a certain sexy farm boy I couldn't quite get off my mind, I sang to myself as I was getting ready.

I was disappointed Levi hadn't called back, but I could always stay with my parents or at a motel if needed. I just wanted to celebrate my progress, and I couldn't think of anyone I'd prefer to do that with more than my friends. I slotted Cliff in that category now too.

Tracy's advice came back to me, and I shook off my thoughts about rushing to define what Cliff and I were to each other.

I was almost to Wilcox when I got a text from Levi saying he and Keya were in Portland shopping. So I quickly called my dad, knowing Mom would never answer a personal call while at work.

"Hello?" he answered, and I smiled at the predictability.

"Didn't Mom tell you not to answer phone calls while you're between patients?"

"I can hang up," he said, but I could hear the humor in his voice.

"I'd prefer if you didn't. Are you going to be home tonight? I'm coming into town and need a place to crash."

"Levi not available, then?"

"What?" I asked innocently, although I knew he had my number.

I heard someone talking in the background and assumed it was Dad's medical assistant. "I'll be right there," he told her.

"Your old room is still your room, although I think it'd make a good dad cave."

"You mean mancave, and no, you already have that in the basement."

He chuckled. "Whatever. You gonna fix supper, then?"

"If you want me to order a pizza and you pay for it when it arrives, then sure, I'm happy to."

"Geez, you're still a brat."

"And you love me. Now go to work before Mom yells at both of us."

"Okay, see you tonight, son."

I'd be stuck at home with my parents tonight, so I decided to go to the farm and see what Levi's parents were up to. And by Levi's parents, I really meant Cliff.

I spotted Cliff the moment I pulled into the driveway. He was hosing down the greenhouse attached to the barn. The seasonal temperatures in Wilcox, Oregon, were the hottest on record, so it was no surprise that Cliff stood in cut-off shorts and no shirt.

Even from a distance, I could see the muscles rippling across his back as he sprayed the water over the glass.

As much as I was enjoying just watching him, I decided to walk down to the barn to see if he needed help.

As soon as he saw me, he smiled, causing my heart to race. "Hey," he said as he turned off the water.

"Hey," I replied, and for the first time, I noticed dark circles under his eyes. Without thinking, I cupped one side of his face and leaned down to kiss him. It was brief—just a tender brush of lips—but we both lingered in our shared space for a long moment.

I fought the urge to wrap my arms around him, both for comfort and to explore all that exposed skin with my palms, but I wasn't sure he was ready for me to get that handsy yet.

"I see you're making progress." I dropped my hand from his face and stepped back to gesture toward the greenhouse.

"Yeah, and you're in time to help me," he said, chuckling. "I got my shade cloth in the mail today and just finished cleaning the windows so I can have a proper shade system instead of just old dirt and grime."

I smiled at him while he showed me the clean glass. Honestly, I couldn't see what he was so excited about. Yeah, it was cleaner than it'd been in a long time, but it was still a nasty old greenhouse on the side of an old barn.

Cliff's enthusiasm was infectious, and it warmed something inside me seeing him so animated. So without comment, I helped him unfold the shade cloth while he talked about his concern that the increased temperatures might kill his plants without it.

We attached the cloth to hooks he'd installed, and I watched as he tucked in the sides and secured it with bungee cords like he'd been doing it his entire life. Of course, he said he'd grown up gardening, so maybe he had.

"Damn, it's hot enough to fry eggs out here," Cliff said, wiping sweat off his forehead. "Now that's done, how about we get out of the sun?"

I followed as he led me into the barn, and what I saw in there utterly shocked me. All the stock tanks he'd bought from Tracy were positioned and filled with water. I could hear the system running, and as my eyes adjusted to the dim light, I could tell the plumbing linking all the tanks together had also been completed.

"Damn, you work fast." I whistled.

"No rest for the wicked," he said with a smirk. "For real, though, Tracy practically giving me all this equipment was the shot in the arm I needed to make short work of it. Now for the big reveal."

I'd seen glimpses of it from outside as I helped put up the shade cloth, but now I could fully appreciate just how intricate the setup was. He'd literally taken cast-off equipment that had been sitting in Tracy's storage shed and transformed it into a fully functional operation.

"Do you already have fish?" I asked after the shock subsided.

He chuckled. "No, it'll be a while yet. I wanted to get the system up and running before I put stock in the tanks."

"Cool," I said as I walked around, inspecting. "So, you done for the day, then?"

Cliff looked around and shrugged. "I mean, I should get more stuff done." When I caught his eye and grinned wickedly at him, he cocked an eyebrow in the way I'd come to adore. "I can be done, though. What do you have in mind?"

"Swimming," I said, and he laughed.

"I'm assuming you don't mean in my plant tanks," he teased, and I rolled my eyes. "So, like, at a pool? I didn't know Wilcox had one."

I tried to look appalled. "Really, dude, what kind of farm kid are you? Haven't you ever been to a swimming hole?"

He chuckled. "We didn't have any in my neck of the woods."

"Grab your swim trunks, and I'll show you the best place in the whole county for a cool dip."

I saw sadness creep across his face and realized he likely hadn't brought any. No doubt something as frivolous as swim trunks would've been the last thing on his mind to grab when fleeing from a fire. I needed to unstick my foot from my mouth, and fast. "As it happens, I need a new pair," I said, hoping he didn't see through me. "If you'd like to come along, we could pop into town to shop real quick."

"That sounds great. I need a pair as well," he said, a bright smile returning to his handsome face.

With that, I followed Cliff into the house to let Sue know he was leaving with me.

"When will you boys be back?" she asked.

"Not sure. We're going to town to grab some swim trunks, then for a dip under the twin bridges between here and Levi's place."

"Want to have dinner with us, then?" she asked, and I had to decline because I'd promised I'd have supper with my parents.

Cliff went upstairs to change out of his sweaty work clothes, and Sue pulled me outside onto the porch.

"Thank goodness you're here," she said. "He's working himself to death, and nothing we say has made a difference."

"What's going on?" I asked, concerned.

She peered through the glass on the front door and, seeing Cliff hadn't come downstairs yet, said, "He got word from his neighbor down in California. They are going to go survey the damage on Monday. He's—"

Sue broke off as she caught sight of Cliff coming down the stairs. When he came out the front door, he smiled at his aunt. "Guess I'll see you later."

"You two have fun and don't worry about hurrying back. I'll put your supper in the microwave if you're late."

It only took a few minutes to drive from the farm to Wilcox and purchase our trunks and a couple of beach towels.

We drove back to the farm, and I parked in Chris and Sue's driveway. We changed into our trunks before I led Cliff down the worn path to the twin covered bridges and my childhood swimming hole. There was rarely anyone around, and knowing Levi and Keya were in Portland meant it was mostly private. That's exactly what I wanted. I just hoped Cliff was on the same page.

It only took a few minutes for Cliff to strip off his shirt and shoes and wade into the cool water.

He sighed as he went in chest-deep, then turned to float on his back. "Damn, this feels good," he said, and I quickly swam over to him. We played around, mostly splashing each other and laughing. The weariness on his face began to subside. Clearly, this was exactly what the guy needed.

I swam under the water then and dunked him. "Hey," he said, coming up for air and splashing me. "That's so not fair."

I laughed and tried to dunk him again, but it wasn't as easy now that he knew what I was up to. We wrestled in the water, then lay back and floated side by side, gazing up at the sky through the canopy.

"It's beautiful here," he said, sounding reverent.

"Yeah, and peaceful too, when Levi and Xander aren't here."

He chuckled. "Levi is a lot. I'll have to take your word for it about your friend Xander."

We floated a while longer and then climbed onto a nearby rock, grabbed our towels, and lay in the dappled shade.

"Do you have any siblings?" I asked. Levi hadn't mentioned it, and I hoped the question didn't seem like I was prying.

"No. I always wanted siblings, but Mom had complications during my birth. I'm not sure of the details, but basically, after I was born, she was done," he said.

I could hear the sadness in Cliff's voice, and I leaned up on my elbow to face him as he spoke.

"I'm an only child too. Until we moved here, I was mostly alone," I said. "Then Levi and I became friends, and after that, I never really felt alone. In a lot of ways, Levi and Xander are like my brothers."

Cliff looked over at me then, longing evident in his expression. "I wish I had someone to...." His voice trailed off and he closed his eyes. I fought the urge to touch him, to run a soothing hand up and down his bare arm in comfort. As strong as he was, he also seemed so fragile at times. "Well, never mind all that. This is a good day. No need to spoil it with a bunch of sad shit."

"Shit you need to talk about?"

"God no. Talking is overrated," he said. In an instant, his serious expression disappeared and he cast me a wicked grin. "However, what we started outside your friend's house the other day might be worth revisiting."

I didn't need to be asked twice. Placing my palm on his firm, tanned chest, I leaned over and let my mouth slide over his.

He wrapped his hand around the back of my neck and pulled me closer, deepening the kiss. "Mmm," I moaned, really getting into it, but then a car rumbled across the bridge above us.

"Damn," I whispered as I broke our kiss and pressed my forehead against his chest. "Can't get past first base with you, it seems."

That made him laugh out loud and sit up. Then he leaned over to whisper, "If you're wanting to play baseball, I'm all in."

My cock took notice, and I would've been happy to caveman him right here in front of God and the world, except I didn't think getting arrested for nudity and public sex was best for either of us right now.

"I'm game. I even have a condom in my car."

Cliff laughed again. "I'm sure you do."

He was about to pull away when I kissed him again. "Don't get me wrong, I want to play," I said quietly into his ear. "And when we go all the way around the bases, I will make you feel *everything*."

That sounded cheesy even to me, but when Cliff blushed and shivered, I knew I'd said the right thing.

"If you want to go around the river bend over there, I'm up for some exploration," he said.

I swallowed hard as I glanced downstream. Unfortunately, as secluded as our little oasis felt, we were still very much public. The sound of another car crossing the bridge confirmed as much. Then I remembered the barn.

"I have another idea. Put your shoes on," I said, and we both quickly dried off, grabbed our stuff, and raced down the riverside path leading to Xander's farm.

The barn that I envisioned converting into a home had remained the same for years. The stalls were still mostly intact, although a few of the gates had fallen over. The tack room that once held saddles and other riding supplies was empty, but someone, probably Xander, had filled it with hay. On more than one occasion, I'd sat in that room, pondering life.

I led Cliff back there and immediately pulled him to me, kissing him hard while rubbing my hands up and down his muscular arms.

"God, I want you," I admitted as we came up for air. I briefly saw Cliff smile before he knelt before me, and I sucked in a breath.

My swim trunks were still damp, but he tugged them down in one movement, releasing my hard cock. Everything about me was excited to know this man.

He glanced up at me, and when we made eye contact, he took my length into his mouth. "Aaah," I moaned and leaned back against a support post to stay upright. I continued gasping as he licked and sucked my shaft. "God, your mouth feels so good, Cliff."

He took me to the root and moaned, making me shiver, and the sound of him taking pleasure in giving it to me fried my brain.

I pulled out of his mouth, kicked off my trunks, and pulled him up to standing, determined not to be the only one receiving a blow job. I desperately needed to taste him too.

He laughed when I sank to my knees and jerked his shorts down in one quick motion, just as he'd done to me. His laughter died on a cry of pleasure when I swallowed his cock all the way to the back of my throat.

God, I loved giving blow jobs. Feeling another man's cock in my mouth was incomparable to anything else.

Cliff's natural masculine scent encircled me, and I buried my nose at the base of his cock, swallowing him down again as I went.

When Cliff stumbled, I grabbed his asscheeks to steady him, then pulled back and motioned him down to my level.

I lined my cock up to his mouth and moaned happily when he took it, then positioned myself over him before taking his cock into mine.

We lay opposite each other on the hay-covered floor and sucked one another into happy oblivion. Sure, the hay scratched a little, but the all-consuming pleasure of being with Cliff outweighed any minor discomfort. Judging by his guttural moans, he was enjoying giving me head as much as I was him.

I could tell he was getting close, and his excited sounds spurred me closer to the edge. In perfect synchronicity, I blew my load down his throat as he did the same. I shuddered twice as my cock emptied. Cliff licked me clean as I swallowed the load he'd given me.

I righted myself so we were facing each other before we both fell onto our backs and lay there enjoying euphoric post-sex bliss.

I finally leaned up on my elbow and looked at Cliff, taking in how gorgeous he was, all blissed out. "That was too fast, but nice."

Cliff chuckled. "It's been a while and, you know, stress. Next time, well, if there's a next time, I'll try to last longer."

"That wasn't a complaint, just an observation." I ran my hand over his pecs and toyed with a nipple, causing him to hum. "And as God is my witness, there *will* be a next time."

Cliff grinned up at me, and the sight made my heart tumble. Then he pulled me on top of him and kissed me. "Then we agree, there will be a take two."

After we kissed for bit longer and the afterglow of our mutual orgasms wore off, lying in the hay really did become unbearable. We got dressed, grabbed our things, and walked hand in hand back to my car, which was still parked at Sue and Chris's place. I opened the car door just as my phone rang. I almost groaned when I saw who it was, but I didn't want to take away from the fantastic experience I'd just had with Cliff.

"Hey, Mom, what's up?" I answered, putting the phone on speaker.

"I hear you're home and coming for supper. Why don't we go to Pete's?" she asked, surprising me.

Pete's drive-up diner was full of saturated fats and simple carbohydrates my mom constantly complained about. I quickly agreed. "I'm with, um, Cliff. He's Sue and Chris's nephew. Do you mind if I invite him?"

"That'd be excellent," she said, but I could hear the note of shock in her voice.

My mom wasn't in any way anti-gay. If I'd sprung a woman on her, she'd have acted the same way. No, Sarah Forest was a woman who planned, and as a result, any partner meeting my parents for the first time would always be a big freaking deal.

"Actually, I can't," Cliff said beside me. "I'm still preoccupied with work, but thank you."

"Mom, never mind about the plus-one. See you tonight." I hung up before she could respond.

"Sorry about that," I said to him, masking my disappointment.

He looked at me funny. "About what?"

"Me springing dinner with my parents on you and Mom being weird."

He shrugged. "It wasn't anything."

"It was, but in her defense, she hates surprises."

Cliff smiled. "It's not a problem, truly. Just so you know, I liked this afternoon's surprise," he said and kissed me again, causing all the blood to flow back down to my nether regions. When Sue opened the door and closed it just as quickly, we both chuckled.

"I should probably go in," Cliff said, and I nodded.

"Probably wise. She's gonna have a bunch of questions."

"Well, we don't have to tell my aunt everything we've been up to, right?" he asked, and the adorable way he scrunched up his face at the prospect made me laugh out loud.

"Only if you promise we'll take another trip around the bases sometime soon."

He leaned up, whispered in my ear, "I'm game whenever you are, slugger," then turned and walked to the front door.

Cliff

I NEEDED that, much more than I'd let myself believe. The quaint setting, the refreshing swim, the hot sixty-nine blow job. It was more like a scene out of one of Brandon's books than real life—at least, my real life.

I sighed at the thought. Since Walt had told me we'd soon be let back in to see what was left of our farms, I'd pretty much fallen apart inside.

I hadn't slept, and when I had, it was one nightmare after another. My aquaponics project kept me busy, but Uncle Chris and Aunt Sue were right—I could only use that to run from reality for so long. I suspected Brandon pulling me away for the afternoon was intended to take my mind off things. To his credit, he'd succeeded with flying colors.

I wished our day together hadn't had to end, because I could've used more of him. I had a lot more plans for him than just a literal quick roll in the hay, but that'd have to wait.

Aunt Sue was smiling the moment I walked into the house. She winked but resisted asking me the twenty questions I knew she had, since she'd seen Brandon and me kissing earlier.

"You still planning to help me prepare supper tonight? Should we make an extra plate?" she asked. "Either way, we best not make your uncle wait. He gets grumpy when he's hungry."

My mom had been a liberated woman in every sense of the word and made it clear that a boy needed to know his way around the kitchen as well as the fields. So I'd had years of training in cooking, and I made a point of helping Aunt Sue here and there when she'd let me.

"Brandon is going out to eat with his parents tonight," I said. "But yes to me helping with supper. I just need to grab a shower. Then I'll be at your command."

She snapped a dish towel at me, telling me to scoot, and I chuckled as I rushed upstairs. As I washed off the remnants of our hay roll, I thought of how amazing it would be to shower with Brandon. Unfortunately I couldn't dwell too much on that or I'd risk supper being late. I cleaned up quickly, dressed, and went downstairs to help.

I'd just pulled a big casserole dish of Aunt Sue's homemade mac and cheese out of the oven when I heard the front door open. Uncle Chris poked his head through the kitchen doorway a moment later.

"Hey, Uncle Chris," I said as I gathered up plates and silverware to help Aunt Sue set the table.

"Well, you look better. Did you finally finish your project?"

I shook my head while Aunt Sue followed me to the table. "No, Brandon came over and whisked him off to the old watering hole," she said. I was surprised that she didn't say anything about the kiss she'd witnessed.

Uncle Chris grinned. "That brings back good memories. Me and my buddies used to swim down there when we were just kids. Was a popular place back then. Truth be known, we'd always hoped to find a few of the ladies lurking around too."

Aunt Sue smiled. "Found you one too, didn't ya?"

Uncle Chris slipped out of his boots, then pulled his wife into his arms. "I caught me quite the mermaid."

"Pfft, mermaid, what you caught is a housekeeper, laundress, and overall workaholic," she teased.

"Mmm, but you do it all so well," he said. Then he kissed her. "You said you always wanted to be a farmer's wife."

"I said that, but I was lying."

Uncle Chris leaned back on his heels and laughed. "Bit late for that, my sweet wife."

"Maybe," she said. Then she kissed him back and sent him to get cleaned up.

My aunt and uncle were as fond of each other as my parents had been. I remembered as a kid, the few times we'd been able to get away to come visit, Uncle Chris and Aunt Sue would sit curled up together on one side of the room and Mom and Dad on the other.

Levi and I were usually in the middle, either playing or arguing about something.

Those were great memories. Sometimes I wished we lived closer.

"Cliff, honey, are you just gonna stare at the plates or pass them out?"

"Oh, sorry," I said. "Just thinking about when we used to visit over the holidays."

Aunt Sue's smile widened. "We all loved those days. It was so hard for your dad to get away for any stretch of time, and we could never leave due to the cows needing to be tended."

"Well, even though it wasn't often, I remember every trip here, and they're good memories."

"Yes, and we're gonna make a whole bunch more too," she replied. Then she dashed into the kitchen to bring in the casserole dish.

"Mmm, I'm ready to dig into that. I'm starving after swimming all afternoon."

"I'm sure you are," Uncle Chris said as he reappeared freshly showered and took his seat. "So, where's Brandon? He seldom misses a meal."

"His parents roped him into going out to eat."

"Oh, that's good. I know he doesn't get to spend much time with them. I was just in to get my annual physical, and his dad said we get to see Brandon more than they do." My uncle chuckled.

"Well, that's 'cause you work the poor boy to death," Aunt Sue said and playfully patted her husband on the shoulder as she served us.

"So, I took a look at that operation you got in the barn," Uncle Chris said, turning to me. "That's an impressive setup you've created."

"Yeah, I got a heck of a deal on the equipment. Otherwise, it would've been mostly piecemeal."

"Speaking of, I talked to our neighbor, and she wants to buy all your beat-up tubs. Reckon she's gonna use them as raised beds or something."

"Really? That's great. I wasn't sure what I was gonna do with them."

"Well, if she takes them, they'll be turned into something remarkable," Aunt Sue said. "I swear that woman can turn pure trash into something beautiful."

"If you don't mind," Uncle Chris said to me, "I'll pay you for them and just give them to her. She supplies us with eggs and vegetables all summer and refuses to take any money, so when we can repay her in other ways, I'm always glad to do it."

"Seeing as I've been eating high on the hog since getting here, how about you give them to her from both of us."

Uncle Chris nodded appreciatively and switched the subject to what was happening at the dairy.

I listened halfheartedly as he complained about the price of milk going down again. The sale of Umpqua Dairy to a company out of California had all the regional dairy farmers up in arms for fear of losing their main buyer. "Been talking to Tillamook, said they might be able to take any surplus milk we have," Uncle Chris said. "It sure is a long drive from here, though. Might not be worth it in the long run."

"Reckon you gotta do what you gotta do for the time being." Aunt Sue grabbed our empty plates and took them to the kitchen.

"Are you concerned you won't be able to keep the farm going?" I asked, but then I gulped at my audacity. It was a conversation my family had frequently. Would we make enough to pay the bills that year? Could—and should—we expand to try to make more, or reduce our operations to save costs? Bankruptcy always seemed to be lurking around every corner. I knew dairies were at just as much risk as the rest of the agriculture market, but I'd never spoken so boldly with my uncle about his business before.

Uncle Chris glanced toward the kitchen to ensure Aunt Sue was still out of earshot before he said, "Son, it's not looking good. All the local dairies are holding on by a shoestring as it is." He sighed deeply and shook his head. "But we'll figure it out one way or another, always do. Generations of this family toiled to keep our dairy churning. Throwing in the towel ain't in my blood. I reckon I'll find the solution that keeps it running another hundred years, just need some patience and time to think."

I nodded, acknowledging the struggle. Mom and Dad had tried to talk me out of farming, but like Uncle Chris, it was in my blood.

Aunt Sue plopped a piece of homemade cherry pie in front of me then, and dang, I could've kissed her where she stood. She handed Uncle Chris a container of whipped cream. He covered his pie with it and then passed it to me. I did the same, which made my aunt chuckle. "Want some pie with that whipped cream?"

"Oh, that's what makes it good," Uncle Chris said.

"Humph, I figured what made it good was the work I put into making it," she replied, her tone sounding more frustrated than teasing.

Uncle Chris apparently caught it too, because a deep crease formed between his brows. "Honey, you feeling overworked?"

She sighed. "Yeah, but don't mind me. Caroline and Kyle were here today telling me about all the amazing places they've traveled to, and I got a little jealous."

Uncle Chris's expression turned from concerned to sad. "Well, if you want to get away, I can probably get the boys to hold down the fort. Just got to get past the early days with the calves and—"

Aunt Sue put her hand up. "Chris, honey, I don't need none of that, I was just being silly. Finish your pie, then we'll go sit on the porch. Temps are supposed to drop tonight in front of a rainstorm that's expected to come in."

"I wouldn't bet on that," Uncle Chris said. Oregon didn't get good rains most summers. Like northern California, the rain came during the fall and winter months. The drought we'd had all winter and spring would likely continue. Add in the intense heat wave we were dealing with this year and, well, that's why I no longer had a farm. Wildfires were raging out of control, and predictions were such that they would just get worse and worse.

I didn't want to think about the devastation I'd have to face soon enough. I was about to help clear the table when I got a call. When I pulled my phone out of my pocket, I saw it was Brandon and hit Accept.

"Hey," I said.

"Hey back. What're you doing right now? Mind if I come over?" he asked.

"Um, well," I said, glancing at the used plates and silverware that I'd planned to help wash.

"Go on," Aunt Sue said, "your uncle and I have this handled."

I nodded my thanks, then stepped out onto the front porch for some privacy. "What do you have in mind?" I asked, blushing because I knew what thoughts were flowing through my own mind.

"My friend owns an old drive-in that's been converted into an RV park but still has the big screen up, and he invited us over. Wanna come watch a movie with me?"

"Sure, that sounds fun, but I can't be out too late."

He laughed. "It's a rerun of the original *Willy Wonka and the Chocolate Factory*, which isn't a long film. But we gotta hurry. They start the movie at dusk."

"Okay. Want to swing by in about fifteen minutes?" I asked. When he agreed, I quickly said bye and rushed back inside to help with the dishes.

Brandon picked me up right on time, and we were only on the road a couple of minutes before he pulled into the entrance to the property across the street from Uncle Chris and Aunt Sue's and kissed me deeply. For a moment, I thought maybe the drive-in was a ruse to get me alone, and I would not have objected. But then he broke the kiss, admitted he needed that again because I'd been on his mind all through dinner with his parents, and pulled back onto the road.

That night we had a lot of fun. It was officially our second date, and an unconventional choice at that. The campers at the converted RV park were mostly older, so there weren't many kids around. Brandon laced our fingers together halfway through the movie and didn't let go.

By the time we were headed back to the dairy, I was happy but ready for bed. When Brandon parked in front of the house, it was my turn to lean over the console to kiss him.

"Thanks for today," I said. "It helped more than you know."

"Anytime. I enjoyed myself too, if that wasn't obvious already." Brandon rubbed the back of his neck. "So, Mom wanted me to ask if you'd join us for supper tomorrow night. She feels bad about the phone call earlier."

I thought about it for a moment, then shook my head. "Brandon, it's a nice gesture, and please thank your mom for inviting me. But honestly, I'm not ready to meet your parents. Hell, I'm barely dealing with life as it is right now. I'm just not ready for… that."

He nodded. "I understand, but I had to ask or I'd never hear the end of it."

I gave him a grateful smile and was about to get out of the car when I remembered Martha telling me I shouldn't be alone when seeing my property for the first time since the fire. "Um, so, my turn to ask you something. What're your plans on Monday?"

"Not sure, why?" Brandon asked.

"I-I've got to go back home and look at my… never mind, it's a bad idea." I opened my door to get out, but Brandon put a hand on my shoulder.

"You're going back to your farm?" he asked.

I nodded. "My old neighbor advised me to not go alone, but it's stupid to ask you. I'll ask Levi. He's on summer break from teaching now, and I'd only be pulling him away from helping at the dairy for a couple days at most."

"No, I mean, if you want to ask Levi, go ahead. But I'd love to go with you."

"Really?" I asked. The word came out as a croak as the packed-down emotions about my farm rose to the surface in a flash.

"Yeah, really," he said in a gentle tone. "What time do you wanna leave?"

I thought for a moment. "I'd like to get there early. Depending on how it goes, we might spend the night and come back the next day?"

I saw a smile play at the corners of Brandon's mouth. A thrill danced around my heart at what might happen on an overnight trip with him. "Why don't we leave at six, then?"

"Monday at the butt crack of dawn it is." I gave him a quick peck on the lips and climbed out of the car.

As Brandon drove away, I was ready to go into total freak-out mode. What made me invite him to go with me to do one of the worst things I've had to do since choosing my parents' caskets?

Oh well, no takebacks now. I would just have to keep my emotions under control as best I could. Maybe he would help me take my mind off things as we drove down and I could spend the evening taking comfort in the arms of a sexy man after the hellish day was over.

Brandon

I WASN'T sure how to handle Cliff not wanting to meet my parents but then inviting me to accompany him to see what remained of his family farm. Maybe it would be easier for him to do it with someone he didn't know very well. Family can sometimes make already-emotional situations worse.

Speaking of which, I expected to face a barrage of questions from my mother when I informed her of Cliff's polite decline the following morning… and she didn't disappoint.

"Why did he turn down an invite to come over?" she asked. "Granted, no one cooks as well as Sue Owens in this town, but I can handle a pot roast and some vegetables."

I fought a smile at my mom's defense of her own cooking. She'd always been a little self-conscious about it, especially since I usually joined the Owens family for supper when I worked on their farm. But Mom wasn't a bad cook. "I don't know, probably because we've just started seeing each other," I said. "I mean, meeting someone's parents isn't exactly third-date material. It's the thing you do when a relationship is getting serious."

"You invited him to share a meal in our home, not walk down the aisle."

I snorted. "Mom, for real, just because Cliff is the first guy I've invited over for supper in eons doesn't mean it's the right time for him to meet you and Dad. He's going through a lot right now, and I'm not gonna push."

"Sounds like you like this one," Dad said from behind his newspaper.

"Maybe," I said, not wanting to divulge too much to my parents just yet. "Anyway, Dad, seriously, who still reads the paper?"

"You leave your father alone. He works hard, and this is his morning ritual."

I rolled my eyes. It was a typical weekend morning at my parents' house. I somehow reverted back to being a teenager, and my mom antagonized me while I antagonized my dad. In the end, we enjoyed teasing each other, and there was never any harm done, but I sometimes wished for the kind of adult relationship other people had with their parents—one in which I could talk to them openly about my hopes and dreams without fear of judgment or of disappointing them again.

I ended up running back up to Eugene that afternoon, because if I was going to spend two days on the road with Cliff, I needed to pack accordingly.

I knew this was going to be a hard time for Cliff, but damn if I wasn't pleased he'd asked me to spend it with him.

Cliff

I WAS not at all surprised to see Uncle Chris and Aunt Sue sitting at the table when I came downstairs Monday morning. They were dairy farmers, and rising before dawn was a normal part of their lives, but this was early even for them. They were there simply to support me, which meant more than they could know.

We sat around the table for a while, mostly in comfortable silence as I drank coffee and my aunt and uncle sipped herbal tea. When I heard a car pull into the driveway, I assumed it was Brandon, so I hugged them both goodbye and headed out.

Aunt Sue rushed into the kitchen and came back carrying a large paper bag that she handed to me. "You boys can eat breakfast on the go. Lunch is in there too."

I blinked back tears. Damn, I was getting emotional already and the day had barely begun. "You're the best, Aunt Sue." I hugged her again.

She and Uncle Chris followed me outside to see us off. "Now you two be safe," Aunt Sue said as Uncle Chris slid an arm around her shoulders.

"Listen, boys," he said, "it's gonna be dangerous down there with all the fire damage. Don't go traipsing all around. You do what you gotta do and get back here as soon as possible."

I knew that was my uncle's way of saying he cared. I nodded and smiled instead of trying to say anything. Even knowing my uncle and aunt cared that much was enough to release the waterworks I wasn't ready for.

I'm not sure what the drive down would've been like without Brandon. He somehow knew I needed my mind taken off why we were making the trip, and he did his best to make it fun and stopped at a few touristy places we could quickly get in and out of. I hadn't even asked him to do all the driving, let alone take his car, but he must have known I wouldn't be in a good frame of mind for doing that either.

Despite the easy drive, I tensed when we pulled into Weaverville. "Pull over at McDonald's," I told Brandon. "My friends are meeting us there."

I'd been texting Walt and Martha off and on since we left Wilcox. They were driving up from San Francisco and needed to know my whereabouts so we would land in Weaverville about the same time, especially with me being farther away.

Sure enough, when we walked into the restaurant, Walt and Martha were already there. "Hey, son," Walt said as I walked toward them. "It's so good to see you." He stood up and pulled me into a bear hug. Then Martha did the same.

"Thanks, you two. This is my friend Brandon. He came with me so I didn't have to travel alone," I said, and both Martha and Walt smiled in that way older people do when they see a new couple.

Despite our somber reason for being here, I chuckled internally. Martha had been playing matchmaker along with my mom since she found out I was gay. Their son was gay as well, and although the man was twenty years older than me and we barely knew each other, they were constantly trying to enlist him into helping find me a man.

"You hungry?" Martha asked.

I shook my head. "No, my aunt gave us way too much food to eat on the way down. We also stopped about an hour ago for ice cream."

"Well, then we best go get this over with," Walt said, and his jolly demeanor slid away.

"Yeah, we probably should," I agreed. "What're the roads like?"

"We were told they've cleared them best they can, but if you're in your old truck, you boys better ride with us."

"We're in Brandon's car, but yeah, we should probably ride with you."

They nodded, and we followed them out. Walt, Martha, and I must've looked like we were walking to the gallows. In a way, we were. We'd be witnessing the death of a life we'd known and loved and could never fully reclaim.

Martha's family had owned their property for generations, and she grew up there, same as I had on our farm. There was no going back to feeling that same peaceful sense of home, or of being completely in tune with the land, even if we rebuilt. That realization lodged in my throat the moment we saw charred trees.

As we drove through the burned-out area, we all fell silent. The smell of burn permeated the truck's air conditioning. Walt stopped at Rhonda Greene's place—what remained of it—and Martha shook her head. "She didn't get out. They found her body after the fire. We came up to attend the funeral a couple weeks ago."

"What? Rhonda was home? Why didn't she evacuate?"

They both shook their heads and shrugged. "No one knows."

Rhonda had been just a few years older than Walt and Martha. Guilt swamped me, thinking of how I'd driven past her place on my way out. It never occurred to me to stop and check if she was still there. As far as any of us knew at the time, she was staying at her sister's place in Redding when the fire ripped through.

I swallowed thickly, and Brandon reached over and held my hand but didn't say anything as Walt drove on. We came to my place first.

Walt and Martha's farm was just over the rise, about a mile and a half away. I used to ride my bike up there and hang out with them when I was young. I wondered if we'd started there, maybe I would've felt more prepared to see my wasteland of a home.

All too soon we reached my old driveway, but downed, burned trees blocked our path. "I'll walk up," I said as I opened the truck door. "No need for you all to—"

"Stop right there," Walt said. "We're in this together. We'll go with you."

I didn't want the older couple to have to navigate the fallen trees, but I wouldn't argue.

I led the way with Brandon close behind me, and Walt and Martha followed him up the winding driveway. The smell of acrid smoke and ash filled our lungs as we walked silently. The place was unrecognizable, but I knew my farm like the back of my hand.

We reached the remnants of the house first, and I was surprised to see tendrils of smoke still rising from the structure this long after the fire. There was nothing left to salvage, just burned timbers.

Bracing myself internally as best I could, I turned to where the old barn had stood. Only piles of ash remained of the place I'd had my first kiss with Jeremiah Stevens and where I built a swing for jumping out of the hayloft, which caused my mom to scream at me for the first and only time I could remember. My memories and a few photos were now the only evidence it had ever existed.

Walt, Martha, and Brandon all stood watching as I made my way from one outbuilding to the next, taking stock of my toasted tractor, the charred equipment, and the scorched metal roofing strewn about. The ribs of the greenhouses shone white and stark against the black soot surrounding them, and I silently thanked God I'd had time enough to save most of the seedlings inside.

Then I walked over to the fields where I'd spent countless hours tending to my crops. I stupidly hoped that maybe, since the fields were open, away from the tree line, the fire would've just singed its edges.

Instead, a wasteland lay before me. What the fire hadn't killed directly, the heat and lack of water had. Only scorched earth remained. Not a single plant had survived.

All the hope I'd secretly been clinging to evaporated in that exact moment. That's when I lost it. "It's all over," I muttered, and I would've fallen to the ground had Brandon not grabbed me.

The tears came unbidden then, and I was unable to stop the anguish that poured out of me. As if losing Mom and Dad wasn't enough. I felt Brandon's strong arms tighten around me, and all I could do was lean into him and let the grief take me.

I don't know how long I stood there and sobbed into Brandon's shoulder. At one point I opened my eyes and thought I saw my parents. It was just my imagination, but their pained expressions only made me cry harder.

When the tears finally subsided and I straightened up, I noticed Walt and Martha were standing beside me and Brandon with glistening eyes. Their hands rested on my shoulders, offering me silent support.

"Okay, I've seen it," I said. "No need to stay here any longer."

Brandon kept his arm securely around me as we walked away from the farmstead. I didn't look back. I didn't want to remember it like that.

We ventured to Walt and Martha's place after that, and what remained of their farm was no different than mine. They held their emotions in check better than I had, though, not that they didn't shed some tears as well. I suspected they'd already gone through some of the grieving process, whereas I'd actively avoided it until today.

When we got back to Weaverville, I was emotionally drained. Walt and Martha hugged me when they dropped us off at McDonald's, where we'd left Brandon's car.

"We're headed back down to San Francisco. We'll text you when we make it home," Martha said, her voice filled with the sorrow we all carried so deeply.

I just nodded and swallowed around the lump in my throat. I couldn't help but wonder if this was the last time I'd see them. I managed a weak smile and waved at the couple who felt like family to me, and they drove out of the parking lot.

"Do you want to drive back to Wilcox tonight?" Brandon asked quietly. "Or would you prefer to stay in a motel?"

"If it's okay with you, I'd rather not drive back today. I'll get us each a room," I said, not realizing what I'd said until Brandon stiffened. "I think I need my own space tonight. Is that okay?"

He nodded and gave me a sad smile, although I could tell it wasn't what he'd hoped for. We drove to a nearby motel and checked in. Brandon helped me bring my luggage in, and I hugged him and thanked him for coming with me.

He didn't try to push for more. Instead he held me tight for a moment, then let me go and left to find his room.

I could still feel the warmth of Brandon's embrace as I stood in the open doorway, not moving. I remained there for several moments as hopelessness swamped me. I'd never felt so alone.

Even after my parents died, I'd still had the farm. I'd still had that tangible connection to them, and an identity. Now I had nothing. I was… nothing.

I shut the door, stumbled to the bed, and collapsed on it fully clothed. I tucked myself into a ball and let grief consume me again.

I'm not sure how long I stayed like that. The light eventually dimmed, and the room was dark when I heard a soft knock on the door.

"Um, yeah?" I asked as I sat up and wiped my nose.

"Cliff, it's Brandon. I've brought pizza."

"Yeah, okay, give me a second." I went into the bathroom and washed my face with cold water. I was still toweling myself off when I opened the door.

"Hey, I thought you might be hungry," Brandon said. "Besides, I'll never hear the end of it if your aunt thinks you starved on my watch." He stepped inside and set the pizza box and napkins on the table. "You okay?"

I shook my head. "No. I'm sorry, Brandon, I shouldn't have asked you to come. I'm—"

"You're grieving, and that's okay. I'm glad to be here with you."

All I could do was nod and wipe away the tear that slipped past my defenses. God, I was a mess, and I knew I looked the part too.

"Thanks," I managed to whisper.

"Now, come on, I won't let you be alone any longer. That's why I'm here. We'll eat pizza and watch bad motel TV."

I chuckled and shrugged. I suspected he was right that I needed to be with someone instead of hiding alone in my room. I'd already made a spectacle of myself, so there was no need to try to hide anything now. In fact, I should readily take advantage of having a pair of strong arms to support me tonight and enjoy it while it lasted, because Brandon would probably go hightailing it as far away from me as possible once we returned to Oregon.

We settled back on the bed as I nibbled at the pizza, my appetite still mostly gone, and watched *Ironman*. At some point, I fell asleep against Brandon, and when I woke up, the TV was off and we were settled on the bed. I was lying in his arms.

I rose up on an elbow. "How long have I been asleep?"

"Not long, thirty minutes or so. Hope you don't mind that I turned the TV off."

"I don't mind," I said, "I should probably turn in, though. I'm not much company anyway."

"Want me to stay?" he asked.

Right at that moment, I could think of nothing I wanted more. I should've said no. I meant to say no. Instead, I nodded and curled back into Brandon's side.

We cuddled for what felt like a long time, until we both really were ready for sleep. He said he hadn't unpacked, and while I brushed my teeth and undressed, he returned to his room to get his things.

I had dozed off by the time Brandon got back, and only woke when I felt the bed dip as he slipped under the sheets and spooned me from behind.

The skin-on-skin contact was comforting. After spending the whole day focusing on everything in my life that'd been stripped away, I spent the night focused solely on the man beside me and how good his body felt pressed up against mine.

I felt safe and secure, and that's the last thing I thought about as I fell asleep.

Brandon

I KNEW this trip would be extremely emotional for Cliff. I guess that's why I was so surprised he asked me to come along. But I tried to make it as pleasant as I could for him, all things considered.

I thought I'd be prepared for the intensity of his grief while he surveyed the burned-out remains of his family farm, but I'd underestimated that. I don't think anyone is prepared for that kind of grief. Hell, I'd wiped away tears and it wasn't even my place. The utter devastation had been overwhelming.

Something primal snapped inside me when Cliff broke down, and I felt an intense need to comfort and protect him. Not that I could protect him from what he was experiencing, but I could at least support him while he went through it.

I stayed with him in the truck while Walt and Martha surveyed the damage to their farm. I watched as Martha leaned into Walt several times and the two comforted one another as they faced so much loss. They reminded me a lot of Levi's parents.

My parents, not so much. Granted, Mom and Dad were strong in their own ways, individually and as a power couple. They built their business, established their practice, and were respected in the community—all admirable things they achieved together. But I rarely saw them vulnerable, and I couldn't remember when I'd ever seen them take comfort from one another.

Sue and Chris Owens, on the other hand, were like two halves of a well-oiled machine that worked in tandem and were powered by unconditional love and faith in one another. I saw that same relationship between Walt and Martha. I had a feeling Cliff would expect to have the same sort of relationship with a lifelong partner, whether he realized it or not.

Was I that kind of person? Could I be that for Cliff? Part of me thought, *Of course*, while another thought of all my selfish qualities.

I'd never had to share my life with anyone. I'd been an only child, and probably a little spoiled. Sure, I considered Levi and Xander my brothers, and we'd certainly squabbled like siblings over the years, but when we got mad at one another, we could all go home until we cooled off. And as far as romantic partners went, well, I'd never gotten that serious with anyone.

It was stupid to contemplate a relationship with someone I'd just met. I valued Tracy's advice on the subject, but that didn't mean I was ready to take that leap with Cliff. Or that he was even remotely ready. But if nothing else, I could be a supportive friend.

Despite the awful circumstances, holding him through the night in that motel bed was probably one of the most intimate experiences of my life. Yes, we were naked, and I couldn't deny reveling in the feel of our bodies pressed together, but it was more than that. Cliff let me see him at his most vulnerable and sought my comfort and reassurance that he'd get through this, that he wasn't alone. I'd be damned if I squandered his trust by putting the moves on him.

I woke up first, so I went out to grab breakfast and brought it back to the room. I remembered Cliff liked coffee from the mornings when I'd gone over to help Chris, but I had no idea how he liked it, so I brought back a pocketful of sugar packets and mini creamers for him.

He was already awake and getting up when I returned. "You feeling better?" I asked, knowing he probably wasn't, but he nodded and gave me a peck on the lips. "Okay, well, just let me know if I can get you anything that'll help."

Cliff gratefully accepted the coffee and assorted fixings, and we sat together on the bed to eat our breakfast. We didn't say much while we ate, but I kept my leg pressed against his in a sort of silent support. I figured if and when he was ready to talk—about his farm or anything else—he would.

"I-I want you to shower with me," he said, not making eye contact. "I just need to feel... *something*...."

I didn't hesitate. I drew him into my arms. "I get it," I whispered into his ear. "I want your body, Cliff, but I also want to help you feel better. Let me take care of you."

He nodded, and we stood up, holding hands, and I led him to the bathroom. I stripped off while he got into the shower, and then

I climbed in behind him. I worked the soap into a lather and gently massaged his muscles, rubbing and caressing every slippery inch of him. I took my time, and Cliff hummed contentedly as I slowly worked the tension out of him.

I fought the urge to bend down and take his hard cock into my mouth, but Cliff needed more than a sexual release right now, and so did I. He needed to be cared for and literally feel that someone cared about him. I knelt and massaged his legs, the globes of his ass, and his taut stomach. He moaned with so much longing that I struggled against the emotions that coursed through me.

I gave myself a quick, cursory scrub and rinse and then we stepped out of the shower. Without asking, I grabbed a towel and dried Cliff off, then wrapped it around his waist and wrapped one around my own. He didn't say anything, but he gave me a smile that spoke to him being more relaxed.

When we made our way back into the room, Cliff sat on the edge of the bed, met my eyes, and surprised the hell out of me. "I want you to make love to me, Brandon, all the way," he confessed. The surprises continued when he grabbed his pants and pulled a condom and a small packet of lube out of the pocket and handed them to me. "Is that okay?"

If actions speak louder than words, my practically tackling him onto the bed was answer enough. Cliff let out a startled laugh, which helped break any tension he felt in asking so directly. I silenced him by ravaging his mouth.

I licked and nipped my way down his body and then sucked his cock. I continued edging while I used the lube to prep him. Since Cliff had handed me the condom, I was confident he wanted me to be the one on top.

I listened intently as he continued to moan, and when he began to buck against my fingers, I knew he was ready. I pulled off his cock, situated myself between his legs, gloved and lubed myself, and then lined my cock up to his hole.

He arched back when I breached his tight ring, and I waited patiently to give him time to adjust and let me in.

Moments later, he began to move ever so slowly up and down the head of my cock, each time taking me in just a bit more.

I watched as Cliff's beautiful body used mine to find the pleasure I knew he must desperately need. Hell, I needed it too. When my cock was halfway into his ass, he stopped moving and met my gaze. "Take me," he whispered, and I didn't hesitate.

We never broke eye contact as I plunged in and out of his hole in a steady rhythm and he arched up in pleasure. I wanted to see him and wanted him to see me, to see how much I felt. I wanted him to know how much I cared.

"God, Brandon," he wailed in a hoarse voice as I picked up speed and thrust harder and deeper.

As I pounded him, I longed to give him the same pleasure he gave me. Cliff's eyes drifted closed as I slowed my pace and peppered kisses along his neck and jawline. Finally I claimed his mouth.

As pleasure overcame him, a tear streaked down his cheek, but I knew he was nearing the release he'd been searching for. I continued to hold him and kiss him as our bodies writhed in the pleasures of being joined.

With both of our climaxes barreling down, I adjusted my position to strike his prostate. Cliff cried out, and as he began to come, he tightened around me just enough to cause my orgasm to hit full force.

All my strength left me, and I fell onto the bed beside him. Moments later, Cliff reached out and grabbed one of our discarded towels, wiped his front down, and removed the spent condom from me. He immediately cuddled into my side, and I dozed with my face nuzzling his neck.

We must've snuggled for over half an hour before he stirred and sighed.

"I'd like to go back to my farm. I, um, I dreamed of my parents last night. I'd—"

"Hey, that's fine," I interrupted as I sat up. I could hear the struggle in his voice. "No explanations necessary. Do you want me to drive you, or do you want to take my car and go alone?"

He thought for a moment, then replied, "Do you mind if I go by myself?"

"No, I don't mind at all. Do you think you'll be back before eleven, or should we check out now?" I asked.

"I'll be back long before then," he said. "I just need to do something."

"Then I'll wait here for you. Take your time."

He nodded and kissed me chastely, then got dressed and left with my keys in his hand.

I didn't know what he needed to do, but I could tell it was important to him. I just hoped whatever it was, it would somehow help the healing process.

CLIFF REMAINED mostly quiet and contemplative on our nonstop drive back to Wilcox. But he did hold my hand the whole way, which I took as a hopeful sign that he was doing all right.

"This is for gas." He pulled money out of his wallet as we pulled up to Sue and Chris's place. "I owe you, Brandon. I really do."

I leaned over, kissed him, and pushed his money back toward him. "It was my pleasure, and all you owe me is another date."

Cliff smiled, kissed me again, and climbed out of my car. As he reached his aunt and uncle's front door, he smiled again and waved at me. Then he disappeared inside.

Something happened for Cliff on the trip. Whether he'd found closure on his old life or resolved to rebuild it from the ground up, I didn't know. But it was something big, and I wondered if it would mean he'd be leaving the area, and what that might mean for us.

That night, as I drove back up to Eugene, I couldn't help but imagine a future with Cliff. It was ridiculous to believe in instant love, but I accepted that I could be ridiculous and even embraced that aspect of my personality.

The little barn across from the Owens place filled my mind, and I could envision us living there together. We'd play to each other's passions and strengths—Cliff working the land and me writing my novels. But would he be truly happy starting life over in Oregon? What if he wanted to return to his land in California? Would I be willing to give up my dream of buying Xander's farm to go be with Cliff?

I got home late, sat down to check my emails, only to find more pressure from my agent about the unfinished manuscripts.

I emailed her back and told her I'd be handcuffed to my computer until everything was done. No doubt the next several days would be intense.

As I lay in bed that night, my mind wandered to my latest manuscript, and seeing the emotions and strong resolve in Cliff had inspired me. I knew exactly what the antagonist demon in the final book would be. A dragon that breathed fire, destroying everything in its path without regard for anything or anyone. That's what my brave and resilient main character was battling against. And that's what he'd vanquish in the end.

Cliff

WHEN I was born, my parents planted a redwood seed they'd collected at the Redwood National and State Parks in our home state. I came to think of it as my special tree as I witnessed it grow taller and stronger as the years passed.

On my fifth birthday, I saw a grove of redwoods for the first time when my parents took me to that same park. I remember my overwhelming feeling of awe as I looked up at what my tree would grow into in a few thousand years if it wasn't cut down or destroyed. Looking back, I think my deep-seated desire to become a grower—a farmer—took root at that exact moment.

As I lay in Brandon's arms in our shared motel room, I dreamed of my mom and dad standing at the base of my special redwood tree. "Did it survive?" I asked, and both my parents shook their heads sadly.

"No, it was still too young," my dad said in the dream.

He pointed at the ground, and I saw that small green seeds had popped out of the tiny cones that fell from the tree every year. Unlike their giant cousins, coast redwoods didn't need fire to release their seeds. But for whatever reason, in the dream, the fire had released the cone, and the seeds spilled onto the ground.

"You think I can get them to grow?" I asked my parents.

I looked at my mom and saw her gazing across our scorched land. "You need to live your life," she said, and suddenly I was standing next to her. "This farm isn't you. It's a part of you, always will be, but you're so much more than any one place, my son. Follow your heart, wherever it leads."

Then I heard my father behind us and turned to see him kneeling next to the seeds. "But you can take a piece of this place with you. Something to remind you of our lives here."

I knew then that my parents were telling me I wouldn't be returning to our farm. I knew it was only a dream, but their message felt real. They were with me, back on the land where we'd spent our lives, but also they were releasing me from any guilt or obligation I might feel to stay.

Brandon had understood I needed to return to the farm one last time on my own, and I felt grateful when he readily agreed to let me take his car.

He'd been so patient and understanding the entire trip, and I was quickly learning that's the kind of man he was. I'd come prepared for being intimate with him, having packed condoms and lube, but I knew I sounded pathetic when I asked him to make love to me. Still, he'd given me exactly what I needed—a connection, a release, and the feeling of being alive—and in a strange way, it helped me let go.

I stopped at a store on my way out of town and bought plastic bags and a small shovel to scoop up the redwood seeds I'd seen in my dream. It never even occurred to me that I wouldn't find them exactly where my parents had shown me the night before.

I pulled Brandon's car up to the driveway and set out on foot toward my special tree. When I reached the dead redwood, now just an assortment of bare branches, I could see it had dropped its seeds before it died.

"Life finds a way," I heard my dad say, and the hairs on the back of my neck stood on end like always when I felt my parents' presence.

I scooped as many seeds as possible into the small plastic bag I'd tucked in my pocket, sealed it, and walked back to the car. I was about to leave when I heard, "Look back."

It was my mom's voice. I hadn't wanted to look back at the property when I visited yesterday, hadn't had the strength. I'd examined the farm then and took stock that there was nothing left to salvage, but I didn't want that vision of the farm seared into my memory. But today was different, and I did as Mom's voice instructed. I looked.

My mind warred with the vibrant landscape in my memories and the barren panorama in full view now—the house, the barn, the greenhouses, the yard with my special redwood at the edge, and the fields full of growing crops. I could still see it all so clearly amid the devastation.

I expelled a ragged breath. "I promise I will remember the good," I said.

It felt like my parents were prodding me to go and to do so with their blessing. A huge chapter of my life had ended, and I doubted I'd be back. Even before coming here, I'd decided to sell the property. I couldn't see myself living here any longer. Walt and Martha surely wouldn't come back either. Other neighbors were already gone or too old to return. The fire had just sped up the inevitable for them.

For me, it rewrote my future. I had absolutely nothing left for me here—no family, neighbors, or even friends I'd grown up with. No one remained.

I felt a calming sense of closure as I gently squeezed the bag of soil and seeds. With any luck they would grow. They represented a new beginning, wherever that might take me.

I PLANTED the redwood seeds beside my uncle's barn, in a sheltered spot that still got plenty of sun. I also installed a small fence around the area so no one would accidentally plow through it. When I showed Uncle Chris, he clapped me on the shoulder and said it looked good, but once those things started to grow, I'd need to move them away from the barn. "You know they grow to be enormous, right?" he asked, teasing.

"Yeah, yeah," I said, letting him have his fun.

He and Aunt Sue left me alone the week after I returned from California, allowing me to meander around at my own pace. I worked on my aquaponics setup and began researching who could supply me with fish once I had a heating system.

My thoughts of Brandon were paramount to all else, even though I kept trying to push them away. I thought of him when I planted the seedlings. He was also the one I wanted to tell each time I made progress on the aquaponics.

When I didn't hear back from him, I felt that much more stuck. Maybe it was serendipity when I opened the email from the county and found the state was offering career development grants for people who had lost their livelihoods due to wildfire. I had spoken to my insurance company, and it would be a while before the payout, so a grant might help.

On a whim I logged on to the website of my alma mater, UC Davis, and searched for aquaponics. I knew they'd offered random classes on the subject when I went to school there, but I hadn't taken any. I'd been so focused on finishing my degree so I could get back to the farm that I hadn't ventured beyond the exact course schedules I needed to graduate.

Looking back, I had missed out on learning some really valuable stuff. UC Davis currently offered several courses on the basics. Without dwelling on it or giving myself time to talk myself out of it, I submitted an online application and sent an email inquiry about the grants. Then I wandered toward the barn, plopped down next to the little fenced-off area, and began talking to my parents. I knew it was silly, but now I'd had the dream with them in it, the seeds felt like a tangible connection to them.

"So, I might have an opportunity to do something… big," I said. "Dad, it could be what we both talked about and researched all those years. But I'll have to start from scratch."

A gentle breeze blew across me, and it felt like confirmation that I was thinking the right way. I might not want to return to the farm, at least not to *that* farm, but I wasn't done with farming.

Several days later, I heard back about the career development grant. I'd explained the situation in my email, and they encouraged me to fill out the paperwork to formally apply and even directed me toward a couple other grants I might qualify for. Suddenly my whimsical idea of returning to school didn't seem so far-fetched.

I immediately wanted to share the news with Brandon, who had still not gotten back in touch with me, so instead I went downstairs and shared my news with my aunt and uncle, who had just sat down for lunch.

"Well, that sounds sensible if you really plan to make a go of this," Uncle Chris said.

"Yeah, I think so too. I'll have to shut down everything I started here, though. That means giving up on the seedlings I brought with me."

"Oh well, son, about that. If you don't plan to use them, I think we can find them a good home."

Had this all happened before I'd gone back and seen the devastation, I never would've been able to part with my plants. But it had already gotten too hot to do much with them other than give them away.

After a quick phone call from Uncle Chris, the neighbor who'd taken the messed-up water tanks readily agreed to accept the seedlings.

"She does what's called square-foot gardening. Imagine cramming fourteen plants together and getting hundreds of pounds of tomatoes out of it," he explained. "No tractor, no tilling, no hoeing, minimal water usage, and one hundred percent organic."

My interest was still firmly in aquaponics, but hearing about the neighbor's approach just went to how much I stood to learn about so many aspects of farming. It only solidified my decision to return to school.

Luckily Chris kept me busy with the dairy. I spent my weeks getting up at the crack of dawn to help Uncle Chris with the dairy. Levi was still on summer break, so he came around quite a bit, but it was nice being able to give him a break from helping so much and just hanging out with my cousin.

All of that almost kept me busy enough to avoid thinking about how Brandon had ghosted me. The keyword being *almost*.

Okay, I thought about him all the time. It was horrifying to think that my emotional outbursts had driven him off. Whether I liked it or not, too much time had passed to hope his lack of contact was because he was too busy. Someone didn't just disappear if they liked you for more than a fuck.

Ugh, I wanted to crawl under a log and hide when I thought of how I'd broken down in front of him, then all but begged him to screw the sadness out of me. Which he had, and then some. Having Brandon inside me felt amazing and beautiful, like broken pieces of me were being stitched back together.

Now I realized just how stupid I'd been. It made my stomach hurt when I thought about it. But here I was, pining for a man who obviously didn't feel the same way about me. Of course, that didn't stop me from asking Levi why Brandon hadn't been around lately, careful not to let my cousin know I'd basically thrown myself at his best friend.

Levi said Brandon was busy working on a huge book deal for his publisher. I didn't press for more information, mostly because I figured it was just Levi's way of not hurting my feelings. I was sure Brandon hadn't told him we had sex. If he had, Levi would've been impossible to deal with. He wanted us to get together almost more than we did. Clearly, more than Brandon did.

I considered texting him, but I no longer saw the point. I could take a hint. The guy didn't want me, and my pride convinced me to leave him alone.

Unfortunately Tracy had been genuinely interested in the aquaponics, so I saw him frequently now, and as much as I liked the guy, each time he showed up, the Brandon wounds broke open again.

I'd been told repeatedly after my parents died that time tended to heal all wounds. Unfortunately, the Brandon wounds seemed to fester instead.

Besides, I had so many other wounds to heal right now, being ghosted by a hot man because I was a stupid overbearing… well whatever I was… those wounds would just have to take a back seat to all the others that were trying to heal.

At the end of the day, I'd have to put my feelings aside until I had the strength to deal with them, and if I was lucky, I'd stop feeling so bad about chasing Brandon away sooner than later. Yeah, like I was lucky enough for that to happen.

Brandon

I LOST myself in my writing, and the summer just slipped away. I wrote, corresponded with my editor and agent, wrote more, slept some, and so went my daily routine. When I remembered to eat, I had meals delivered rather than spend the time grocery shopping and cooking.

I ended up rewriting the first book to add the dragon character, and I made the other antagonists of the series subservient to her. I'd write, rewrite, start editing the next book, and then come back and rewrite the first. I did that so many times, everything else around me became a blur.

But Cliff never left my thoughts. My fantasy character and the real man merged in my mind, and I lost all track of reality between the two.

Aleean was the character I based on Cliff. In my story, he was a young teenager when he lost his parents. He didn't know then what had destroyed his village. There was talk that it'd been a dragon, but no one could confirm it.

As I wrote I kept thinking of Cliff and his sensitive nature. Caring and unassuming, Aleean had been forced to join the king's military guard when he was the last of his people, and that's where he and Cliff diverged.

But I added other components into the story that hit close to home, like a wise older dairyman I based on Chris and a wacky friend that I named Levi, since I based the character entirely on him. He might make me change that later, but considering his students might love the novel, I couldn't imagine he would.

Then there was Aleean's bold and rather clueless love interest, who bore a striking resemblance to me at times, not that I'd ever admit it.

By the time I completed revisions on the third novel, I was emotionally whipped. My first phone call was to Levi. "I finished it. The whole series," I said when he answered his phone.

"Like *finish* finished?" he asked.

"Well, I've got to send it to my beta readers, but yeah. My work is mostly done. Oh, and I need your okay to use your name for one of the characters."

"Um, dude, tell me you didn't."

"I totally did, and you're gonna love him. He's just as funny and wacky in the brain as you are."

Levi laughed. "Do I get to read it first?"

"Yeah, I was hoping you'd be one of my betas. I'd like your opinion as a schoolteacher, since this is YA fiction."

"Okay, send them over. When are you coming back to the farm?" he asked.

I chuckled as I looked at the clothes I'd been wearing since… well, I wasn't sure how long. Showers and new underwear seemed to be the only clean routines I'd managed lately.

"I'm not sure what comes next. I literally just finished the last book, and you were my first call."

"Can you come tomorrow? It's Saturday, in case you didn't know."

"Of course I know it's Saturday." I had no idea what day it was, but damned if I was going to let Levi mock me about it. "I'll verify that my agent doesn't need me for anything else, but I think that's fine. I need to check in with my folks too, so it'd be good to come visit. Mind if I stay with you?"

"That'd be great. We have some news to share that includes you."

"Wait, why would it include me? Are… are you okay? Is Keya all right?"

I had just spent weeks writing a three-part fantasy series where a dragon wreaks havoc worldwide. People in my story died left and right, and my hero only barely survived. My mind was not in a good place to digest any sort of heavy real-life information.

"We're fine. Just come down tomorrow if you can."

"Okay, I'll text when I'm leaving here," I said, and he hung up before I could ask about Cliff. Oh well, I guessed I'd see him soon enough and find out for myself.

I sent the manuscripts to my agent and editor with a gift certificate for Starbucks for both of them. I said I'm sorry, like, one hundred times, because my rewriting of the series was going to seriously inconvenience them. Especially my editor. I told them I needed to have the beta readers spend some time on the stories before we officially did the final edits. My agent immediately wrote back that I was a pain in her ass. Of course, that just made me laugh. I wrote back, "Trust me, it's worth the rewrite!"

Classes didn't begin until the end of September, which meant I would have a full month with no pressures on me other than hanging out on the farm with Cliff.

I closed my laptop and went into the bathroom to shower. It was going to be an epic few weeks.

Cliff

"CLIFF," MY aunt yelled up the stairs, "Levi and Keya want us all to come over to their place tonight. Can you make it?"

"Yeah, sounds good. I'm gonna get a shower and hose off the cow stench first, though."

I'd just gotten back from helping Uncle Chris milk the cows and was literally covered in poo. I heard Aunt Sue chuckling downstairs. I'm sure my uncle had already told her that one of the cows had backed up on me, forcing me to jump out of her way and land right in the poop tray that ran along the side of the milking barn.

That particular cow was known to do that to the workers, and she was huge, so I didn't have much choice. As I shook off the liquid shit, I looked at my uncle and said, "I hate cows. For real, I'm a crop farmer for a reason."

He laughed so hard I thought he would throw up. I could admit how funny the sight must've been, though I was grateful Levi hadn't witnessed it or I'd never live it down. Clearly cattle farming, especially dairy farming, was not for me.

I stripped outside, tossed my clothes in the washer, and immediately turned it on to wash, as Aunt Sue had instructed me to do whenever my clothes were soiled. Luckily, I could sprint up the back stairs without being seen in my underwear.

I showered as quickly as I could and came down to meet my aunt and uncle. "So, you all gussied up and ready to roll?" Aunt Sue asked.

Uncle Chris snickered, and I rolled my eyes but couldn't completely hide my grin. As stoic as they seemed sometimes, it was obvious Levi had inherited his teasing sense of humor from the both of them.

I followed them to their antique pickup and scooted into the middle. That was pretty much how I rode when we went anywhere.

It reminded me of when I'd ridden with my parents in the old GMC pickup that burned in the fire.

During my teen years, I dreamed of fixing that old truck up into a hot rod. But it was uncomfortable, just like this one, so I never seriously considered it as an adult.

We pulled up in front of Levi and Keya's a few minutes later, and I followed my aunt and uncle inside. I froze when I saw Brandon sitting in the living room.

Shit, this is awkward, I thought.

My cousin noticed, of course. He always freaking noticed things.

"You all come eat," Keya said. She and Levi had prepared a huge meal that could rival Aunt Sue's cooking.

Keya's mom had passed away when she was young, but her father, who still lived in the area, sat on the sofa, talking to Brandon.

We all moved to the dining room, where Levi was directing everyone toward particular chairs. I moved to the seat he pointed to and, to my horror, realized he'd put me next to Brandon. The table easily accommodated all of us, even if it was a bit snug.

Levi helped serve, which made me proud of my cousin. Having grown up with a mom who commanded ownership of the kitchen, it was a relief to see he didn't have the same expectations for his wife.

I smiled politely at Brandon and accepted plates that were passed around without making eye contact. "What's wrong?" he finally whispered as everyone began to dig into the food.

"Nothing," I said and stuffed my mouth with a homemade roll. "Mmm, y'all, this is delicious."

Keya looked at Levi and grinned. "My dear husband got a little of his cooking talent from his mom. That's Sue's recipe," she said.

Aunt Sue beamed and reached for one of the rolls. I smiled at how gullible my aunt was regarding Levi and Keya. She clearly adored them.

While we ate, Levi got everyone's attention and said he and Keya had an announcement to make. "We're going to start a winery," Keya blurted, and Levi sighed.

"You stole my thunder," Levi whined, though it sounded more like teasing.

She chuckled. "I couldn't help it. I'm so excited."

"So this is what includes me?" Brandon asked, smirking. "I'm free labor?"

Everyone laughed, including me. Poor Brandon might not be interested in me, but he was a great friend to Levi and even Uncle Chris, helping out whenever needed. My uncle couldn't say enough good things about him. I just wished he and I had never gotten involved so we could've avoided the awkwardness between us now.

"Well, yes," Keya said. "Your free labor is going to be appreciated, but that's not why we invited you all here."

She let the information settle, and we all looked around the table, everyone clueless. Then Levi jumped up and announced, "We're pregnant."

Keya rolled her eyes and pulled her husband to her side. "Now who stole all the thunder?" she said, then kissed him sweetly.

The room erupted, and I found myself smiling so hard it hurt as the new grandparents-to-be encircled the couple. "When's the baby due? Do you know the sex?" Keya's dad and Aunt Sue were volleying questions at them one after the other.

Keya and Levi did their best to answer through their happy tears. Uncle Chris looked stunned, and I reached over and lightly punched his right arm. "So, what should we call you now?" I asked, grinning at him. "Gramps, Pop, or Pawpaw?"

"Listen here, son, I can still turn you over my knee," he said, quietly enough that I didn't think anyone else could hear.

But Brandon leaned in and said, "Believe him when he says that," which got a chuckle from my uncle.

"Ask him about the time I kicked his butt at arm wrestling," Uncle Chris said. Before I could respond, Keya came over and pulled him into a hug. "Oh, I'm so happy for you kids. I can't believe it, though. I'm going to be a grandpa."

"Yeah? Imagine being the one making the baby."

Uncle Chris laughed and kissed his daughter-in-law on the cheek. "You'll do it like a champ."

When everyone settled back down to the meal, Levi looked over at Brandon and me, and taking Keya's hand, he said, "We'd like both of you to be the baby's godparents."

I stared at my cousin, shocked. "Me?" I asked.

"Of course you," Levi said. "We want you to play an active part in our kid's life, Cliff. They'll be blessed to count you as a role model."

I swallowed thickly. His words had caught me completely off guard. "I'd be honored to be the baby's godfather."

Keya wiped a tear as Brandon and I came around the table and embraced them both. A rush of emotions threatened to swallow me whole. I really wasn't without family, and tonight, Levi and Keya proved it. They'd never know how much that meant to me, especially at a time when I'd lost so much.

After the meal, I decided to go for a walk around the property, and Keya jumped at the chance to show me their soon-to-be winery.

We hadn't even made it outside when Aunt Sue grabbed Keya's arm and pulled her into the kitchen. "Okay, now tell me again when the due date is?"

I was smiling when I went out onto the porch and found Brandon sitting alone, looking smug.

"So, apparently, we're gonna be godparents together," he said. "Levi sure goes to extremes with his matchmaking efforts. He managed to hitch us together for life without getting married."

I knew Brandon was joking, and to avoid making things even more awkward, I smiled and sat on the porch steps. "Yeah, apparently. Should we set up who will spoil him or her and when? I plan to be the one who feeds them too much candy while babysitting and then lets their parents deal with the sugar rush."

Brandon chuckled. "I should be the one to get them drunk on their twenty-first birthday. It'll be like coming full-circle, since I took Levi drinking when he became legal too."

"Really? Oh, that had to be epic."

"You have no idea," Brandon said and laughed happily. "Sometimes it pays to be the oldest, even if it's only by a couple months."

I leaned back against the rail and smiled. "It's a good night. I'm really happy for them."

"Yeah, me too. I thought they'd invited me to celebrate finishing my series."

"Really?" I asked. "You finished already? Don't books take years to write?"

"They can, but I've been working on this series for a while. Having crushing deadline pressure is a good motivator too."

"Well, congrats to you too, then. It's a night of celebration."

Brandon smiled, got up, and came over to sit next to me. "You're the inspiration that made it possible," he said.

"Me? How?" I asked.

"Your fortitude while facing the fire damage. You're so strong and brave, Cliff. I couldn't help but be inspired by you."

I humphed. "You must be thinking of someone else. I was an emotional basket case, even drove you off," I said and immediately regretted it. So much for not being awkward.

"What? Drove me off? Why would you think that?"

I turned to face him, and annoyance surged through me. "Dude, I haven't heard from you in weeks. The last time we spoke was when you dropped me off after, well, after I blubbered all over you and all but begged you for sex." I quickly looked around to make sure we were still alone.

"It's not what you think, and you didn't beg me for sex," he said, quieter than I'd been a moment earlier. I stood up and turned to go back inside, but Brandon put a hand out to stop me. "Cliff, listen, it really isn't what you think. I didn't abandon you. You're literally all I've thought about since I dropped you off. It's just that I lose track of time when I'm writing. Like I said, I was very inspired."

I sighed. "Brandon, you don't have to protect my feelings, but respecting them would've been nice. If you wanted to end things, you could've just said so."

"I'll prove it to you. Tell me your email address," he demanded. "I'll send you the manuscripts. Then you'll see what I mean."

I collapsed back onto the step next to him and, feeling exasperated, rattled off my email as he typed it into his phone.

"Please just read the books and let me know what you think. I intentionally did not write anything personal about you. Keep in mind, my main character is a teenager, but I think you'll see some of yourself in him. That's my hope, anyway."

"Okay, I'll read them," I promised, which seemed to appease him. "Tonight's been a lot. I think I'll walk back to my aunt and uncle's."

"Can I drive you?" Brandon asked.

"Thanks, but I need some time to myself, and they aren't going to be interested in leaving anytime soon."

We both stood, and Brandon smiled as he looked through the farmhouse window at the family, who were still talking ninety miles an hour.

I gestured toward the house when I caught Aunt Sue's eye.

She smiled and waved me off.

I stepped off the porch and started to walk away when I felt Brandon's hand on my arm. "Cliff, I'm sorry if I gave you the impression I'm not interested. Truth is, I'm *very* interested. I like everything about you." He sighed heavily and dropped his hand to his side. "Take a look at the manuscripts. Then, if you're willing to give me another chance, I'd… I'd really like one."

I smiled but didn't respond. I honestly didn't see a future with Brandon and me. Our lives were already heading in different directions, only he didn't know it. I'd be leaving for California in a few weeks to start classes at UC Davis. Whether or not I'd permanently relocate to Oregon after that, I didn't know.

Brandon

"How the hell have I fucked this up so bad?" I asked Levi as he sat across from me at the little diner that served food that tasted like used rubber but somehow made pies from heaven.

"So let me get this straight. You went on a trip together, enjoyed fooling around, and then didn't even text him?" Levi asked. "Tell me how that's not ghosting."

I gave him a look. "You know how I get when I'm in the zone. I don't even know if it's day or night sometimes."

He shrugged. "I have to tell you, I don't think my cousin is a second chances sort of guy. If he thought you weren't interested, he's probably already shut that door. Can't say I blame him either. You sorta blew it, dude."

I sighed. "Well, maybe I can weasel my way back in," I said, managing a charming smile, even though I wasn't feeling it.

"Did he tell you he's leaving?" Levi asked.

That brought me up short. "Leaving? Why? When?" I asked, nervous.

"Not sure, couple of weeks, I'd guess. He's going back to school to learn about this aquaponics thing."

"Shit," I said. "I need to set things right, at least. Can you help me fix it? I mean, you don't want your kid's godfather to end up alone and regretful, right?"

Levi shook his head. "You are hopeless, man. I'm not sure what I can do to help. I can tell him you feel like the idiot you are, but that's probably not going to persuade him. You need to convince him to meet with you and talk."

I sighed and dug into my overcooked omelet. I listened, miserable at how stupid I'd been, as Levi told me his dad had agreed to keep the dairy operation going while Cliff was away. Even my pseudo-uncle Tracy had agreed to come help from time to time, which was news to me. Apparently he and Chris had gotten on really well when Tracy came to tour Cliff's aquaponics setup. Knowing how unsocial Tracy was, just finding out he'd connected like he had with Chris and Cliff illustrated how much I had dropped the ball.

Fortunately, the conversation shifted to the baby and then to the winery. Keya was an avid wine connoisseur, so it wasn't surprising that she'd convinced Levi to consider it. It'd be fun to watch them develop the land Chris had purchased around their house.

I knew Chris desperately wanted his son to follow in his footsteps. Being a dairy farmer was never in the cards for Levi; he just didn't want that life. But creating a different way to tie him to the land would satisfy Chris. That made me happy as I thought about my dream of one day putting down roots on the land neighboring theirs.

"Two Bridges Winery," Levi said, and I stared at him blankly. "Dude, are you even paying attention?"

"Give me a break. It's been an intense few weeks. Anyway, what's Two Bridges Winery?"

"The name of our place," he said, shaking his head. "It is cool, right?"

"Very fitting, given your proximity to them. But you know those bridges look like they might collapse at any moment. If you're serious and expect people to come to the winery in droves, you should see if the state can fix them up."

He nodded. "Yeah, Keya's already begun talking to the county commission about that. The bridges officially belong to the county highway department."

Levi and Keya's place wasn't easily accessible without the bridges, not for an influx of tourists, anyway. The route to their farm wound around a mountain, and a huge rock blocked the main road into that area. Identical covered bridges had been built many decades ago to bypass the boulder, and while still quaint and functional, they'd seen better days.

"The bridges were renovated in the nineties, so the highway department is convinced both are structurally sound, but they don't have the budget to paint either one, this year or next."

"Can we paint them?" I asked.

"That's what I asked, and the commissioner said, and I quote, 'I can't endorse vandalism, even if it's a historically accurate blue that matches the original paint job.'"

I laughed. "Okay, well, that sounds like tacit agreement, at least. How about we ask Xander to help us? I need to call him anyway and catch up on his life since we've all been busy this summer. Besides, he probably has a crew who can finish them both in one day."

"Please, you mean you want him 'cause he won't spill the beans when we get in trouble," Levi said, and I smirked in confirmation.

Levi grabbed the tab just as the server placed it on our table. "This is on me 'cause you are the bestest godfather-to-be best friend I got."

I chuckled. "Wonderful grammar, English teacher. Okay, let me see if I can get in touch with Xander before we start buying paint."

As soon as we left the diner, I pulled up Xander's number and called. "Hey, Xan," I said when he answered. "What's happening? Are you in the big city?"

"Hey, buddy. I've got a job in Salem next week, but was thinking of heading to Wilcox for the weekend. Why? You visiting our old stomping grounds?"

"Yeah, Levi and I just had breakfast at the diner. Hey, do you remember the two covered bridges down by his place?"

"Of course, how could I forget? I'm not gonna meet you there for another try, though, if that's why you're calling," he said, which made me laugh out loud. Our one attempt at sex had been terrible for both of us.

"Dude, that ship sailed down that same damn river, as have my days stealing kisses under old bridges." Of course I blushed as I thought of doing that with Cliff not so long ago, and with a much more agreeable outcome than when Xander and I had tried. "Anyway," I quickly said to get those dueling images out of my head, "I wondered if you could meet me and Levi at the first bridge."

"Okay, I can be there in a few hours. Should I pack my swim trunks? You guys planning to toss me in the river or something?"

"Or something." I laughed. "At least Levi will be with me, so you don't have to be afraid I'm gonna jump your ugly-ass bones."

"Dude, you didn't think I was ugly when—"

"Stop, you're on speakerphone," I said as Levi burst out laughing.

"Levi has seen my bare ass running in and out of that river enough times to know I've got an admirable backside," Xander said. "Anyway, see you both soon."

"Whatever. See you at the bridge."

I hung up, shaking my head. "That dude needs a husband." I looked up to see Levi with his eyebrow cocked. "What? Not everyone is husband material, but our friend needs someone to keep him stable."

"That wasn't you, though," Levi said with understanding, since he'd been my sounding board as Xander and I had tried to work through our differences.

"Definitely not me, but he can sure as hell paint a building, and that's what we need about now."

"Oh, wait," Levi said. "I told Cliff I'd meet him and Dad to discuss the aquaponics and fish stuff. You willing to go with me? We can walk to the bridges from there."

I smiled, happy to have any excuse to spend time with Cliff. "Yeah, that sounds perfect."

Cliff

I HADN'T meant to keep the aquaponics operation running. I figured when I started school, that would end my big experiment until I could get enough education to do it right. But one visit from Tracy Morris, coupled with my uncle, cousin, and even Aunt Sue ganging up on me to say they could keep it going so the tiny fry could grow while I was learning, changed that.

Despite Tracy being a total stoner and Uncle Chris being somewhat religious, the two hit it off the moment they met. I never would've guessed that in a million years. So, in my final weeks on the farm, I worked to set up the operation so it was easy for them to maintain.

I'd just finished checking the water pH to confirm for the umpteenth time that it remained consistent when Levi pulled up with Brandon behind him. I backed into the barn, hoping they hadn't spotted me, and went back to checking the connections and equipment. There was plenty to do while I waited for them to leave.

Unfortunately, luck wasn't on my side. Levi came into the barn with Brandon close on his heels. "Hey, how's it going?" Levi asked.

I rarely got upset with my cousin, even when he was annoying. So I let go of my frustration and pasted on a smile. "Hey, guys, what's up?" I asked, ignoring Levi's question.

"We're going to meet a painter over at the covered bridges. We thought we could get away with painting them since they're sort of off the beaten path."

I cocked my eyebrow but didn't ask for details. I'd rather not know if they were doing it without permission. And if Levi was involved, anything was possible. Plausible deniability came to my mind.

"Cool," I responded, pretending to be checking out the connections.

"Come with us," Brandon said. "It'll be fun, and you can meet one of our oldest friends. He's a professional contractor and an annoying history buff. He'll probably spout a bunch of obscure bridge factoids at you."

I chuckled. "Okay, I guess," I said, imagining Xander dressed like an old man with a pipe and funny hat who liked to talk about the history of this area. That could be entertaining.

I followed Levi and Brandon across the paddock toward the bridges, taking in the beauty of the area surrounding us. It wasn't home yet, not that I'd ever make it such, but it was a place I was beginning to love. Being here with my aunt, uncle, and cousin only added to that feeling.

When we arrived at one of the bridges, no one else was around. Trying not to think about the kissing fest Brandon and I had under this bridge at the beginning of summer, I wandered around to get a feel for the architecture. It was solid on the inside, unlike what you'd expect from the peeling paint on the exterior. A little window spanned the entire bridge to let light in, which gave a picturesque view of the river below.

I was coming out the opposite side when a new, rather expensive-looking pickup pulled up. This must be the friend Brandon mentioned, though I didn't expect the guy to be driving such a new rig.

I reached the other side of the bridge just in time to see a model-like bodybuilder grab Brandon in a hug. I stood rooted on the edge of the bridge, unable to tear my eyes away from the two handsome men locked in an embrace. They appeared to make a much better couple than Brandon and I would have.

Then the newly arrived hunk caught sight of me, and his face broke out into a mischievous grin. "Well now, who is this?" he asked.

Brandon and Levi turned toward me. Brandon's expression turned dark, but Levi smiled. "That's Cliff, my cousin. Cliff, this is Xander, a buddy of Brandon's and mine from our high school days."

I took the giant's hand, which he shook like he was trying to seal a deal with me. "Nice to meet you, Cliff," he said, and as clueless as I usually was when men flirted with me, even I could see he was.

"Same," I said as I removed my hand and stepped away from him and the mountain of trouble a man like that could bring.

"So, um," Brandon said behind us, "the bridge?"

Xander's gaze held mine for several more moments; then he turned toward Brandon. "Yeah, the old Petterson Bridges."

Highly attractive men like Xander were almost too pretty, too put together for my taste. I had an innate distrust of perfection. I guessed too many years working the land had taught me to understand how seldom perfection existed in nature. I preferred men who were naturally bigger, more squarely built than me, and who had a rugged quality—men who took care of themselves more to feel healthy than for their looks, men like Brandon.

Once Xander's gaze focused on something other than me, I enjoyed his story. "The Pettersons were a family who moved to the area a few generations back. You see that big rock there?" he asked, pointing at an enormous boulder on the other side of the river. "There was a small gold rush here back when settlers first arrived. The Pettersons were convinced there was gold in that mountain, so they blew that thing off the side of the cliff, effectively blocking all access to their farm right over there."

Xander chuckled and winked at me as he said that last bit. When he did, out of the corner of my eye, I noticed Brandon stiffen beside me. "The family had been finding gold in the river down there. With their earnings, they decided the best thing they could do was build not just one bridge across the river, but two."

Xander walked to the river's edge and gestured for me to follow; then he pointed at the side of the bridge. "You see this blue color? It's almost faded, but originally, both bridges were Victorian blue, which was unusual for bridges of the time. Covered bridges are covered simply because water can't rot the wood if it can't reach the foundations. Most of the time, they were either painted white or red, because those colors were affordable. The Pettersons were a different sort, though. With their newly acquired wealth, they wanted to show off, so after a trip to San Francisco, they decided to paint their bridges the expensive blue color."

In his deep baritone voice, Xander rambled on about the family, an old graveyard where most of them were buried, and an old mansion that burned in the nineteen twenties—all stuff that would've been interesting to me if he hadn't stood so freaking close.

"How do you know all this?" I asked, taking the opportunity to step away from him because he was invading my personal space.

Xander smirked and gave me some more room, clearly picking up on my discomfort. "Well, that'd be because my last name is Petterson. This all belonged to my third great-grandfather."

"Don't let him fool you," Levi said. "He's always been a history geek, even in high school."

"Which is why I started working out," Xander added. "Got tired of getting bullied."

"Cool," I said, unconsciously moving toward where Brandon stood, glowering at his friend.

I saw when Xander must've figured out Brandon and I were an item, of sorts. His face fell for an instant, but he quickly recovered. I hated that I'd accidentally given him the wrong idea, but I didn't think I'd actively encouraged him either.

Xander swiftly shifted the conversation and began telling Levi how much he'd charge to paint the bridges, saying something about giving him a discount since he'd be helping preserve his family's legacy.

While Levi and Xander talked shop, I continued to explore the bridge. Brandon kept an eye on me and stayed fairly close, maybe to ensure I didn't get too close to Xander, although I could pretend he was concerned I'd fall into the river. In any case, it felt nice just being near him again, even if our relationship was in an awkward spot.

Sexy men need to be on the back burner, I thought. Then I laughed inside because Brandon on my back burner was exactly what I would've preferred.

Brandon

I'M NOT usually the jealous type. For real, I tend to be live and let live, but when Xander started flirting with Cliff, I saw red. I'd had just about enough when Cliff came over and stood next to me, all but telling Xander to back off.

Luckily the big lug was smart enough to get the hint.

Cliff was one of those rare guys who sent my already-enamored heart into overdrive. I needed to figure out a plan to win him back.

After Levi and Xander discussed paint cost estimates, we all parted ways. They headed to the paint store in town, Cliff walked back to Chris's farm, and I decided to take lunch to my parents at their clinic. I hadn't done that in a while.

Wilcox had two options for eating out—the diner I'd eaten at with Levi that morning, which had mostly unremarkable food, and an Italian restaurant, which had pasta to die for when I was a kid. But the last time I ate there, the food was beyond horrible.

Since I wasn't in the mood to drive clear to Eugene and back for decent takeout, I decided to do the next best thing. Mom was a health nut. Dad, less so, but he was still health-conscious. That made my best bet Kay's Grocery.

I preferred Kay's, especially for fresh, locally grown produce. I picked up Mom's favorite dressing and Dad's sunflower seeds and grabbed some lettuce and grilled chicken breasts cut into chunks for a salad. Then I headed to the clinic.

I walked in and almost ran face-first into Dalton O'Dell and a very angry little boy. "Dalton? Is that you?" I asked just as the toddler kicked him in the shin.

"Ouch, Max, that hurt," he said as the kid made a beeline for the small play area in a corner of the waiting room.

Dalton watched the little boy in frustration, then rolled his eyes at me and shrugged. He and I had been in Ag class together in high school. He'd sat right across from me, and we'd become pretty good friends.

"I am now the proud guardian of that little terror and his sister. I moved back about a year ago. What brings you back to town?"

"I'm still working for the U of O in Eugene. I'm only down here to help my friend Levi on his farm. Do you remember him?" I asked.

He nodded and filled me in on how he'd been awarded guardianship of his bestie, Lizzie's, kids. I remembered her from school. We hadn't chatted very long when Dad's medical assistant came out and called them back.

"Hey, why don't you come over and visit sometime? There still aren't many gay guys in Wilcox. It might be fun to hang out, if you don't mind two very active and opinionated kids running around," he said.

"I'd like that. Oh, can I bring a friend? He's also gay. It's Levi's cousin."

"Sure. Sorry, gotta go back," he said as he rounded up the little boy.

"I'll leave my number with the receptionist," I said as he disappeared through the door.

The woman behind the front desk was smiling at me when I turned around. "A friend?" she asked.

"Yeah, we went to high school together. Can you hand him my number when he comes back out?"

She took the paper on which I'd written my number and name, and I slipped in back with the groceries and unloaded them just as Mom walked into the break room. "Hey, what's all this?" she asked.

"Just wanted to bring you and Dad lunch."

"Why?" she asked.

"Mom, I don't need a reason to be nice, do I?"

She shook her head, and I saw the skepticism. Okay, note to self, I needed to raise my game here if Mom thought I only did nice things for them when I needed something.

I thought about how Cliff had lost his parents, and suddenly I was overwhelmed by how much I took mine for granted. I pulled Mom into a hug, which she resisted at first, then quickly leaned into.

When I pulled back, she looked at me for several moments and then asked, "What's going on, Brandon?"

"Realizing I've been taking you and Dad for granted is all. I'm gonna stop doing that now. Anyway, there's lunch." I leaned over and kissed her cheek like she used to do me when I was little. "Mind if I stay with you guys tonight?"

She shook her head, and I could tell she was shocked by my realization. Mom was a hard person. She'd fought to get to the level she was professionally. I might've felt left out of the equation as a kid, but I never doubted my parents loved or wanted me.

When I got back to their house, I crashed on my old bed, and with my hands behind my head, I pondered the day. I knew I needed to be a better... whatever Cliff and I were, but I also needed to be a better son.

My phone dinged, and I smiled when I saw the message.

Dalton: *If you're serious about getting together, we're free tomorrow night.*

Me: *Sounds good. I'll need your address.*

Dalton: *Sending that momentarily. Bring your friend too. Just make sure he knows it's kid-central here.*

Me: *LOL, sounds good. I'll see what I can do.*

When I received Dalton's address, I texted Cliff.

Me: *Hey, I've just been invited to hang out with an old high school friend. Dalton is gay and stuck here in Wilcox with a couple kids. Wanna go with me?*

I watched the dots come and go several times before he finally responded.

Cliff: *Maybe. Let me think about it.*

I gave him the thumbs-up, happy to not get an out-and-out no. It might be stupid to invite him to meet a friend and his family just because we're all gay, but hell, Wilcox was a small town and could be hard if you're LGBTQ and had no support.

Dalton was cool in high school, and I assumed he still was. It couldn't hurt to make more friends anyway, right? Granted, I didn't live here and Cliff was moving back to California, but hanging out could make for a fun night. Who knows, maybe we could spend more time together when I went down to visit. That's assuming Cliff would still want to see me.

Cliff

IT SEEMED strange that Brandon had invited me to visit people I didn't know. I hadn't hung out with many gay people in general. I'd lived in the middle of nowhere, and where I grew up had a few lesbian families but no gay people that I knew of.

So, feeling like I should at least try to be friendly, I texted Brandon back and agreed to go. Aunt Sue was friends with one of the guy's parents, so she filled me in on his backstory. Apparently the kids' mom had died and given custody of her kids to her high school sweetheart, who was gay. As if that wasn't interesting enough, now the mom's brother was the guy's fiancé.

Who knew sleepy Wilcox would be such a small-town soap opera?

Brandon pulled up at five thirty. I couldn't help but smile when I saw him, which was a welcome change from the melancholy I had felt so often in the past year.

"Hey," I said as I climbed into his car. I stopped short when I started to lean over for a kiss.

"Um, hey." He sounded surprised. Clearly he had noticed my faux pas. "You're in a good mood. What's going on?"

"Just feeling thankful for having people in my life who care about me," I admitted. "Uncle Chris and Aunt Sue, Levi and Keya… and you. Thanks for inviting me to meet your friend."

"Hold on," Brandon said. He unbuckled his seat belt to lean in and claim my mouth, and I moaned into the kiss. I didn't resist. I resigned myself to deal with the consequences of letting him back in.

When he pulled away, he said. "I do care about you, Cliff."

We sat there, looking into each other's eyes a moment, and then I broke the silence. "Are we gonna be late?" I asked, though I could've used a lot more kisses.

Brandon winked at me as we fastened our seatbelts and pulled out of the driveway.

Dalton met us at his front door. He smiled and shook our hands.

"Hey, I'm Dalton O'Dell. "This is my fiancé, Pierce Simms," he said as a good-looking man came to the door behind him.

"Honey, this is my high school Ag buddy, Brandon Forest, and his friend."

Brandon shook Pierce's hand, then turned to me. "My friend, Cliff Anderson."

Just then, a huge ruckus drew our attention, and a little boy came barreling in and grasped Pierce's leg. Seconds later, an older girl with a huge head of hair came in behind him.

When she saw us, she stopped short. "Who are you?" she asked, pointing at Brandon.

He smiled down at her. "I'm Brandon, and this is Cliff."

She looked up at him, then over at me, and shrugged. Then she rushed after her brother. "Give me back my toy," she demanded, grabbing a block from him.

I talked to Dalton and Pierce as the little boy came back with the block and pulled Brandon down to show him. When the little girl came over, clearly upset the boy had her block, Brandon asked if they'd like to show him their other toys.

Both kids nodded and pulled him into the next room. It was fun to see Brandon playing with the kids. The guy was a natural, and that set something off inside me that I wasn't prepared for. I already had it bad for the man. He was sweet, smart, sexy as all get out, and I liked his personality, but this sent his likeability factor through the roof.

Remember he ghosted you, I quickly reminded myself. Besides, *When did I start wanting kids?* I wondered. I guessed one day I'd have at least one, but I'd never really thought about it beyond that. As I watched Brandon with the children, I was becoming one of those guys planning their wedding before the good stuff happened—time to pull back on all that. Or maybe not.

After my parents were killed, I was alone on our backwoods farm—still loving farming, still happy to be there, but very much alone.

Wilcox had the farm life I loved, but it also had people, not just a couple of kind neighbors. I looked at the kids and the little family that encircled them. It was more support than my folks had ever had. Dad's family rarely made an appearance in our lives, and while Aunt Sue and Uncle Chris were close to my parents and me, we hardly ever saw them.

I looked at Brandon, still smiling and playing, and realized I could easily see myself with someone like him. I needed family, friends, and connections, and I could build on that here in Wilcox. Just too bad he and I weren't right for each other.

And I needed to learn about aquaponics to ensure I would have a future in farming and be able to support a family of my own one day. As I spent an evening with a fun gay couple, as well as their very energetic children, I began to think maybe I could learn what I needed to in another way without leaving everything I cared about behind again.

Brandon

"WOW, THEY'RE great people," Cliff said as we left Dalton's house. "Thanks for inviting me to come along."

"Yeah, I'm glad we came. Dalton's always been a little cooler than most, but now he seems right in his element."

As soon as we were in my car, Cliff reached over and took my hand. "You seemed to be in your element too. So, kids, huh?"

I shrugged. "Well, I never really thought about it, but I could see myself having kids. Just, you know, I don't want to raise a child how my parents did. Not that I didn't turn out all right, but they were always too busy for me. If I ever have kids, I want to be around and be involved, maybe even stay home with them."

That statement shocked me as soon as I said it. I had never considered the possibility of being a stay-at-home dad before. Now that I thought about it, I felt how real that was for me. It didn't mean I couldn't also be like Chris and Sue, raising a family on my own farm. I logged that new realization in my brain to think about later.

I seriously needed to figure out how to make my book-selling business profitable, because I suddenly could imagine my entire future—husband, kids, animals, writing, and living a contented farm life.

"So, would you be willing to move back to Wilcox to raise a family?" Cliff asked, pulling me out of my thoughts.

"Yeah, of course. I've always known I'd eventually settle down here, hopefully on that property I want to buy from Xander. This is my home."

Cliff smiled and nodded. "I think it might be mine as well. I like it here. It feels right."

I leaned over and kissed him. Then I put the car in gear. "Are you up for another adventure?" I asked.

Cliff frowned. "Listen, we should talk first. I, well, I read your novels, and they are really great. I get it, you were busy and all, and yes, I saw myself in the characters...."

He paused, looking down at his hands. "I, well, I'm interested in, you know, continuing, 'cause I like you, but I want to take things slower, okay?"

I squeezed his hand, and when he turned to me, I smiled. "You take as long as you like."

"Thanks." Cliff smiled. "But we still get to have sex and stuff, though, right?"

"Oh yeah," I said, and I kissed him. Had we not been sitting in Dalton and Pierce's driveway, I'd have been happy to show him exactly what I thought about that.

I pulled back and said, "Okay. You willing to let me show you something?"

His smile got even bigger. "Are we going to go make babies?"

I nearly choked as I barked out a laugh. "That could be more fun than what I'm thinking, although I'm pretty sure we don't have the right equipment."

Cliff chuckled. "What did you have in mind?"

"I think I forgot. Your suggestion sounds better anyway."

Cliff leaned over and bumped my arm. "There's time for that. Take me on your adventure."

I drove toward Chris and Sue's, but before we reached their place, I turned onto Xander's property. I wanted to share more of my dreams with Cliff about living there. I wanted to help him see what I envisioned here long-term.

I pulled into the driveway, drove past the dilapidated house, and parked in front of the barn. "Come with me," I said as I got out and walked toward the barn. "You remember Xander?"

Cliff frowned a bit but nodded. Poor Xander had made a bad impression on him. Too bad because Xander really was a nice guy, but I was secretly glad Cliff wasn't interested in him. "Xander inherited this place years ago. It belonged to his aunt. When we were still teenagers, I asked him if he'd sell it to me one day, and he told me he would. So I've been working toward that dream ever since. In fact, I've already put down a deposit."

I couldn't read Cliff's expression as I opened the barn door, so I proceeded to explain what I had in mind. "I want to transform this old barn into my home. See how open it is to the top? The hayloft was removed because Xander's uncle used to work on large equipment here. I want to restore half of the hayloft, up to here," I said, pointing to the middle of the space. "Imagine a huge kitchen back there, under where the loft would extend. Then a bedroom over there in the corner, and a bathroom here." Cliff followed me around as I continued to excitedly describe a detailed layout of my dream home. "I'd make this the primary bedroom, with an en suite. The kids' room would be upstairs, but the rest would be open, where the dining and living rooms are. I could even see a fireplace and maybe a—"

I didn't get the words out before Cliff was on me. His kiss was intense, demanding, and I relished it. "Damn," I said when he pulled back. "Home design turn you on, or just dusty old barns?" I was going for playful, but when our eyes met, Cliff looked on the verge of tears.

"I love it," he whispered. "I used to tell my parents I would turn our barn into a house, and they just thought it was some fanciful notion. But I can totally see it here. Thank goodness it's not as big as Uncle Chris's barn, though. No one needs that many kids."

I laughed as I pulled him into my arms. "About that brilliant idea of making babies, why don't we revisit the tack room?" I asked, waggling my eyebrows. Then I led him to the back room he and I had already christened.

Cliff

THE FIRST time I had sex with Brandon was in the back of that old barn. Having a repeat there was sexy as hell, especially after he'd just explained how important the place was to him. I doubted he'd ever be able to look at that tack room without thinking about our rolls in the hay. The thought made me smile.

I would've preferred to spend the night with him, but he said he had to return to his parents' house. After I read his incredible novels, I'd been thinking about him a lot. I had intended to make a bigger deal about giving him another chance, but then I saw him with those kids. Something inside me had clicked, and all I could do was ask for things to go slow.

I laughed at myself. I was much more easily influenced by a sexy man than I'd even realized. Besides, if I was going to go to school, the time was ticking before I'd have to leave. But I was beginning to rethink that as well. God, I hated being so fucking wishy-washy.

That night I lay in bed thinking about my future. By morning I'd figured out I couldn't go back to California. I simply couldn't throw away everything I'd gained—the community, the family, the guy. But I still needed the classes.

Even though it was still the wee hours of the morning, I couldn't sleep, so I opened my laptop. I searched for online aquaponics-related courses offered through UC Davis or California's agricultural extension office, and I found a flood of information. So I bookmarked several webpages to look at later when I wasn't so tired.

I climbed back into bed and closed my eyes, and just before I fell asleep, it was as if I could hear my dad. "Keep the faith, son. The right path will fall before you. When it's time, you'll know." I fell asleep hoping he was right.

I woke up the next morning feeling better and more hopeful about life in general than I had since I'd lost my parents over a year ago. I had a life I had begun to cherish, and despite the difficult night, I decided to embrace it.

As soon as I entered the kitchen, I hugged Aunt Sue. She hugged me back gently and shoved me toward the coffee pot. I grabbed a mug of coffee, doctored it up, and gulped it down. Then I headed out to help with milking the cows.

I met up with Uncle Chris later while I was checking on my aquaponics system. "I've been meaning to talk to you. There's been a change of plans," I told him. "I, well, I don't want to leave, Uncle Chris. I just got the equipment up and running, and I feel like I've found my place here with you, Aunt Sue, Levi, and Keya."

My uncle cocked an eyebrow at me, I suspect because I didn't mention Brandon in that list, although I was thinking of him too.

"So you're not going to do the training, then? I thought it was important to you that you get a more formal education about all this," Uncle Chris said, gesturing toward my setup.

"I'm still going to try to, but not in California. I left home to go to college once, and I was miserable. I don't want to do that again if I can help it. I know it's probably an imposition having me here long-term, so I plan to start looking at apartments in town."

"Stop right there. You will be doing no such thing. This is your home as long as you need it, and neither your aunt nor I think you being here is an imposition. You've been nothing but helpful since arriving. Besides, we want you here. We'd prefer you to be here where we can help you instead of so far away."

In his own way, Uncle Chris had just said he and Aunt Sue loved me, and I cleared my throat before a lump could form there. "You're sure you don't mind? At least let me pay for groceries once in a while. I've got a big mouth to feed, after all."

Uncle Chris just laughed. "Come on in, and we'll eat our oatmeal. Sue said she's made you some bacon to help it go down. Then I need your help with the cows. Someone is coming to look at them later this morning."

"Look at them?" I asked, but he had already walked inside.

When we were seated around the table, Uncle Chris told Aunt Sue the news about me staying, and she grinned, stood up, and kissed me on the head. "I was hoping you'd come to your senses."

She grabbed the coffee pot and refilled my cup. I knew for a fact she was busying herself to hide her emotions because I tended to do the same thing.

Brandon

"REALLY? THEY'RE ready to take it on?"

"Brandon, they have been ready all along. It's you who's been dragging your feet. I had to do some heavy negotiating, but they finally came around to the advance your books deserve."

I expected her to say they'd agreed to a low amount, but then she told me what they'd agreed to and I almost dropped the phone. "What? They agreed to that much?"

"Well, of course they did," she said, as if this sort of thing happened to authors every day. "They should've paid more, but you're still new."

"Yeah," I agreed, "there's no guarantee my books will find readers either. They're really taking a chance on me."

"Brandon, listen to me," she said in the authoritative tone that always snapped me to attention. "I've been in this business longer than most. I love it, and it's been good to me. I've seen a hell of a lot of books cross my desk, and I've gotten pretty damned good at picking out the winners. This series is a winner. I recommend you go out and celebrate, then put that ass of yours in a desk chair and start writing the next series. You're only as good as your last novel, and if your books do as well as I think they will, you'll need to pump the next ones out faster. Welcome to the world of being a successful author."

I sat, stunned by her words. Could I really do this full-time? Was this the confirmation I'd been waiting for to make that leap?

"Brandon? You still there?"

"Yeah, sorry, got caught up in the moment."

She chuckled with her deep, cigarette-stained voice. "This is the fun part. Enjoy it, but don't rest on your laurels too long. I'll send the contract over, and you get it signed. You should be hearing from them soon."

"Yes, ma'am, and thank you." I hung up to another chuckle.

I felt like I'd just won the biggest lottery jackpot in history. I never thought I'd make it this far. As a professor of English, I knew that the number of authors who actually got published traditionally was minimal at best, regardless of their talents and skills for writing and storytelling. The ones who could make a living at it were even fewer. I'd just received an invitation to become one of that elite.

I leaned back in my chair and thought about Xander's farm property. Way back he'd considered turning the land into a housing suburb, but his mother had nixed that, saying it'd been his family's land and he needed to respect that. To this day I remained thankful to her for putting the brakes on that idea.

I'd given Xander a thousand bucks as a sort of downpayment to keep him from selling the property to someone else. The amount was a drop in the bucket, but enough to convey to my friend how serious I was about buying the place as soon as I could afford it. I'd always wanted to live close to the Owens family, and still did. Only now that scenario included their hunk of a nephew.

I didn't think. On impulse, I picked the phone up and called Xander. "Hey, what's up? I need to talk to you about something."

"Dude, tell me you're not calling to rag on me for not having that bridge done yet. It's not even been two days."

"No, but you will be doing that soon, right?"

"Of course I will," he said. "You can cool your jets, though. The paint is still on order."

"Okay, well, that's not the reason I called, anyway. You know that property that belonged to your aunt? The five acres over by Sue and Chris Owens?"

"You mean the old farm you drool over every time you set foot on it?" Xander teased, and I could practically hear him smirking into the phone.

"That's the one. I'm ready to buy it outright."

"Ah, man. What brought this about? I've been holding it for you for, what, five years?" he asked.

I rolled my eyes. "Try nine," I said, but the way Xander chuckled told me he knew exactly how long it'd been.

"You told me ten thousand an acre, but that was a while ago. Things have gone up in the area, so what's your price."

"Nope, you already put money down, and our deal stands. The place has unofficially been yours since the day you did that. Fifty grand, and I'll sign the deed."

"Are you sure, Xander? I know it's worth more…."

"I'm sure. Now, I'll have my attorney draw up an agreement and send it over."

I shouldn't be surprised. Xander really was a great friend, but he was also a businessman. The price of land in the area had gone crazy over the past few years, and I was honestly expecting him to renegotiate for double or even triple what I'd offered. He could certainly get it if he put the place on the market, not that he needed the money. Of course, that would put an end to my plans. Luckily Xander had made a killing since he left Wilcox. He dabbled in real estate and then ran a huge construction company up north. I'm guessing that's why he was being so generous. That and I really had put money down. Not that we had a written contract or anything.

"What are you gonna do with the place? You still want to turn that barn into a house or something?"

"That's the plan, but it'll be a while before I can afford that. Step one is buying it, not sure the order of events after that."

Xander paused for a few moments, then said, "When you're ready to convert the barn, let me know. Aunt Greta was my best buddy when I was a kid. She was the first family member I came out to. I regretted her old house wasn't salvageable, but it'd mean a lot to me if that barn could be saved. If I can help you renovate it, I'll do what I can."

I smiled. Xander could be a lot, but he was a great guy. "Thanks, man. I appreciate it."

When we hung up, I relaxed in my chair and let out the breath I'd been holding. I was really doing this. I was about to become a landowner. Yeah, I was also about to use up my entire savings, not to mention my advance, but it'd be money well spent.

That farm had been my dream since high school. So many of my best memories were tied to that piece of land. Levi and I had hung out in the abandoned barn as kids, even before we became best friends with Xander, and I had already made new memories there with Cliff. The place represented my past, and even though Cliff had made it clear I was far from out of the woods for inadvertently ghosting him, I thought of him as my future. Now that I could afford it, the little farm would soon be something I could actually call mine.

Cliff

I SIGHED with relief as I read through the more detailed information UC Davis had sent me about its online courses. The program I wanted to take had an entirely web-based option, which was ideal. It included the possibility of touring active aquaponic operations in Southern California, which was also doable.

I had some sticker shock at the overall price tag, but then I remembered I'd been awarded the career development grant for wildfire victims, along with some other grant funding. Money might still be tight, but the whole venture wouldn't be nearly as expensive as if I'd been planning to attend on campus.

Just to make sure I fully understood it all, I read through the paperwork a second time. Then I went downstairs and told Aunt Sue my news. "I can do all the courses online and only have to go down to California a few times a year for some field trips and such. I can't tell you how relieved I am that I can do all of that and stay here."

She grinned at me, as if it didn't surprise her in the slightest. "These things have a way of working out. Why don't you go on out to the dairy and tell your uncle? He's been concerned about what you were going to do about classes."

I kissed her cheek and rushed outside. An older man I didn't recognize was talking with Uncle Chris as I approached the milking barn. The cows hadn't been released into the fields like usual, and several other men were inspecting them in the holding pen.

"I can't believe after all these years you're finally selling," I heard the man say to Uncle Chris as I came within hearing range.

I froze. Uncle Chris selling his cows? No, I must've misunderstood.

He glanced over at me and smiled, sadness etched on his features. "There's a time for all things, and this is my time."

I stood back and listened as my uncle negotiated away his entire herd. I gleaned enough from their conversation to learn the man already had a large operation and sold exclusively to the Tillamook Creamery.

Uncle Chris, being the upstanding farmer he was, also negotiated for the cows' new owner to employ as many of his workers as were willing to relocate. When they discussed the equipment, I listened carefully. I had a sick feeling this could be the start of my uncle selling the entire farm, although the sale of the land never came up between the two.

I was too paralyzed to leave, too caught up in what I'd learned, so I stuck around and helped release the cows after everyone left.

Once we were alone, Uncle Chris spoke first. "Come with me," he said, and we walked toward the milking barn.

"Every year, dairy farmers are forced to think about how to become more efficient. It's been like trimming fat off a bone-thin heifer, and it only gets more difficult to manage. I'm tired, son. Your aunt is too, and Levi has no interest in farming. I don't want to let go of this land. The Owens family was the first to farm it after this area was settled. Before that, it was used by Keya's ancestors. That's quite a legacy for my grandbaby, don't you think?" he asked, and I nodded, unsure why he was telling me all this.

He turned and looked at the immaculately clean barn. A feat that still surprised me, considering how nasty it'd been while the cows were in it. "The fact is, I know more than a few farmers who've lost their britches running that rat race. If I decided to keep going, I'd have to borrow money, expand and grow the business, find new customers, and still maybe end up in the red. Or I can sell."

I nodded, fully aware most modern-day farmers faced the same concerns, but that didn't ease the knot in my stomach. "So you're selling?" I asked.

He glanced skyward and stared long and hard at the barn's rafters. "Your aunt and I were discussing it before you came to stay. We had to make some hard decisions with the impending loss of our best milk buyer. Ultimately, we decided we didn't want to borrow more money. Then you offered us a great solution, which I hope you'll consider."

I frowned in confusion. "What does selling your farm have to do with me?" I asked.

"When your dad started talking about aquaponics, I thought he'd lost his mind." Uncle Chris chuckled at the memory. "He told me all about taking you and your mama to Kansas City to tour some old dairy that'd been converted to an aquaponics operation selling basil. He was so danged excited, said he wanted to chat about it, one old farmer to another, so he called me." My uncle shook his head fondly. "That was well over a decade ago, and I always kept that in mind and joked with your aunt that if the dairy ever failed, we could grow basil. Now that doesn't seem quite as far-fetched as it used to."

He pointed around the huge barn and winked at me. "With my girls gone to Tillamook, there'll be a lot of empty real estate around here soon. That buddy of Brandon's, Tracy, made me an offer last time he was here. Said he wants to invest in our setup. Your setup, that is. He wants to see if we can get the aquaponics thing to work in a closed system so he can grow his marijuana."

"You want us to grow pot?" I said, shocked.

Uncle Chris doubled over from laughing so hard. "Boy, no, your aunt would kill us both. But there's a lot to this aquaponics thing, or so I'm learning—equipment, heating costs, and keeping the fish stable and balanced. Not to mention feeding them. If we're going to make a go of this, we've got to do it right. This family doesn't do anything half-assed."

For thirty minutes Uncle Chris shared his ideas for creating a sustainable system, along with separating the two barns into distinct areas. "Grow tilapia in one, catfish in the other," he said. "At harvest, you'll use the remnants of one fish to feed the other." Clearly, my uncle had already given this new venture a ton of thought.

My head spun. "Let's back up a second. You want to make me your business partner? Why would you do that when you own the farm and already have a plan in mind?"

"I'm too old to start all this new stuff myself. I don't even want to do that, Cliff, but you have your mind set on it," he said. "You're my nephew, and I want to support you in this. Besides, it's a good idea, much better than me chasing my tail trying to turn my dairy farm into a glorified computer that milks cows."

I couldn't help but laugh. I'd watched a video recently of a guy in California who was touring new dairies, and one of them really was just a vast computerized milking parlor. Not something my uncle would be interested in.

"You know, we'll be pretty computerized too," I said, mostly to get a rise out of him, but he didn't take the bait.

"There's a big difference between a machine keeping fish water at the right temperature and a robot milking a damned cow. I just don't have the energy for all that," he said, and the fact that he cussed told me exactly how frustrated he must be.

"Okay." I looked my uncle in the face. "A hundred percent yes to your offer. If I'm going into business with someone, I can't think of anyone I'd rather work with than you."

Uncle Chris smiled and reached out his hand. Emotions caught in my throat as I reached over and shook it. Not once had my uncle shaken my hand on an issue. People who didn't work in these environments couldn't understand the significance of a farmer, one as proud as my uncle, giving his word by shaking your hand. It was a big deal.

"Okay, well, you best figure out how to take them classes, 'cause we're gonna need you on top of your game."

"Already got that ball rolling. Figure I can do it all online."

Uncle Chris sighed but smiled. "Everything is computers. Well, if you can learn online, that means you can still work here. Why don't we schedule a time for Tracy to come down and have dinner with us? We'll talk about all the basics and get a business plan written up."

Just like that, my life changed course yet again. But this time it was in a direction I'd wanted to go but didn't know was possible. Uncle Chris had made it possible by changing his own dream for his farm, and I'd be forever grateful.

But nothing about setting it up was going to be easy. I had jumped into aquaponics feet first because I needed something to keep me busy while dealing with the loss of the farm and my parents, and it felt like I was honoring my dad in pursuing it. Never in a million years would I have thought it would lead to converting Uncle Chris's farm.

"Uncle Chris, if we do this, I want to explore how we can keep the farm going if the aquaponics doesn't work out. We best avoid finding ourselves in the same situation years down the road as we are now with the dairy operation."

"You're on board with this idea and fixing to stay for the long haul. That's half the battle won already," my uncle said, sounding relieved. "We'll figure all the rest out in time. Always do."

"I believe we will, Uncle Chris. You know I'll do everything I can to make that happen."

Brandon

I PURPOSEFULLY didn't mention purchasing Xander's land to anyone right away, not even Levi. I was too afraid Xander might back out of our deal before we'd signed on the dotted line. Although I was dying to tell everyone, I just carried on like normal and spent most of my last days of summer at the farm helping Chris and Cliff shut down the dairy business.

That news hadn't come as a complete shock, but it was still a sad process. Levi even shed a few tears about it when he and I were alone. "I-I can't do it, Brandon, and I feel so guilty. Dairying is all Dad has ever known. He had to sell all his cows because of me."

I put my arm around my bestie and pulled him close. "Listen, Levi, not even your dad expects you to become a farmer. He knew you never wanted that life. He's doing the right thing for all of you, especially his new grandbaby. He's keeping the land in the family and he's still farming, just in a different way now."

"Yeah, I know you're right." He swiped at his wet eyes. We sat silently as we stared over the river from the window of the covered bridge. So many of our life troubles had been resolved while we stood on that bridge, hashing things out.

"Anyway," Levi continued, "I'm glad Cliff and Dad have found a way to keep it all going."

I nodded but didn't respond. My heart was so full of excitement, happiness, and concern that I'd screw things up again with Cliff that the subject of him living here permanently was one I couldn't even talk about.

When Keya arrived, I hugged her and left them alone so they could continue the conversation. Keya was the calming force in Levi's life. She was as steady as anyone I'd ever met. If anyone could help Levi leave his guilt behind, it'd be her.

I was strolling across an empty pasture toward Xander's barn when my phone dinged—my bank notifying me that the payment from my publisher had been deposited. I jumped up and down, whooped, and called Xander immediately. "Dude, it's time. The money's in the bank. Let's close this thing!"

Xander chuckled. "Okay, I'll call the title company. I've already asked them to begin the process. I'll let you know when it's time to come in and sign paperwork."

"Cool, thanks. I can't believe this is finally happening for real. I'd do a darn cartwheel if I didn't think I might land in an old cow pie."

"Where are you right now?" Xander asked.

"Oh, at your barn." I laughed when Xander snorted. "Well, my barn now, I guess."

"I should've known. Okay, stay put. I'm coming over. I have a proposal."

I kicked back on an old bench outside the two sliding barn doors and leaned back against the building to wait for Xander. I was just about to doze off when I glanced up to see Cliff walking my way.

The quick jump of my heart in that moment had become routine whenever I saw him.

"Hey, I saw Levi and Keya, and they said you'd walked this way. I thought maybe you'd be down for touring the tack room again." He winked at me.

I jumped up and took his mouth with mine. When he deepened the kiss, I reluctantly pulled back. "Can I get a rain check on that great idea? Xander's on his way over, and I don't share."

Cliff blushed at the insinuation, and I grinned, even though I was actually dead serious. "Oh well, I should get back," he said. "I didn't mean to stick my nose into whatever you're meeting him about."

"No, Cliff, wait. Xander is a close friend, and I know he came on strong, but I promise you, he's a good guy."

Cliff sighed. "Pushy men always send me running in the opposite direction. I don't have much experience with guys, being stuck in the middle of nowhere my entire life, but in college, I had a few that pushed too hard. If Xander comes on to me like that again, I might not be able to stop myself from putting him in his place. But it… it's not him, it's me."

"Trust me, if he comes on to you, knowing we're an item, I'll do all the putting him in place."

Cliff grinned, leaned up, and kissed me again. "Too bad we don't have time to visit the tack room, though."

Just then, Xander's huge truck rumbled down the driveway. To his credit, when Xander saw Cliff and me standing close, he didn't even blink an eye. For all his cockiness, I knew he'd back off the minute he grasped where things stood.

"Hey, Cliff, good to see you again. Brandon, I have something I want to chat with you about."

Cliff began to leave, but I grabbed hold of his hand and pulled him toward the truck. Xander opened the tailgate and then unfolded some pieces of paper and laid them out. "I told you my aunt Greta and I were close and that I'd like to help with the barn conversion. Now that you're gonna be the official owner, here's some drawings I had made up."

Cliff looked up at me and then over at Xander, clearly catching the part about me buying the place. He moved closer to Xander and examined the drawings.

"Oh, that's cool," he said as Xander explained how his architect had divided the barn into livable spaces.

"That's amazing." I leaned in for a look. "Why did you do all this?"

Xander paused, then sighed. "Truth?"

I nodded.

"I had these drawn up when you told me your idea, years ago. I didn't know if you'd ever buy the land, and back then, I was fixing up houses here in Wilcox. I was dating an architect for a while, and even though the guy was shit as a boyfriend, he did good work. I brought him here, explained what you had in mind, and he drew these up free of charge. You mad?"

I snorted. "No, not mad, and I'm not surprised either. Why didn't you show me before now, though?" I asked.

"'Cause I didn't want you to think I was stepping on your toes. You were buried in college classes at the time and barely made enough money to pay for that ratty apartment of yours, much less all this. I'm sorry," he quickly apologized.

Cliff's smile grew as he examined the blueprints.

"No need to be sorry. You're right, I couldn't come near buying this place before now. It's just luck and a hell of a lot of work writing my books that finally got me there."

"Can we go look in the barn with these?" Cliff asked.

Xander winked at me, and I nodded. "Yeah, let's go look."

There were things I'd change. My ideas of what I wanted had evolved some over the years, and the guy who drew it up had made things uber-modern with country elements on the side. That was not my style. From what Cliff said and the questions he asked, he felt the same. But the blueprints were a solid starting point that needed some tweaking.

"The kitchen is probably too small," I said as I looked over Cliff's shoulder. He leaned back against me slightly, enough that I could tell he was really into this. "I plan on doing a lot of cooking here, and if we're building it from scratch, it needs to be made for practical use. The bedroom down here seems too spacious. It's a nice layout, but do I really need a living room inside my bedroom?"

When I shook my head, Cliff showed us how we could move the wall a few feet, taking space from the oversized bedroom to make the kitchen larger. "It flows better into the living space too. You're gonna want your sight lines to show the land."

I was watching him when he looked up, and I wondered how he knew that. He must've seen the question on my face because he answered me without my asking. "My mom redesigned the farmhouse I grew up in. My dad made fun of her for it, saying they spent her entire inheritance on it, but she'd made it so every room on the first level looked out over the land. If you're gonna live in the middle of nowhere, working the land until you are so tired you can barely move, you should be able to enjoy it from every angle."

Sadness momentarily showed on his features before he looked back at the drawings. "If you move this wall, you'll be able to see the farm while working in the kitchen. Some have the old doors on automatic tracks so you can open and shut them from inside, but regardless, the view from the front of the barn is something I'd take full advantage of too."

I leaned over and kissed him, and he blushed awkwardly in front of Xander. "Your ideas are right with mine," I said as I pulled him close. I didn't give a shit if Xander saw me kissing Cliff. He already knew we were together, no sense in hiding it.

Xander cleared his throat and said, "Well, I'll leave these with you, but my proposal is I can have my crew come out and remove the old house. I'll have to rent equipment, but if you pay for that, I'll provide the labor."

"Really?" I forced myself to look away from Cliff.

"Yeah, it's almost like finally putting my aunt to rest. That old house needs to be dealt with for liability reasons and because it's an eyesore. Last thing you'll want to see with all your panoramic views is that old heap."

I nodded. "I'm happy to contribute. Just tell me how much."

"Sounds like a plan, my friend." Xander clapped me on the back and shook Cliff's hand.

Once he was gone, I looked at Cliff, who was back studying the drawings. "I didn't want to tell anyone about buying the place until it was a reality. I wasn't purposefully keeping it from you."

Cliff glanced up and smiled. "Brandon, your business is your own. I don't expect you to get permission just because we're screwing around."

"But we aren't just screwing around, or did I get that wrong?"

He looked down at the drawings, but I could tell he was thinking. "No," he said quietly.

"Listen, I know what I said the other night about going slow, but Brandon, that's because you really hurt my feelings when you gho… um, well, when you disappeared."

I tried to say something, but he stopped me. "What I feel for you… yeah, it's more than screwing around, at least for me. But I don't want to push you into a relationship if you're not ready for it. I know I'm screwed up…."

I reached over and drew him into my embrace to stop the stupid comment about him being screwed up. We ended up crumpling the blueprints between our chests, but nothing mattered to me except Cliff.

With effort, I pulled back. I wanted to get all this off my chest. "Listen, I like you a lot. If you feel something, you don't have to hide that from me, okay?"

"Same for you, right?"

I grinned and pecked him on the lips. "Yeah, same for me. Now," I said. I found the drawing of where the tack room had been turned into the primary suite. "Shall we explore the main bedroom, just to, you know, get a feel for it?"

Cliff laughed and led me by the hand to our little hay-covered love nest.

Cliff

I'D COME over hoping for a little roll in the hay, but I got so much more. Apparently Brandon and I were officially a couple now, and the barn conversion Xander had secretly designed was epic.

I could easily see a life there with Brandon. The house would be amazing—spectacular even—but there was more than just a building here. There was us, building a life together.

My heart had begun to wrap itself around the idea of Brandon early on. I could see that clearly now. During the trip to the farm, when things had been so hard, I had begun to see Brandon as a part of me, a part of my journey.

Things had solidified between us since then, albeit not without misunderstandings. After we made love on the hay in the back of the barn, I absently stroked his bare chest and sighed. "I'm ready," I admitted. "To meet your parents, I mean. You know I didn't do that when your mom invited me over before, but if we're, you know, boyfriends, it's important."

Brandon's chest rumbled in a chuckle. "You sure you're ready for that? I mean, we've only been official for a couple hours, and my parents are a lot. Not saying Mom will have us shopping for rings before supper's over, but who knows?"

"My parents were a lot too, in their own way. I miss them every day." I quickly went on before emotions got the better of me. "Anyway, I'd like to meet your mom and dad, if the invitation still stands."

Brandon pulled me on top of him and rutted his now-spent cock into mine. "If you're ready, I'll set it up. Shall I invite them over here?"

I laughed. "That's totally up to you, but if you want my opinion, this should be our special place. I mean, at least the tack room."

"Okay, deal," Brandon said. He stood and brought me up with him. "I see you here, you know?"

My eyes must've grown huge, because he snorted. "Don't freak out. I'm not dropping to one knee right now or anything. But I wanted you to know that if this continues, well… I'm bumbling this up…."

I took his face in my hands and kissed him. "You're not bumbling anything up. Thanks for saying that. I don't think we should rush things, though. Let's see what happens, but yeah, I see myself here too."

We dressed and did our best to remove the hay from our hair. Then we returned to Uncle Chris and Aunt Sue's.

Brandon excused himself not long after, saying he needed to get back to his parents' place. My heart sped up, knowing he would speak with them about us. My dad's family never liked my mom, and as a result, it caused problems for them. It's one of the reasons I never saw that side of the family growing up. Now, as an adult, there just wasn't a relationship there.

So I understood how important it was to meet the parents and make a good impression. If they didn't like me, that could be a major challenge in my relationship with Brandon. Luckily my family— Uncle Chris, Aunt Sue, Levi, and Keya—loved Brandon, so even if his parents hated me, we'd still have family when….

Wow. When we what? Got married? Yeah, I couldn't deny that's exactly what I was thinking. I wanted to be Brandon's husband.

I was a broken man less than six months ago, a man with no future and a past burned to ash. Now I was surrounded by people who loved me, including a man I'd clearly fallen in love with.

Brandon

MOM STARED at me a bit too long, then glanced down at the tablet she used at night for reading. "It's serious, then?" Dad asked.

"Yeah, it's serious," I responded. "Cliff's my boyfriend, and I can see a future with him, here in Wilcox."

I wondered what was going through Mom's head. I knew she was supportive of me as a gay man—we'd worked through all that when I came out in high school—but she seemed hesitant now, and I couldn't quite tell why.

"Mom?" I asked, causing her to put the tablet down and sigh. My father was a straight shooter, and I had some of that in me as well. No sense beating around the bush. "Anything you want to tell me?"

"Son, Brandon, I—" She got up, walked to the window, and stared at the cute little park between the clinic and their home. "You know I grew up on a ranch, that I left that life, right?"

I nodded, unsure where she was headed. "You never really told me why you left, just that you'd always wanted to go into medicine."

She came back over and put her hand on my shoulder as she sat down. "First, I'm more than excited to meet Cliff. Since you and he started making eyes at one another, the entire town has made a point of telling me he's 'made of good stock, that one,'" she said, mimicking at least three townspeople I could imagine saying that very thing. "This isn't about him, but I left that life because I saw it as a dead end. We were dirt poor. So poor, we sometimes didn't even have enough food. My dad was too proud for food stamps or government handouts."

She paused, and I could tell she was thinking about those hard times. I felt a surge of compassion for my mother just then. How had I never known what she'd gone through growing up?

"We barely survived," she continued, "even after I went to college, taking the grants and loans my dad got so angry about. That's neither here nor there, but even after I left, they struggled. Your grandparents were good people too, but they struggled their entire lives. In the end, if it hadn't been for your dad and me helping to support them, they'd have ended up destitute and homeless. Your boyfriend, he's rooted in that life. Even Sue Owens said as much when we chatted. If you marry him, that's the life you'll have. You understand that, right?"

I knew my grandparents had been extremely poor, and that Mom and Dad had supported them financially in their final years. Mom was born when they were both quite old, so they died when I was little, but I still remembered those conversations between my parents about money.

"I understand, Mom, and I appreciate your concern. I truly do. I know you're trying to look out for me. But I'm not without options," I said, ready to finally share my book deal with them. "I sold my YA series to a publisher. I'm not making millions, but I've got my foot in the door on a solid career as a full-time author. Even if Cliff and I get more serious, I don't have to depend on him for my living."

From her expression, I could tell she hadn't considered that. She studied her nails for a moment, then looked over at me. "I guess country life is in your blood." She laughed with a slightly bitter edge to it. "Mine too, as much as I railed against it. I couldn't bear working in the bigger cities. Your poor father agreed to practice here in Wilcox, mostly because I begged him to move to a small town."

That shocked me. I always figured Dad was the one who decided to move us here.

"Son, just promise me this. Make sure you never have to rely solely on the farm to survive. I don't want you to go through what my parents and grandparents had to. That life was hard before. Now it's virtually impossible."

I leaned over and bumped her shoulder with mine. "Mom, Cliff is clever—smarter than the average guy—and what he and Chris are doing, it's pretty phenomenal. But like I said, I have my own life and career, and I did just get a nice advance on my books."

That seemed to mollify her, and for the first time, I saw more of my mother than I think I ever had. She was a strong woman, fighting to keep her career alive and struggling to continue her education and keep her business afloat. It made so much more sense to me now why she was the way she was.

I had to think more about it, but I was beginning to understand why she'd put so much emphasis, time, and energy into her work, sometimes to the detriment of her own family. If she had gone hungry as a kid, it made sense that she'd show her love through providing for her own child what she'd gone without.

"You said you got an advance?" Dad chimed in. "I didn't realize you'd finished your books."

"Ugh, yeah. Okay, since Mom opened up, I should do the same."

I admitted I'd been hesitant to communicate much about my books, partly out of fear they'd think it a waste of time and in case it all went nowhere in the end anyway. The shock on their faces, followed by the hurt, told me I'd read them wrong.

That night, we worked through a lot of unresolved family shit. I'd already decided to be a better son, which obviously had a learning curve, but I didn't think they understood just how emotionally abandoned I felt growing up.

I hadn't understood why Mom, in particular, focused so much on her work. Knowing now took some of the sting away, but hurt feelings ran deep. Still, we all went to bed that evening in a completely different, healthier place.

I brought Cliff over to meet them two nights later, and it couldn't have been a better experience. Mom cut up with him, getting more than a few smiles out of all of us, and it's like our earlier talk had lifted a weight from her shoulders.

Dad was his typical laid-back self, and when he began talking about his best friend, Tracy, he and Cliff found common ground in sharing stories. Tracy was a lot, but my father loved him, and Cliff clearly had an affinity for him as well.

That night I talked Cliff into coming back to Eugene with me. Before I knew where things stood with my books, or with Cliff, or Xander's farm, I had agreed to teach fall semester at the university. School started the following week, and I wanted a few days to spend alone with Cliff. Making love in the tack room was fun the few times we'd done it, but I really wanted him in my bed.

Cliff

I HAD no idea why Brandon made such a big deal about his parents. I loved them the minute we met. His mother informed me she grew up on a ranch south of Medford. Then she teased me constantly. His dad was laid-back but funny as hell. He reminded me a bit of Tracy, minus the pot-smoking.

I could totally see why the two men were such good friends. Their personalities were very similar, even though their career paths differed by a country mile. Of course, when I told Mr. Forest that, he looked over his glasses and asked, "What makes them so different? I prescribe meds. He dispenses them."

Brandon's mom snorted but didn't say anything. "Fair point," I conceded, and Brandon winked at me.

On the heels of meeting Brandon's family, he whisked me off for a weekend in Eugene.

His apartment was small and looked more like somewhere a college student lived than a professor. But I'd barely had time to look around the place when he began to undress me as he walked me backward toward his bedroom.

"Mm, slow down. I'm going to land on my ass." I laughed, and he pulled back.

"Your ass is exactly where I'm headed." He slowed our walk but picked up the pace in kissing up and down my neck.

I chuckled and let him continue to undress me as I did the same with him. We were both fully naked by the time we reached his bed, and we stood a moment, drinking in the sight of each other. Then he stepped closer and wrapped his hand around my cock. I moaned happily, tucked my mouth into his neck, and sucked.

Brandon smelled so good—like dark chocolate and vanilla. His scent always seemed to bring me to the edge.

I ran my hands up his back as he pulled me closer and ground his hard, erect cock into me.

"Can I fuck you?" Brandon whispered in my ear. My already-hard cock twitched.

I nodded. "Yeah, but… it's been a while, so you'll have to be gentle with me."

Brandon smiled and rested his forehead against mine. "I will always be gentle with you," he said. Then his smile turned wicked and he added, "Unless you want it rough."

I laughed. "Let's start gentle and see what happens."

At that, the time for talk was over, and Brandon laid me out on the bed and proceeded to kiss down my torso, all the way to my cock.

Before taking me in his mouth, he tilted his head up. When our eyes met, he languidly licked up and down my shaft, savoring me, then sucked me in deep.

"Aaah," I exclaimed. "Oh God, Brandon."

Pleasure flowed through my veins as he assaulted my cock with every suck and bobbed hungrily up and down my length until I thought I might come.

I put my hands in his hair and tugged. "I'm about to blow," I all but whined. He chuckled, but he slowed his pace.

I couldn't resist bucking into his mouth a few times, but to save me from ending this sooner than I was ready, I managed to roll him over onto his back. When my cock slipped from his mouth, I climbed atop him and slowly rubbed my body up and down his until his cock struck me between my balls and ass.

"You are so hot," I whispered as I ran my hands all over his glorious body, exploring. He bucked against me, seeking friction and sending pleasure through me as I leaned over and tasted his lips again.

He grabbed my ass and spread my cheeks. Then he slipped his cock up against my hole to tease me. "God, I want you, Cliff. I want you so bad," he said.

I was so turned on, I would've pressed down and taken him in dry had he not stopped me. "Got protection?" I asked, and he grinned and nodded toward his side table.

I leaned over and reached inside the drawer to pull out condoms and lube. "We'll need this and all of these." I smirked, holding up the lube and the entire box of condoms.

I slipped a condom over Brandon's cock and lubed him up, then prepped my ass before I crawled back on top of him and slowly pressed his throbbing cock inside me.

We both moaned as I took him deeper and deeper, all the way down to the root. Then he thrust gently and my brain scrambled.

We exchanged indecipherable grunts and whimpers as he set a gentle but steady pace, thrusting deeply into me again and again, setting all my nerve endings on fire.

"Fuck, Cliff, you feel good on my cock," Brandon moaned. I looked into his eyes and saw the same need I'd felt reflected in his.

Just then Brandon shifted and his cock hit my prostate. It sent an electrical charge through me. "Fuck," I yelled. "Harder, please. I need harder!"

I leaned back and closed my eyes, enjoying the sensation of being taken in a way that seemed to fill my soul as much as my ass.

Brandon continued thrusting into me, harder and harder, until I rolled off him and onto my back. "I need more of you than that," I said, and he smiled.

He quickly positioned himself between my legs, draped both ankles over a shoulder, and thrust all the way inside. The sensation felt like my nerve endings had exploded.

A thin layer of sweat formed on his forehead as his cock rammed into me at an unrelenting pace. He was putting his whole body into the effort, holding nothing back, and I luxuriated in the pleasure.

His moans intensified, and then he slowed and grinned down at me. "I'm close," he whispered. I nodded, a bit disappointed because I wasn't, but I should've known Brandon wouldn't leave me hanging. Instead, he shifted, found my prostate again, and bucked into it with punishing speed.

I yelled out as my cock shot out white ropes of cum all over my stomach and chest.

"Cliff." He sounded out of breath. "Goddamn, that was… the… the best."

"For me too," I said, my heart still beating wildly.

We held each other for a long time, neither of us ready to let the other go. Feelings whirled through me even as my heart rate slowed and my cock slowly softened. I was completely and totally head over heels for this man.

Late Sunday I begrudgingly returned to the farm, not because I didn't love it, but because I knew I would miss Brandon.

His classes started in a couple days and mine began next week, and while I should've been excited about the latter, I hated what it meant. I'd gotten way too used to having Brandon around and now we found ourselves in a long-distance relationship of sorts. Ironically Brandon found out he'd be teaching mostly online courses this term. He lamented about only having one in-person writing class—he preferred to have a live audience when he taught—but said he should be able to visit more often as a result. I grabbed that silver lining with both hands.

Still, it was hard to say goodbye to him after spending the weekend wrapped in his arms. I tried not to pout when he dropped me off at the farm. The place had a different feel now that the cows were gone, but there was still a peacefulness to it. I took solace in that and tried not to think about how miserable I'd be missing Brandon.

After supper with the family, I went for a short walk outside. Uncle Chris and Levi must've had the same idea because they joined me out near the old paddock.

"Gonna be hard when they start dismantling the barns," Uncle Chris said as his gaze roamed over the wide expanse of the pasture.

"You're sure about all this?" Levi asked him.

"You having a change of heart, son? Wanting to take on the farmer's life?" Uncle Chris laughed, then snorted when Levi's face twisted. "No change of heart. It's time. I know this is a big change and feels sad, end of an era and all that, but we really should be celebrating. It's a new beginning. Right, my darlin'?" he said as Aunt Sue came out and stood with us.

She didn't respond, just looked toward the now-empty paddock. As far as I knew, there had never been a time in the past hundred years where cows weren't on this land.

It was sad to watch a century of dairy farming come to an end, but there was comfort in knowing that, at the end of the day, my family was doing what was right for them.

Later that week Tracy visited and spent the day with Uncle Chris and me, wandering through the now-empty milking barns. We discussed how to set up the systems on a budget so as not to overextend ourselves.

"The first year is all about the fish anyway," I said as we discussed using the tanks Tracy had sold us, plus the rest he wasn't using. "If we can get the fish established, we can focus on the crop production later."

"You still need to use the crops, though," Tracy said. "Otherwise, you'll have to filter the water."

"Yeah, but we can use crops we aren't going to sell that can be fed to the fish. I read about using microgreens to supplement their diet."

We talked the subject to death, then Aunt Sue fed us, and we talked it to death some more.

I was just about to climb into bed when I got a call from Brandon. I quickly slipped my shoes back on and went outside as I answered the phone. "Hold on, I'm going to head to the barn for some privacy," I said.

Brandon chuckled, knowing my reason for doing that was because our conversations could get pretty dirty. "Okay, I'm in a safe place," I said as I entered the barn and closed the door behind me.

"Good, 'cause I have news."

"Yeah?" I asked. "Good news?"

"I think so. They canceled my creative writing class, and I agreed to take on my colleague's online freshman English class, provided they let me work exclusively from home. So I'll be teaching exclusively online and don't need to maintain in-person office hours, which means I can work from Wilcox."

"Damn, that's great news," I said. "Where are you going to live?"

"Well, that requires another conversation. I know you need to be at the farm, but I… I think we should move in together. If I'm going to be in Wilcox, I want to be with you, all the time."

"Yes," I yelped, then laughed at myself. "Okay, how can we make it happen?"

We discussed options for renting an apartment, and I cringed, knowing I couldn't afford much since the insurance company had yet to pay up and my grants only covered school-related expenses. "Let's play it by ear. I don't have much income until I get the payout, but—"

"Don't worry about that. We'll make it work. If you're willing, we can figure out the details later."

I was *so* willing. I wanted everything that went with loving Brandon.

That night I fell asleep thinking about how much my life had changed. I'd survived a string of horrible things, but I'd come out the other side, and now I was about to move in with my dream guy. Sometimes life really could surprise you.

Brandon

OUR HEART-TO-HEART over Cliff opened things up for my parents and me. They liked him almost as much as I did, which was a relief. Had their meeting not gone well, I wouldn't have given him up, but it surprised me how much I wanted their blessing.

I also told my parents about closing on Xander's property, and they actually took a Friday afternoon off to tour the place with me. I wanted Cliff to be there too, but he was busy with his own schooling. And I was still hesitant about rushing him into things, so that was always in the back of my mind.

But I told him I was closing and asked if he'd celebrate with me that night. My parents had planned a picnic at the property after the closing, and I asked him, Levi, Keya, Xander, and Chris and Sue to join us.

We'd just spread out the blankets when Xander pulled into the driveway, and in his typical dramatic way, pulling a trailer with a massive bulldozer on it.

"What's this?" I asked as I walked over to where he parked.

"I didn't want to leave you with that mess." He pointed at the dilapidated house.

"Xander, you don't have to do that. I mean, I do own it now."

He laughed. "Brandon, we agreed. Besides, that house belonged to my aunt. She's probably rolling in her grave knowing I've left it in a shambles like that. I'd feel better knowing we put all that to rest."

I looked at him and saw the sadness there. I didn't know his aunt's story, except Xander had shared enough to let me know hers had been less than a stellar life.

"Okay, yeah, it would be nice, but like we discussed, I'll cover the cost of the equipment, though."

Xander smiled. "Sure. I'll have my crew show up tomorrow. Shouldn't take them too long. Oh, and Levi," he shouted over my shoulder, "we can start on the bridge painting tomorrow too."

Levi gave him a thumbs-up, and then he dove back into whatever he was talking about with my parents.

"Um, one last thing." Xander grinned and then looked down. "I don't want you to get mad, and I can cancel it, but we checked the septic tank the week before last, and it's viable. The well still works, and the electric company said all we have to do is get the pole stabilized and you can have power here. No idea about internet. I knew you'd probably want to put a trailer here or something until the barn is inhabitable."

My mouth dropped open. "Really? Thank you, Xander. You're a great friend."

He smiled. "Here's where you might get mad." Xander could never stop when he was ahead.

"Xander, what did you do?" I asked, and he laughed out loud.

"Damn, you know me too well. Okay, so you said today, during the closing, that you were looking for a place to stay here in Wilcox. I know your mom said you can stay with them, but I'm guessing," he said, switching to a whisper, "this is more about you having alone time with Cliff. So I convinced my buddy who owns a few construction trailers in town to let us park one here. Getting the septic inspected and the electricity turned on won't cost much. Then you can be here, you know, on your own land."

I didn't know what to say. Cliff had come up behind us and slipped his hand into mine. I looked at him and thought about how amazing it would be to have him here with me. It was a dream come true.

"Xander, it might be too much. I mean you—"

"No," he interrupted me. "You don't understand how much it means to me, knowing you are the one who will be living here. My aunt Greta was a good woman. She was like the grandmother I didn't have. I want this place to be a happy one, full of energy and life, and I think you two will make it that."

I nodded, and Xander clapped me on the back and then left Cliff and me to go say hello to everyone. Cliff pulled me aside, pretending he wanted to walk around the house. When we were on the other side, he said, "I have some money saved, and if you want me to live here with you, I want to help with some of the expenses to set up the construction trailer."

"No, Cliff, this is—"

"This is your land, I get that, but I'd be paying you rent if I stayed here anyway. Let me help out a bit."

I smiled at him. "Okay, but don't let it put you in a bind. We'll figure out how much it all costs before I commit, but yeah, it'd be nice to have a place to stay here on-site."

I pulled him into a hug and then took my time kissing him. Finally, we rejoined the group and talked about the costs with Xander. When Mom and Dad interjected that they would cover the costs of the trailer, I was shocked. "Really? I mean, we, um, I can handle it."

Mom looked at Cliff and chuckled. "It's the least we can do, Brandon. You've never asked us for anything. Please, let us contribute to you realizing a dream."

I glanced at Cliff and then back at them. The day was overwhelming. So much generosity, first from my friend, then Cliff, and now my parents, who just a few days ago I thought would be dead set against me buying the property.

I hugged them both. "I don't know what to say, other than thank you."

We stayed until the sun set, then went over to Chris and Sue's for homemade pie.

The entire day had been one I'd never forget. I don't think I'd ever felt so embraced by loved ones. Not only was I going to own my own property, but I was going to share it with someone I cared a lot about—someone I'd already fallen in love with. That was a gift I'd never even dared to dream of.

Cliff

I STOOD next to Brandon and Xander and watched as the dozer pushed down the old house. Xander had already told us he and his family had removed all the valuables when a falling tree destroyed the roof years ago. Nothing that remained inside was worth saving, so a huge dump truck had arrived that morning to haul the entire thing away.

While the house was being demolished, Xander had a crew repaint the bridges. I still didn't know how much trouble Levi and Xander would get into for doing that to public property without formal permission, and I was a bit concerned about it.

Around noon the dozer pulled down the final part of the house. The porch had already been destroyed by the fallen tree, so it was just a matter of removing it. Just as the pieces were being loaded into the dump truck, a metal box fell from the debris and rolled onto the ground.

Xander waved the dozer driver down just in time to stop him from driving over the box, destroying it and whatever contents were inside.

Brandon and I gathered around Xander as he opened the box and withdrew a small book bound in leather. Plastic wrap around the book indicated that whatever it was must've been important to whoever owned it.

Xander gasped when he opened the book and saw the writing. "It's Aunt Greta's journal," he said, and I watched as a tear slipped out of the big guy's eyes and down his cheeks. "Sorry, guys, today's been so emotional, and now this."

Brandon squeezed his shoulder. I was reticent about Xander. Even after all he'd done for Brandon, our first meeting had put me off. But seeing him so emotional over his aunt's journal touched me.

"Why don't you take that home and read it there? It must be pretty personal if she hid it away."

Xander smiled at me and nodded. "Yeah, thanks. That's probably best. We still have a lot of work to do around here."

He wrapped the journal, slipped it back into the box, and placed it in his truck.

Brandon and I gave him space and walked down to see the progress on the bridges.

"Wow," I said as we came to where the crew was already packing up. "This is amazing. Who knew a coat of paint could make such a difference?"

Brandon leaned into me. "It's been an amazing couple of days, huh?" he asked, and I smiled.

"Yeah, and how are you doing with all of it? There's been a lot happening."

He beamed. "Terrific. You and I are going to have a place to live here in Wilcox. What's not to be excited about?"

"Tell me about it. I have no words to express how ready I am. I love my aunt and uncle with everything I have in me, but I am so ready for my own space again. Even if it's just a construction trailer, having you there with me, I'm all in."

He laughed. "Well, if experience is any indication, your aunt will be over here quite often anyway. She was at Levi's place daily for the first few months. I think letting go is hard for Sue."

"I have no doubt, but I'll be there every day anyway, with the farm stuff. Oh, Tracy is coming this week to finalize things with Uncle Chris and me. Do you want to be a part of all that? I mean, I know you're officially not into it and—"

"Stop. Cliff, I want to be a part of your life. Of course, if you want me, then I want to be there. Besides, someone has to watch Tracy. He may seem like a stoner hippie who grows pot for kicks, but he's a businessman through and through. But I'm immune to his bullshit, so if you're making decisions, I might be able to help you navigate some of that."

I snickered. I already knew there was a sly element to Tracy, but both Uncle Chris and I were farmers deep down. It took more than a few fancy words and smooth maneuvers to convince us to sign on the bottom line. Tracy had already had to deal with that, and of course he'd backed down from some of his more unfriendly terms. Not that anything he proposed was over-the-top inappropriate. Just that margins were always tight, and growing marijuana during a boom hadn't shown him how tight those could be.

We walked back to the property just as Xander sent his guys off with the equipment and the remains of the old house. "We have about an hour before the crew comes to work on the utilities and another couple of hours before the construction trailer arrives. Just so you know, I had the dozer guy level the ground here, but it's been so dry. The ground is hard, so I don't think you'll need to put gravel down. Up to you, though. I can have them hold the trailer if you do."

Brandon surveyed the ground while I quickly dialed the same guy who'd delivered the gravel for the greenhouse. And even though it was Saturday, he agreed to bring a load out.

"Hey," I said just as Brandon told Xander he didn't think it was necessary. "I've got a gravel guy who can deliver a load today. Brandon, if it rains, this will be a mess otherwise. If you don't mind, I'll happily pay for a few loads to keep things from becoming muddy."

My boyfriend smiled and nodded, which was good since the guy had already agreed to deliver in the next hour. The gravel company was just down the road, making it convenient.

"Meanwhile, Sue invited us to lunch," Brandon said, and Xander whooped.

"I was hoping she would. That woman has a gift in the kitchen," he said.

We just nodded in agreement.

The rest of the day went smoothly. The gravel guy brought two loads before the trailer arrived, which ensured a firm foundation for our temporary home. Xander's crew hooked up all the utilities except power, but they got the pole up and ready for the electric company to come out and attach everything.

I laughed when I walked into the construction trailer. It was basic. It didn't even have a stove, just a microwave and a small refrigerator, like a dorm room. It was still perfect for us for now.

Uncle Chris and Aunt Sue showed up a bit later and offered to loan us some of their extra furniture, including the bed I was sleeping on. By the time Brandon's parents arrived, our place was set up.

"Just needs power and it'll be the perfect little love nest," Levi said with a wink, causing me to blush. Damn him, that's exactly what I was thinking, but I sure as hell wasn't going to say it in front of my aunt and uncle or Brandon's parents.

Brandon's dad just snorted, but thankfully no one commented.

Brandon

IT TOOK a few days, but we had electricity and satellite internet set up in time for Cliff's online classes to start. But I had to go over to my parents' on Monday to ensure I had a good enough internet connection for *my* classes.

As luck would have it, most of Cliff's classes were in the evenings, and all but one of mine was during the day, so while Cliff was working his uncle's farm, I had the trailer to myself. It was a great trade-off, especially at night.

Some evenings he came home with plates from Sue's kitchen, another norm for us, especially after I rushed over a few times between classes to help Chris load equipment. Sue told us she'd feed us if I offered free labor. On this particular night, Cliff placed the plates on the countertop, then pulled me outside and into the old barn.

I knew instantly what he had in mind as he drew me toward the tack room. I laughed at what I hadn't been expecting. Cliff had swept a lot of the hay out and put a camping mattress on the floor. "I thought this might be a bit more comfortable," he said. Then, when I sat down, he pulled out a bottle of wine and two glasses from behind one of the posts.

"What's all this for?" I asked.

Cliff blushed as he handed me a wineglass and poured some for each of us.

"I… well, I love you, and I know it's probably too early to say that, but it's, you know, like, I thought I should tell you 'cause it's eating me up that I'm not being honest about it. And if you don't want or feel ready to say it back—"

I ended his rambling with my mouth and slid my free hand around the back of his head to deepen the kiss. Then I put my glass down, did the same with his, and crawled on top of him, pinning him to the mattress. "I love you too, Cliff, so much. I don't know how it happened so fast, but I've fallen hard for you. I think I fall more in love with you every day we're together."

"For real?" he asked, and I could see a flicker of doubt in his eyes.

I wanted to show him with my body rather than with words, but I needed to erase his uncertainty first. "Truth?" I asked, and he nodded. "I think I fell in love with you the moment I saw you chatting with that woman and her kids outside the ice cream shop."

Cliff laughed. "That seems so random."

I shrugged. "You were so sweet and gracious with your time and didn't even realize the woman was flirting with you. It was endearing, and it gave me a hint as to the kind of man you are."

"I probably fell in love with you before, but I began to admit it to myself when I saw you with Dalton and Pierce's kids," he admitted. "I love how kind you are to other people. How kind you've always been to me, even when my entire life had fallen apart."

I took his hand and kissed the back of it. "You are and were always easy to love, Cliff. Your sadness didn't keep me from falling for you. If I'm honest, your strength of character through all that was so impressive. You're a stronger man than me. I have to admit that."

"Pfft," Cliff muttered. "You've chased your dream of being an author and have actually done it. Do you know how few people have done that? Pursuing that takes its own kind of strength, let alone achieving it."

I chuckled. "Okay, it's not a competition, we're both strong, but I still want you to know how impressed I was, and I'm so glad I get to tell you how much I love you now."

Cliff pulled me back down on top of him and proceeded to kiss me from head to toe, and then some.

After a couple rounds of lovemaking, Cliff and I were back in the trailer, sitting on our bed, legs entwined, when Xander called, asking if he could come by. "I've got something I want to share with you two now that you own Aunt Greta's property."

I looked at Cliff, who was listening on speaker, and he shrugged. "Yeah, come on over, we're just doing homework," even though our homework was mostly making out.

"I'll bring pizza. See you in a bit," Xander said and hung up.

"What's that all about?" Cliff asked as he started dressing.

"I'm guessing it's about what he found in that journal."

"Oh yeah, I forgot about that," he said. Then he picked up his book and began reading.

When Xander arrived we went outside to sit at the patio table my parents had brought over because we had little room to eat inside. Xander's expression was serious in a way he never seemed to be around me.

"Hey, what's up?" I asked as soon as we all sat down.

"Well, you know how I told you my aunt Greta was the first person I came out to? She was always so accepting of me, so understanding, and I never really thought anything of it other than feeling relieved at the time that I didn't have to hide who I was."

I nodded, prompting him to go on, and glanced at Cliff, who appeared to be listening intently. "She was married to a man who treated her poorly, and his kids treated her even worse. Before that, though, she lived here after her parents died and was what my mom called a spinster." He paused and looked down at the journal he'd brought with him. "I guess there's always things you don't know about people, even those you're closest to. Here," he said and handed the journal to us, where he'd marked a page, "read this."

My dearest, I know I can't tell you in person, so I will write it here in my private journal.

I don't understand where my love and passion for you comes from. We are both from this tiny nothing of a town. Like you've said, our family roots are so deeply set in the soil that you can't tear yourself away.

Tonight, when we argued, and you told me you would never leave Wilcox, I gave up hope. We can't be together here, Helen. The town, our families, would tear us apart. I know you think the world has changed, but the way the country passes laws, even changing state constitutions, tells me it's not changed that much.

I want you. I hunger for you as I have never hungered for anything ever. I have spent the past twenty years dreaming of the day when you and I can lie in each other's arms and stare at the stars, free of fear and judgment, and simply feel free to love.

I've dreamed of the mornings when I can wake up in your arms and not have to rush away to satisfy some family drama. That can be had in Portland or Seattle, I know it can. I truly will never understand why you refuse to go away with me.

Helen, my beloved, even now, I can't stem the tears. You've made your decision, and I must accept it.

Wilfred Crook asked me to marry him, and I've decided to say yes. I believe this is the best decision. It gets me out of Wilcox and away from what I can't have—you. Maybe in time I will learn to love him. Maybe in time I will stop burning so passionately for my true love.

I know I'm bitter, but as I write this, I hope your Healy roots were worth throwing me aside. I don't believe I will ever be able to forgive you for choosing that over me, but maybe you never loved me as much as I do you.

I go now to start the next chapter of my life, but even as bitter as I feel, I know, my sweet Helen, I will never forget you. And I will never stop loving you, much as that pains me to commit to paper.

May the life you've chosen be worth it.

With all my broken heart,

Greta

I looked up from reading just as Cliff blew out a deep breath. "My God, that's sad. Do either of you know Helen?" he asked.

Both Xander and I nodded. "Yeah, she lives in town and works at the hardware store," Xander said.

"Have you shown her this?" he asked, and Xander frowned.

"No, I couldn't and won't. I showed Mom, and she agreed. It would do no good now. Aunt Greta died of a broken heart. I didn't see it until I read the journal. The man she married was no good, but it's like she was resigned to an unhappy life anyway."

"Yeah, I guess that explains why she didn't care if the house was fixed or not," I said, thinking about what Xander had told me about when the tree fell on her home.

"I think the destruction of the house represented her heart," he said sadly. "Anyway, I wanted to show you so you can see again how much it means to me that you now own the place and you're both living here together. Not only do you love one another, but you're a gay couple. You're living your life in a way Aunt Greta and her lover, Helen, couldn't."

I nodded and reached over to squeeze my friend's hand. "I'm sorry for your aunt, Xander. Things were bad back then. Still are in some ways, but I'm grateful we were born later and can live our lives openly." I put my arm around Cliff and scooted closer. "I can't imagine having to hide how I feel about the man I love. It would eat me up inside."

Xander sighed. "Yeah, and I think that's exactly what it did to Aunt Greta." He looked down at the journal. "I was going to leave this with you, but if you don't mind, I-I sorta think I should keep it now."

Cliff was the one to reach over now and pat Xander's hand. "You keep it. Maybe one day you can share it with the woman your aunt loved. Or just keep it as something that speaks to how deeply your family could love. Meanwhile, this one and I will do our best to change the legacy of this land. Right?" he asked as he looked at me.

I gave him a smile, and we all sat together for a bit, giving Xander time to be with friends since it was clear he was struggling to manage his emotions.

Xander excused himself after a few minutes and thanked us for letting him share his aunt's journal with us. I'd known Xander since high school and had never seen him so upset. I guess if I'd been in his situation and learned my favorite aunt had been hurt like that, I'd be upset too.

Abandoning our schoolwork a while longer, Cliff and I lay cuddled up in the tack room, talking about Helen and Greta. "What would it have been like for us back then? Do you think we'd have given up on love for the sake of our homes and families, or run off together?" I asked.

"I don't know, Brandon," Cliff admitted. "I-I loved my farm, and I hated it when I was forced to move to go to college, but that was for a defined set of time. But then, that wasn't a choice between the farm or love. I'd have been hard-pressed to choose back then, I think."

I rolled over and tickled him. "You'd have totally chosen the farm," I said.

"Hey, not necessarily. Besides, I wouldn't have had to. My mom was a hippie, and my dad was cool. I wouldn't have had to hide, even back then. I lived in California, not that far from San Francisco. It's not anywhere near as liberal as there, but it's close enough. I doubt I'd have had to choose."

"Same. My uncle Joe is out and a total player. My parents were always cool. Well, Mom had to come around to the idea a little bit, but even when she was concerned, she wasn't a jerk about it or anything. I never felt like I had to hide who I was from anyone, family included."

"It's kinda hard to understand what life must've really been like, huh?"

I leaned over and kissed the tender skin of his neck. Then I kissed up his chin and eventually took his mouth. "I think we honor the past by living our lives to the fullest, appreciating the sacrifices made by those who went before us, and loving each other with all we have in us."

Cliff smiled up at me. "That's very poetic, Mr. Writer Man."

I laughed and ran my hands down the length of his body. "I'll show you poetic," I said, then took my sweet time sending him into ecstasy.

Cliff

THE STORY of Helen and Greta struck me hard. The thing that hit the hardest was feeling the pain in Greta's writing—how utterly heartbroken she was when Helen refused to run off with her. I tried not to show it to Brandon, but the truth was, I was Helen in that scenario.

I'd lived my life on the farm and never had any intention of leaving. Would I have abandoned the farm for the sake of love? At the time, back when I still had the farm, I don't think I could've easily answered that question.

But fate had a different plan for me. So instead of whiling my life away on the farm in the mountains of north central California, I was living here … and with a man who I loved more than I even thought possible.

Speaking of loving couples, I'd never seen Uncle Chris and Aunt Sue as sweet on each other as they'd been my last few visits to the farm. Although I knew they'd never tell me as much, I was convinced they were happy to have the house to themselves. In addition to me moving out, Uncle Chris didn't have as many farm responsibilities now, fewer things that pulled him out of the house at the crack of dawn and kept him busy until the late hours. No doubt the two were rekindling their relationship as a result of him simply being home more.

Even my financial future was looking bright. I'd called the insurance company last Friday, since Walt told me he and Martha had already received their payout. I found out mine was supposed to be paid out the following week. It didn't mean I was suddenly rich, but the money would ensure I could pursue my dreams here on Uncle Chris's farm without worry.

I had just finished my online session in sustainable agriculture when my phone buzzed. I groaned when I saw the caller ID.

"Hello," I answered, even though I knew it was my dad's brother and I would rather have avoided the man altogether.

"Hello, is this Cliff?"

"Yes, Uncle Sim, it's me."

I knew I was being short. I hadn't seen or heard from him in years, and the son of a bitch hadn't even shown up to my parents' funeral. What could he possibly want now?

"Cliff, I wanted to speak to you about your parents' farm, the one that burned in Weaverville."

I didn't respond, and I had to work hard to maintain my cool. The nerve of him to call after everything had happened, and that's the first thing he wants to say to me? Not once had he acknowledged all the losses I'd suffered, much less what happened to his own damned brother.

"Cliff, you still there?"

"Yes, I'm here. What did you want to discuss?"

"What're your plans with that property? I've seen pictures of it. There doesn't appear to be much, if anything, to salvage."

"Uncle Sim, why do you want to know?" No need to pretend like I cared what he thought. Best to get down to business.

"I want to buy it from you, Cliff. I have plans."

I saw red and hung up without saying another word. Damn, I was angry, but underneath that, I was hurt and sad. Dad's family had ostracized him, and therefore me, for as long as I'd been alive. I barely knew them. It hurt to think about how that must've felt for him, choosing his best life and being punished for it. And now he was gone, and those vultures were circling overhead.

I immediately thought of Helen. She had chosen not to leave, and it had cost her too. But instead of losing family, she lost love. Granted, we didn't have her side of the story to know how she felt at the time, but again, I was forced to think about the consequences of the choices we make.

I glanced at my phone when it rang again, but seeing it was Uncle Sim calling back, I ignored it and then blocked his number. I knew I'd probably sell eventually, but God help me, not to him.

I knew Brandon was busy, and since my only daytime class was today, I usually stayed at the farm, puttering around if I didn't have homework. But after that phone call, I needed some alone time to sort through my feelings.

I left our trailer and made a detour to the barn. Despite all of my anger and frustration, seeing the little tack room set up for our lovemaking made me smile. Brandon really did make me happy. When I glanced over and saw the blueprints sitting next to the mattress where we'd left them, I decided to let my dreaming distract me.

Since Xander had given Brandon the drawings, we'd pored over them, making changes and envisioning what it all might look like one day.

I could see in my mind's eye the open floor plan, with rustic wood adorning the space and overstuffed leather furniture placed strategically to take advantage of the beauty of the surrounding landscape. There would be a huge kitchen, which I knew Brandon wanted, and the tack room, which was already a special place for us, would remain our primary space. The room we first made love in would become our bedroom, and envisioning our first night sleeping there in an actual bed made me shiver.

I didn't know how much the barn renovation would cost, but my insurance payout would likely cover a healthy chunk, if not all of it. Mom and Dad had insurance coverage not only for the house but also for the barn and outbuildings. They had a separate policy for the crops. As much as I shared in Brandon's dream of converting the barn, I wrestled with the idea of pouring a significant amount of money into something I didn't own. Granted, Brandon and I were a couple and planning a future here together, but it's not like my name was on the deed.

That, and the aquaponics business was also going to cost money, and I had already agreed to fund part of it. Tracy and Uncle Chris had accepted the money I had saved as part of the initial investment. But farms were notorious for sneaky costs, and I expected plenty of those in our new venture.

I looked around the barn, then at the plans, and sighed. I had several options, and choices to make, but none seemed like easy decisions. "You can sell the land," I heard my father say, and even though it was clearly in my head, I looked around the room as if he were standing there.

"Uncle Sim is such an ass, Dad. He didn't even come to your funeral, your own brother. I can't turn our family farm over to him, even if he is technically family and even if it's no longer a farm."

There was no reply, and I huffed in frustration. Mostly because my dad wasn't wrong. I'd seen the appraisal for the amount of land I owned, which was significant even in its burned-out state. If I sold the property, it would put enough money in my pocket to renovate the barn and leave the money I received in the insurance payout sitting comfortably in my bank account.

Brandon and I would be set and never have to think about when the next financial shoe would drop. My parents had taught me to be smart with money, mostly because they never had much, but a nest egg was something to protect with your life, as they always advised me.

I walked over to my aunt and uncle's house and found them sitting across from one another at the table, talking.

"I think I might need an attorney," I said when they looked up.

"Why?" Aunt Sue asked, concerned.

"I'm going to sell my land to my dad's family, but I plan to make them pay through the nose for it."

Uncle Chris snorted, but Aunt Sue tutted. "Now, now, they are still family."

"No, *you* are family. They're just blood relations. But I need the money because I've decided to ask Brandon to marry me and I want to ensure we have a solid start to our lives."

Aunt Sue's eyes bulged and she squealed. Then she jumped up and pulled me into a hug so tight I thought I might burst a blood vessel. She let me go just so Uncle Chris could do the same thing.

"Oh, son, that boy's a good one. You won't find one much better." He hugged me again. I hadn't seen them this surprised and excited since Levi and Keya announced they were expecting.

The whole thing made me misty-eyed, but I didn't hide it. These people were my family. They'd been here at my very lowest, when I didn't think my life would have a purpose again. Now I was sharing probably one of the most significant moments in my life with them.

I glanced around the room, and although I couldn't see them, I could feel my parents there, celebrating with me as well.

Brandon

TEACHING ONLINE had its challenges, but the good mostly outweighed the bad. The one thing that truly made it all worth it was the guy who walked into the barn while I was teaching, then headed for Chris and Sue's place a short time later. Something was up with Cliff, and I couldn't wait for class to end to find out what.

I'd just stepped outside to head over there when a sheriff's car pulled up. I smiled when Aaron Langley got out. "Hey, buddy, long time no see."

Aaron smiled back, then sighed. "Hey, Brandon, sorry, I'm here on official business."

"Oh?" I asked, my hackles rising.

"The county highway department is demanding we investigate who vandalized the two covered bridges over by Levi's place."

"Vandalized?" I had to work hard not to smirk. "What kind of vandalism? Kids tagging it with graffiti like we tried to do that one time?"

He frowned, clearly not as amused as I was. Aaron had been hell on wheels back in high school, but apparently, he'd tamed some in the intervening years. "Someone painted them," he said.

"Oh really?" I asked, putting my hand on my chest like I was clutching pearls. "Sounds serious. It's a wonder you didn't come blazing in here with your lights on and siren blaring."

"Brandon, stop playing. I know it was one of y'all. I also know the commissioner is plenty mad about it."

"Well, don't you figure the commissioner should've put some money into keeping them painted? Seems like whoever did it actually helped preserve those bridges for a few more years, at least."

"Not for me to say," Aaron said. "So, you aren't talking?"

"Ain't got much to say about it, no."

He sighed deeply and held his breath. Then he let it out and his cheeks deflated. I sort of felt sorry for Aaron, knowing it was a ridiculous thing for him to have to chase down, since the bridges were anything but vandalized. I knew Levi had paid a pretty penny to get them painted too, even with Xander's discount.

"Well, if you figure out who did it, let them know they'll have to face the county. Could even be jail time," he said.

I nodded, serious now. I didn't want Levi or Xander to go to jail over doing what amounted to a community service.

When Aaron left I called Levi, and he answered, saying a sheriff's car had just pulled up at his place. "Until you've spoken to an attorney, just plead the Fifth," I advised him.

"Gotcha," he said. "Hey, Aaron, what drags you out here?" Then he hung up on me.

Damn, I hoped this didn't boil over. Wilcox and the outlying areas could be funny that way. Some issues that should drive county officials batty didn't seem to faze them, but something like this could send every department into overdrive.

Xander being the local golden boy worked in our favor, though. I had to think that, if and when the townsfolks learned he was involved, they'd rally around our little group and it'd all blow over. I hoped we'd be able to laugh about it someday.

Cliff

NOW THAT I'd decided to ask Brandon to marry me, even if it was in the heat of the moment, my mind was made up. I just had to figure out how to make it work financially.

Aunt Sue referred me to a local attorney named Jason. Apparently he worked for Dalton's uncle Tim, and within fifteen minutes, my aunt had given me a full family history lesson. I heard all about who was related to whom, and how Jason was a year or two older than Levi and Brandon, grew up in town, and had moved back this year to do real estate law.

"Thanks for the referral, Aunt Sue." I went outside to call him.

Jason seemed friendly enough on the phone. He walked me through my options, then promised to give me a fair estimate of my land before the fire. By the time I drove to my appointment with him, I knew roughly how much my property was worth, and it wasn't a small amount. A neighbor or two had sold their farms in the past couple years and made small fortunes. I had no idea why my dad's brother wanted the farm, and honestly, I didn't care.

I'd be sending him my price. If Uncle Sim didn't want to pay it, he could go back to ignoring me like he'd done most of my life.

I walked into an old, paneled office straight out of the 1980s, and smiled fondly. Some things in small towns never changed.

Jason came out and met me. He shook my hand. "So, tell me about your uncle," he said when I sat down.

I relayed my own short family history lesson, including my uncle's decades-long estrangement from my parents and the fact he hadn't shown up at their funeral or spoken to me after the fire. "So, if he wants the place, it'll cost him."

Jason smiled. "Understood. These were comparable properties before the wildfire."

He pointed at some papers on his desk. They showed two neighboring farms I remembered had sold, and I was surprised to see they'd fetched significantly more than I'd heard. "How could they be worth that much? In the middle of nowhere?" I asked.

Jason shrugged. "There's lots of hiking, fishing, and other outdoor activities in the region. It's a tourist draw. There aren't many parcels of land as big as yours either. If you had sold with the farm intact, you could've easily brought in that much."

"And now, after the fire?" I asked.

He did some calculations and showed me a price reduction for the buildings, reflecting almost exactly what the insurance company had agreed to pay me.

"I doubt my uncle will want to pay what I'm asking, especially since I'm going to make him pay the pre-reduction amount. If I'm guessing correctly, he wants to get it for a steal and thinks he can manipulate me into it. I honestly don't care what he does with it. I've made peace with leaving the land behind, and I'd rather not speak with him again. If you can send him my price and ask that he speak only to you, it'll be worth whatever you charge to represent me."

Jason nodded. "Okay, I've got some paperwork for you to sign, making me your official representative. Then I'll work up the proposal and send it to the address you gave me."

"Yeah, you might wanna check that too. It's the last known residence I have for my uncle, but I don't know if it's current. That was just what my mom had written in her address book."

"Don't worry. I can track down his actual address. It was nice to meet you, Cliff. My boss tells me you made quite the impression hanging out with his nephew's little ones recently."

"Yeah, that was a fun time. Dalton and Pierce are nice guys, and they're raising a couple of great kids."

Jason nodded. "I don't know them well, although I should. There aren't many of us in town, after all."

I chuckled to myself because he'd just outed himself to me. "No, there's not, but on the bright side," I said, standing up, "there's more here than where I'm selling that land."

Jason laughed and stood to shake my hand again. "That's something, I guess. I'll let you know when I've mailed this out," he said before I left.

Jason was another one of those almost-too-good-looking guys. I wondered why Xander and he had never become a thing. I'd have to ask Brandon. For now, I felt like I'd made some headway. Hopefully I wouldn't end up regretting it.

Brandon

CHRIS WAS clearly upset with Levi as he stared his son down. "Tell me again why you didn't go through the proper channels?"

Keya sighed. "Because Don Joseph told me himself that private citizens offering to do it or pay for it would never be approved. But what choice did we have? If the bridges didn't get painted, we would have no hope of securing funding to start the winery. We're trying to create a whole experience for tourists, and those things were an eyesore."

"Funding? Why didn't you come to me?" he asked.

It was awkward, and I regretted being there. Not that I hadn't heard Chris rip Levi a new one before. Hell, he'd ripped me one or two in the past as well. I tried not to chuckle at the memory.

"Dad, you're selling. Of course we weren't going to come to you."

Chris shook his head and looked over at Sue, who sighed. "Levi, this is serious, son. They sent a deputy sheriff over here. You know you'll have to face this."

He nodded, but the expression on Levi's face was clear. He didn't care. He'd decided to paint the bridges, got some friends to help him, and that was that. I agreed it shouldn't be a big deal, but I didn't dare say so.

"I've called Tim. He's going to meet with us tomorrow to discuss your options." Sue looked at me. "Xander needs to meet us there as well."

Levi nodded and took Keya's hand as they walked out. I can't say I blamed them. Being fussed at by your parents when you were a grown man was hard to swallow, and I knew that from experience.

Once they were gone, Chris sat across from Cliff and me, laced his fingers, and stared at his hands. "Boys, I know you don't want to hear this, but I'm going to say it anyway. Don't make enemies out here. Life can be hard enough without having to watch your back all the time. You might not want to, but you should try to stay within the confines of the law. If you can't get them to work with you, there's always the troublemakers to help you get things fixed."

Sue sat next to him and smiled. "They aren't troublemakers, they're peacemakers, and if I'd known Levi and Keya were struggling to get approval, I'd have gone to meet them. They'd have done their thing, and stuff would've happened. It always does."

Cliff and I nodded, not really having anything to say other than they were probably right. Xander and Levi rarely did things by the book. The few times we'd gotten into real trouble in school, it was because one or both of them threw caution to the wind.

Sue finally got up, went to the kitchen, brought back two pieces of pie, and set one in front of each of us. Then she went back to get one slice for her and Chris to share. Poor Chris, I knew he wasn't too happy about that.

They changed the subject as we ate dessert, and we talked about farm stuff and Tracy's ideas about expanding the new tanks into the almost-cleared dairy barns.

By the time Cliff and I got home, I was exhausted—mostly mentally after all the conflict.

Cliff snuggled into me, not speaking much, but I lay awake thinking about what Chris had said. I wasn't one to color outside the lines. I usually stayed well within the confines of the law, and I suspected Cliff worked too hard to ever get into much trouble.

Hopefully whatever this brought about for Levi wouldn't create much of a problem for his and Keya's business plans. Not that they needed permission to grow grapes, but I didn't know if they required a license to make wine. I assumed they needed one to have a tasting room, at least.

The next day Sue called and asked if we could come over, because Tim and Jason had contacted her early and said they were stopping by before work hours. "Tim said he wants to meet with all of us since we knew they were going to paint the bridges. I've called Xander's mom, and she's getting him up too."

I chuckled because it was typical of when we were teenagers. If we got in trouble, there was usually a three-way crossing where our families came together to give us kids a good talking to.

Cliff was already awake, so I followed him to Chris and Sue's. I didn't have my first class until nine, and since the sun had yet to appear, we had more than enough time to work through this before I had to return.

A huge breakfast awaited us when we arrived, but few of us had an appetite. Even Chris barely nibbled on his oatmeal. Attorneys calling for an early client meeting couldn't be a good sign, and I think we were all feeling it.

But when Tim and Jason showed up, I could tell Jason was enjoying himself way too much for this to be a serious matter. I didn't know Jason well, mostly just by association. He'd been around when we were all growing up, but he was a little older and hung out with a different crowd than Levi, Xander, and me.

Unlike the rest of us, Tim dug into Sue's biscuits, eggs, and gravy and asked questions between bites. Sometimes Jason would chime in with a question or two.

"Well," Tim finally said as he sat back and patted his tummy, "you will probably get fined, and they could hold you in jail for a few days. Defacing the bridges is what they'd charge you with, and luckily, that's only a misdemeanor. Regardless, we'll argue your side with the county if we have to, and we can take it to court if they really want to raise a stink. I think we'd probably have even better luck there for getting charges dropped."

They left after that, and Chris shook his head. "Well, that's that. Levi, I need to see you in the barn," he said and walked out.

I glanced at Xander and had to bite my tongue not to laugh. The barn was where you got a full-on lecture about bad behavior. Luckily, the two of us had avoided it all these years.

We left soon after, mostly so I could shower and appear presentable for my online class that morning.

"So, that was something," Cliff said as we entered the trailer.

"Oh, it's nothing Levi hasn't had to deal with before."

"Uncle Chris seemed pretty angry."

"You think so? Seemed to me he was having a hard time not laughing, especially when Jason and Tim slipped up and smiled. It's kinda serious, but no, when your uncle gets mad, it's obvious. Trust me."

"Seen that a lot, then?" Cliff teased, and I nudged him with my elbow.

"Not a lot, but he's chewed me out pretty good before. Remind me never to tell you about it."

Cliff laughed, and I could tell he wanted to ask a million questions, but luckily I had to get ready for work. He did too. Tracy was coming down today to look at the mostly empty barns. They were planning how much to get started on, given their limited budget, so it would be a busy day for Cliff as well.

By the time I was done with classes later that day, Cliff came home to tell me Tim had talked Levi into coming clean with the county. "I think they'd have loved to charge him, but apparently," Cliff said, smiling, "Aunt Sue contacted those so-called troublemakers, and they've called a county meeting over at the town hall Friday night."

"Your aunt doesn't play around. She wasn't wrong either. Keya and Levi should've just talked to her about the commissioner dragging his feet. I'm sure this will put a wrench in the commissioner's plans," I said.

"Hopefully draw attention to the dilapidated infrastructure too. Sorry, quoting Aunt Sue."

I laughed and hugged him to me. "I hope it works out, but for now, I fixed us a frozen pizza. Not as good as Sue's cooking, but tonight I want you all to myself."

"Aah," Cliff moaned as I sucked his earlobe into my mouth. "Pizza for two sounds delicious."

Cliff

LEVI'S TROUBLES were amusing. I tried not to be a goof about it like Brandon and Xander, but it was funny nonetheless. Xander and Levi made a full confession, not that everyone didn't already know it was them.

Aaron, the sheriff's deputy who'd questioned everyone, later came by the farm and asked Levi to go to the sheriff's office to make a statement. Apparently Xander had to as well.

According to Aunt Sue, the "twin bridges scandal," as she called it, was the talk of the town.

I didn't have much time to dwell on it since Tracy and Uncle Chris were in the middle of a heavy negotiation for most of the day.

By Wednesday I was ready for the week to end. Aunt Sue was all in a tizzy over the Friday town hall meeting. Levi and Keya avoided everyone, Brandon was buried in work, and I was stressed out by proxy.

I wasn't surprised by Jason's update on the offer we'd sent my uncle.

"He said he wouldn't pay that much and that it isn't worth it since the fire destroyed everything. He came back with a counteroffer."

"No need to tell me, Jason, you can send back my refusal. My initial asking was final, not open for negotiation. Uncle Sim can take it or leave it."

I knew it was childish, but a big part of me hoped my uncle just walked away. Even though I said I didn't care about who bought it, I didn't necessarily want my uncle to own the land he chastised my father for keeping. When the will was read after my grandparents' deaths, Uncle Sim had inherited a large bank account and Dad inherited the farm. It'd been a much better deal for my uncle, but then my dad had only ever wanted the farm, and he made the most of it.

Dad never talked about his brother much, and I'd only met him a handful of times. Dad's half sister, who was much older than him, lived in San Francisco near Uncle Sim, and I'd never met her.

All I knew was that they'd both shunned Dad when he decided not to sell up and move. I'd never really known why things had been the way they were.

I honestly thought that was the end of my uncle's meddling, and I decided I'd ask Jason if he knew a good realtor who could list the property for me.

I got the phone call the next morning. "Cliff, your uncle just contacted me. He said he'll take it."

"Pfft, that man is a piece of work. So he's willing to pay the full price after all?"

"Yep, said the money could be transferred into your account when you're ready. If you want, I can get things going on the title transfer. You don't have any liens against it, do you?"

"No, those were paid off before... well, before it became mine."

"Okay, it should be pretty simple. I'll let you know when you need to come in and sign the paperwork."

"Thanks. Hey, see you in town tonight."

Jason laughed out loud, probably because he hadn't expected me to say that. "Oh, tonight is going to be epic. I'm going to guess the entire county will be there to see Ms. Healy hand Commissioner Jones his ass."

"Really? Ms. Helen Healy?"

"Yeah, she's mad as a hornet, and it's not at Levi or Xander. Should be a good show."

I laughed. Small towns get their entertainment in odd places, but hearing the name of the woman from Xander's aunt Greta's journal caught my attention. Funny how that was the thing I'd glommed on to, not the sale of my parents' farm to my estranged uncle.

I'd have to think about that later, since I still had a few chores to finish on the tanks. I was concerned that the ones farthest from the pump might not get enough oxygen, so I wanted to monitor that closely. Luckily the fry were in the upper tanks, but within three months, they would be big enough that we'd need to use all of them. When that time came, we couldn't afford any of the tanks not to be working properly.

Brandon

CLIFF TOLD me what Jason said about tonight's town hall meeting, and because I'd had a hell of a week teaching, I was actually looking forward to the distraction. I got there late because one of my students had a major breakdown over a paper that wasn't even due for another week and a half, so when I arrived, I had to sit on the other side of the room from the family.

I'd just sat down when the commissioner called the meeting to order and knocked his gavel on the table. Ms. Helen Healy stood up and walked to the lectern.

"Ms. Healy, we'll get to questions in a moment."

"I don't have a question, young man," she said, squaring the middle-aged man with a look that could kill. "I'm the one who called this meeting, and therefore, I'm the one who will be speaking. Now do you have a problem with that?"

The commissioner deflated in front of her. I'd known Ms. Healy as long as I could remember, and she'd always been a sweet woman with a quick wit and an even quicker word of kindness. I'd never seen her like this, and I suspected at least half the town was thinking the same.

"Very well, Ms. Healy, you have the floor."

"Thank you." She turned to address the room. "As you may know, my family were the first settlers to come to Umpqua Valley. My ancestor was a trader with the tribe that occupied this area at the time. Then, when they were driven off this land, my family were the first to lay claim to it."

She waited a moment and looked out at the crowd. I guessed she likely recognized every single person in the room by name, except maybe Cliff. "I'm an old woman, but even as I stand here, in the last days of this lifetime, I take great pride in my heritage, my town, and in this county. It shames me that we've waited until now to address the serious deterioration of our town and county's infrastructure. I was here in the nineties when so-called investors wanted to swoop into Wilcox to tear down our old historic buildings, and I stood with the community to root them out. We fought them and we won. I was also here when we came together and had most of our old covered bridges repaired and painted. That was over thirty years ago, and we've allowed a new problem to seep into our midst. We've allowed those we voted into office to ignore the basic needs of our fine home."

She drew a folder from her rather large purse and opened it. Then she leaned back into the mic. "I had that sweet young librarian, Jonas, pull up some statistics for me."

For the next few minutes, she talked about how Oregon sported a lot of covered bridges at one time, but most had deteriorated beyond saving or been torn down. She went on to talk about the history of the local bridges and their importance, then and now.

I was anything but a history buff, but Ms. Healy held my attention as she built her argument. Finally, she once again addressed the now rather red-faced commissioner. "Sir, this is not just your county, it's ours," she said to thunderous applause. "What those boys, Levi Owens and Xander Petterson, did was unorthodox. However, I will remind those gathered that Xander's ancestors built both those bridges. If anyone had a right to paint them, it was him."

"Now, Ms. Healy, it's not our place to ignore the law."

"No, but it is our place to demand that you do your job," She slammed her fist on the lectern. "And if you plan to prosecute those boys for doing what you haven't, then I promise you this—not only will I fight you with every ounce of strength I have left in me, but you'll find most of the citizens in this room feel much the same as I."

The commissioner looked frozen in place. He didn't speak, but the nod Ms. Healy gave indicated that was exactly what she was expecting.

"Now, here's my proposal, and I'm going to call for a vote," she said, glancing again at the commissioner to see if he would challenge her. When he didn't, she smiled ever so slightly. "We need to fix our covered bridges, and I know we don't have the budget. But I've looked over said budget and I think a large part of that is priorities. Frankly our county has put money in places it shouldn't have. Regardless, the time to hold elected officials accountable for that is later. For now, we need to come up with revenues for our beautiful covered bridges or risk losing them. I spoke to Linda Thwart, our county treasurer, and she assures me we won't need much to maintain them. Our town attorney, Tim, assures me your vote tonight should be enough to get a levy placed on the ballot. Mr. Commissioner," Ms. Healy said, obviously using his title to put him further in his place, "I assume your office is capable of figuring out how much of a levy we need to ensure our bridges stay maintained?"

"Yes, ma'am," he said, which earned another curt nod from her.

"Okay. Jasmine, make sure you record this in the minutes. All those in favor of adding a levy to the next ballot to ensure our beautiful covered bridges are maintained into the future, please raise your hands."

The woman I assumed was Jasmine stood up and began counting. That lasted a while, but everyone kept their hands raised. When she nodded, Ms. Healy asked who was opposed. Not one hand went up.

"Well, Mr. Commissioner, that appears to be a unanimous decision. Now if there's nothing else?"

She waited, and when no one responded, she slapped her hand on the lectern and said, "Peggy said she's made extra pies and is selling them for two dollars a slice at the diner. So let's get out of here and go enjoy us some pie."

I had never experienced anything like that before. I laughed as the crowd rose and began to mill out of the meeting room. As soon as I could make my way over, I walked toward where Levi, Keya, and Xander stood with Chris, Sue, and Cliff.

"Now I can understand why your aunt was so taken with Ms. Healy," I said quietly to Xander, and I froze when I heard her voice behind me.

"And pray tell, what do you lot know of that?" she asked.

Xander gave me the stink eye but looked at Ms. Healy and explained we'd found his aunt Greta's journal.

For several long moments, it looked like she was going to lay into us about reading it, but as emotions warred across her face, I could tell when she finally came to terms with what he'd said.

"I-I'd very much like to see that journal, if you don't mind," she finally said, her expression showing nothing but sadness.

She left after that, and Xander punched me on the arm—hard. "Sorry," I said.

He rolled his eyes at me and left behind her. I assumed to set up a meeting time. "Well, shit," I said and got slapped on the very same arm by Sue.

"Watch your voice, Brandon. We aren't on the farm. We're in a respectable and important building."

"Yes, ma'am," I said, and when she turned around, I stuck my tongue out at Levi, who was having way too much fun at my expense.

Cliff

FALL DISAPPEARED in a flurry of leaves and happy moments. Uncle Chris and Aunt Sue were in excellent spirits, and when the last of the dairy equipment was removed, they left for a week's vacation to Disneyland. They wanted to experience it before families with kids took over during holiday breaks. Aunt Sue had always wanted to go, even as a little girl.

Levi and Keya were nesting. We saw less and less of them as they prepared for the arrival of their little one. Occasionally Brandon and I would cook or buy pizza and take it over there, just to make sure they knew we still existed.

I hadn't found the right time to ask Brandon to marry me, but the longer time passed, the more I wanted to. Unfortunately the school term had been a bear for him. I wasn't sure how long he would want to continue teaching, at least virtually, but we hadn't discussed his plans for spring semester yet. On the other hand, I loved my online classes and had already learned so much.

After Thanksgiving I sat down with Aunt Sue and Uncle Chris and told them my plans. "Fall semester will be over next week, and he'll be free of teaching and stress for a while. That's when I want to pop the question."

Aunt Sue hugged me. "Son, just let it happen like it's supposed to. Sometimes you can't push these things. That boy loves you. Anyone with eyes can see that."

I smiled at her. "I love him so much, Aunt Sue. I'm surprised at how much sometimes," I admitted, and she winked at me.

"I know the feeling." She glanced toward the living room, where Uncle Chris sat reading a newspaper.

Brandon

BY THE time fall semester came to an end, I'd decided I was done teaching. The added stress of teaching virtually, trying to juggle classes and still be involved on the farm, let alone fulfill my writing obligations, was just too much.

I'd even called my agent to get a feel for whether she thought my books would sell.

"Do you think I can do this full-time?"

"Listen, Brandon," she interrupted me. "I'm going to tell you what I've told every author I've ever worked with. The industry is unpredictable. Your books will likely sell like hotcakes, and if your publisher disagreed, they'd never have given you such a lucrative advance, but even they know it's a gamble. Your other books are selling very well, so you're in a good position right now, but we just have to see what happens with the new release. As they say, don't quit your day job." She chuckled at her own joke.

But that's exactly what I wanted to do. My new release was scheduled for April and was already getting some positive feedback. "Actually, I think I'm going to do just that," I told her. "I can probably afford it if I'm frugal."

"Then you should be frugal and get me another series as good as the one you just wrote. I've told you before, you're only as successful as your last book."

I laughed because she said that every freaking time we spoke. "Yes, you've mentioned it."

"Okay, well, I'll let you get back to it. But Brandon, don't put yourself in such a stressful situation that you stop writing. Whatever you do, that needs to be your main focus."

I hung up, knowing she was right, since my university job had already become stressful enough to prevent me from writing. Decision made, I picked up the phone and called Human Resources to tell them

I was either taking the spring semester off entirely or committing to teaching only a couple of classes. They confirmed the next day that I would be off the schedule next term, which was a relief.

If not for Cliff, I would've regretted buying Xander's land. Looking back, I should've put that advance aside for a rainy day— like the very rainy day I was facing right now. But I couldn't regret it, not when that part of my life was so amazing. Nothing I'd ever experienced was as wonderful as having that man in my arms every night.

I waited until we met up for lunch in the trailer to broach the subject with Cliff. "So, I'm taking next semester off. I know we should've talked about it before I contacted HR, but you already know how hard these last few months were for me teaching. Besides, I need to focus on my books," I said, mostly as a way to avoid telling him I'd be stupid-ass broke.

He listened and then kissed me, and he seemed excited that I'd be around more now, even when I told him I'd have to keep expenses down until royalties for the books came in.

He hugged me tight, dug into his food, and then rushed out of the house to work. I shook my head. "Well, that went better than I expected," I said aloud to no one.

After lunch I turned on my laptop and opened a blank Word document.

The cold winds of Ramoria tore through the tiny village of Emblor....

And just like that, my next series was started.

Cliff

"YOU CAN have it done that fast?" I asked the guy Xander had introduced me to.

The man chuckled. "Son, I'll start work on it now," he said as he shooed Xander and me out the front door.

"Xander, this is amazing. Thanks. Hopefully, all this will work out and Brandon will want to, you know, marry me and share his barn with me."

"Rumor has it he's been sharing his *barn* with you already."

I gave him a friendly shove. I hadn't liked Xander at first. That was more on me than him, though. He'd just shown interest, but now that I look back on it, I had already decided Brandon was the only man for me.

I'd told Uncle Chris my plan to finance the barn conversion by selling my property to my dad's brother. The sale had gone through without a hitch, and somehow I felt at peace about it. I secretly hoped Uncle Sim would keep the farm in the family, even if it wasn't through my line now. He had a daughter I'd never met. Perhaps the property would be passed down to her one day.

I had so much riding on Brandon saying yes. Not just the marriage and the barn conversion, but building upon the life I'd already carved out for myself here in Oregon. A life he was inextricably linked with, between our shared dreams, everyone we both considered family, and our expanding friends group that included Xander, Dalton, Pierce, and Jason, not to mention the older generation as well. I tried to convince myself that if Brandon said no, that he wasn't ready, we'd still be okay. But just that thought ripped my heart to shreds.

It was Levi's idea to get a painting made that showed what the barn conversion would look like once complete. Xander knew an artist—a guy who had to be significantly older than Uncle Chris and

Aunt Sue. He was wiry and bald, and his clothes were covered in paint. I could only imagine that was pretty much his life.

The guy's wife was exactly the opposite—taller than him, slim, with huge teased hair that made her seem even taller and clothes that looked like she'd traveled to Paris to purchase them. The opposites-attract couple made me chuckle.

We might not look as opposite as those two, but Brandon and I had some opposite energy—me a farmer who worked with his hands, him a professor who wrote amazing stories. And by amazing, I mean "rip my heart out, sweet, he really got me as a person when he wrote me into his series" kind of stories.

I received a phone call the following week telling me the painting was ready, and it blew me away. I hoped Brandon would have a similar reaction to it. The artist had somehow captured my hope for the future—my hope to be with and love my man for the rest of my life.

He had even added little touches of artistic license that gave the barn house a genuinely homey feel—like where we might plant shrubs and perennial flowers along the side. I could almost see the kids playing in the front yard, swinging from the vast branches of one of the redwood trees.

I still had hope that my little redwood seeds would sprout, although they'd yet to make an appearance, not that they would in the middle of winter. But I had already scoped out areas around the property where I'd plant them. I didn't want to lose those trees. They represented way too much. I hoped we'd get at least two.

I hugged the artist and struggled to keep my emotions from taking over. He helped me secure the painting so the not-quite-cured paint wouldn't rub off, and then he and his wife wrapped it in the most beautiful gift wrapping I'd ever seen.

It was still two whole days until Christmas, and I was fit to be tied. I wanted to do this, to ask Brandon to be my forever lover, my lifelong companion, my spouse, and give him the painting that represented all of our shared dreams. The uncertainty that came with waiting never went well for me, so I tried to focus on work.

Having learned a lot in my first semester of classes, I was confident in our choice of herbs for our operation. Basil, thyme, oregano, and parsley had already been planted in trays in anticipation of being transferred to the aquaponics system.

The fry were big enough that we had to fill all the tanks, which meant we couldn't continue to filter sufficient water with the system we'd chosen. We needed the plants in place to begin doing their job of keeping the tanks clean, not to mention growing and giving us an income.

I laughed at myself as I geeked out and thanked all that was good that the project kept me busy until Christmas Day.

Brandon and I had eggnog and a little rum on Christmas Eve. Then we went to a candle-lighting service with his parents. Well, maybe his father had a bit too much rum, because it seemed he almost let the cat out of the bag about the proposal, although he wasn't actually aware of my plans.

"When are you boys going to tie the knot?" he asked.

I choked on my eggnog, and Brandon clapped me on the back.

"What, is marrying me so scary that you'd rather inhale eggnog instead?" he teased.

"Are you proposing?" I asked, and Brandon waggled his eyebrows and kissed me.

I kept my mouth shut after that, but I swear his mom winked at me when Brandon wasn't looking. I'm sure Aunt Sue had probably spilled the beans.

On Christmas Day, we all gathered at Aunt Sue and Uncle Chris's place, including Brandon's parents. I was bouncing off the walls in anticipation and almost knocked myself out when I bumped my head on the stair railing behind my chair when Aunt Sue announced it was time to open presents.

Levi snorted, and I gave him my most intimidating "say a word and you die" look.

"Why don't we let Brandon go first," Uncle Chris announced, and all eyes flew to me. Although I was thankful he was going to let me get it over with, for a moment I was afraid I might puke up the Christmas meal we'd just eaten.

We'd pulled the chairs into the living room, and the entire family surrounded the tree. Brandon sat between his father and mother, who I now believed knew what was going on. Otherwise they'd have let me sit next to him.

I grabbed the framed painting, and Brandon looked nervously around him as he finally realized this was a moment. Of course Levi and Keya standing on opposite sides of the room filming us with their phones might've given him a clue.

I handed him the gift, and he opened it and exclaimed with joy, just as I hoped he would. "Cliff," he said, the shock obvious on his face. "It's our barn. I… this is beautiful. It's just as I've envisioned it too."

He pulled me down for a kiss, and then I stood back up but stayed close. "There's actually more to it. I… I'd like to, um," I babbled, losing my nerve. Like an idiot I finished with, "I'd like to help you finance turning it into our home."

Brandon smiled, and a tear slipped from his eye and rolled down his face. He got up and hugged me, and before I could get the words out that I'd practiced countless times, the man dropped down on his knee.

"In that case, Cliff, would you consider being my husband?"

He pulled a box out of his pocket and opened it, revealing a beautiful white gold band etched with leaves. "You're asking me to marry you?" I asked. I knew I sounded incredulous, but I couldn't help it.

Brandon smiled nervously and nodded.

I leaned my head back and laughed, pulled the box out of my pocket, and opened it. Then I knelt beside him.

"Great minds think alike," I said as shock registered on his face.

"You were proposing?"

"Trying to," I admitted.

We were both laughing when Brandon pulled me to him and kissed me deeply as our family applauded all around us. "That's a yes, by the way," I whispered when we pulled back, both of us wiping the tears from our cheeks.

"Yeah, that's definitely a yes from me as well."

The rest of the evening went by in a blur. As soon as the final gifts were unwrapped, Brandon and I rushed home and christened our new status as fiancés.

"I love you, Cliff," Brandon spooned me from behind as we lay exhausted.

"Not as much as I love you," I said, and he tickled me.

"Maybe we should just call it a draw," he whispered into my ear, and we fell asleep wrapped in each other's arms.

Epilogue—Cliff

THE FARM was covered in ribbons, thanks to Keya. Little Lilly, who was lovingly named after one of Keya's great aunts, snuggled happily against her mom in the baby sling Keya wore anytime she wasn't sitting.

I'd wanted a May Day wedding. I chose the date mainly because it'd been Mom's favorite holiday. She used to decorate the yard and invite the neighbors over, saying it was the holiday when we celebrated life. That's definitely the way I saw our wedding—as a celebration of life.

We'd moved back to Uncle Chris and Aunt Sue's home since, even with the gravel we'd put around the construction trailer, the area around the barn was dug up and muddy. I'd finally thrown my hands up and threatened to get a hotel room until it was done when my aunt and uncle generously offered us their home.

Dalton's parents had managed to talk the pair into spending a month in Arizona with them. Since I was here to handle the farm, they'd agreed, giving us the privacy we needed as we prepared for the wedding.

Brandon and I wore matching white tuxes. "So many people," I whispered as Aunt Sue tucked and patted me, making me look like the picture-perfect groom.

Brandon was in the greenhouse, surrounded by all my fish tanks, with his parents, who I assumed were doing the same for him.

"Oh, honey, the town loves you boys and wants to see the two of you hitched. Besides, it never hurts to have a big crowd. You get more presents this way," she teased.

We were about to leave for the ceremony when we both stopped short. The hairs on the back of my neck stood up, and Aunt Sue reached over, took my hand, and squeezed it.

"She's wanting you to know she's here." Aunt Sue quickly dabbed her eye using a hankie she pulled out of her dress pocket.

"Thanks, Mom," I whispered. I'd hoped my parents would be here. I needed them to be. Just one last time, I wanted to know they were with me on one of the most important days of my life.

Aunt Sue nudged me forward, and I walked out of the house and toward my future—a future with a man I loved so deeply, it sometimes hurt.

Brandon stood waiting for me at the back of the crowd. When I reached him, the little chamber orchestra Xander had found and helped us hire began to play.

Our guests all stood, and I had to catch my breath. It was overwhelming, having so many people there supporting us, including some folks I'd just gotten to know in the year since I'd arrived in Wilcox.

When I reached Brandon, he squeezed my hand, and I leaned into him.

"Who stands for these two today?" the minister asked, and Uncle Chris, Aunt Sue, and Brandon's parents answered in unison, "We do."

I couldn't hold back the tears as the minister led us through the ceremony.

I wasn't one for speaking vows, but I'd promised everything to Brandon in private the night before. "Brandon, I love you and will always love you. You are my life, my soul. I… I don't have the words to tell you how much you've lifted me and made life better," I said as he held me close in our bed.

"Cliff, I want to be your person for the rest of my life," he said. "You are my life too, one that hadn't fully started living until the day I met you." He had to stop speaking as he wiped his tears. "You make life worth living and dreams worth dreaming. Thank you for making my biggest dream come true in finding you."

With our vows spoken the night before, the minister finished the required ritual and requested that we exchange rings.

As Brandon leaned down to kiss me, I felt my soul mix with his. Our lives completed their intertwining as we became life spouses. I wanted to reach out, embrace the man, and never let go, but there was a massive crowd of people watching. So, for now, I settled for a chaste kiss as the minister announced, "I now introduce you to Brandon and Cliff Anderson-Forest."

Just hearing that made my heart sing as we walked down the aisle toward the back of the house, where Aunt Sue and people I barely knew had come together to cater a feast fit for kings.

Brandon took my hand again and led me through the house. The crowd began to come toward us. That night we celebrated with our family and packed to fly to Hawaii for our honeymoon.

The next morning I brought my luggage down while Brandon finished getting ready, and his parents, who were driving us to the airport, finished eating the huge meal Aunt Sue had cooked for us.

I walked around the farmstead and allowed myself to remember the night I'd arrived, broken and damaged beyond repair, or so I thought.

It'd only been a year since I pulled my truck and trailer into the driveway, covered with ash, smoke, and loss. Now I was here surrounded by loved ones and a new husband I already cherished with every ounce of my heart.

Brandon found me outside, staring down at three little seedlings that had just popped up through the ground. "They grew," I said and felt a chill cover me. I looked up into the eyes of the man I loved and said, "The redwoods, the one from my home, they came up…."

"Your parents?" he asked, and my breath caught as I nodded.

Brandon held me then as the quiet stillness of morning seeped into our bones. He continued holding my hand as we drove away, heading for the airport, and I could feel all the sadness I'd held deep inside since I arrived flowing away as I embraced a life of happiness with the man sitting beside me.

Brandon

HAWAII WAS beautiful, and our gay-friendly resort allowed Cliff and me to spend our time curled around one another, even when we were sitting by the pool or on the beach. At night we made love, not worrying about anything other than giving pleasure to each other.

I almost wished we could stay like that for longer, but eventually, duty called us back to back home.

We'd been home a week when I opened an envelope from my publisher with a statement of how much money I'd earned since the release. My eyes must've bugged out of my head, and I had to sit down, causing Sue and Cliff to rush to my side.

"Brandon, are you okay?" Sue asked, and all I could do was show them the statement.

"For the love of God, this is what you earned?" Cliff asked.

I nodded and swallowed hard. Thanks to Cliff's generosity, I hadn't returned to teaching and had focused solely on my new books. Not that I did much writing before the wedding, even though I tried.

I hadn't expected to make any money from the books, at least not for a while, since the advance had been so significant, but damn. They were selling so much better than even my agent had predicted. I wondered if she'd known and hadn't contacted me because I was on my honeymoon.

Cliff pulled me into his arms and kissed me. Then we embraced Sue, and the three of us danced around the room until Chris came in and asked what the commotion was about.

Sue handed him the statement, and I laughed hard when Chris's mouth fell open. "For your books?" he asked, and I just nodded, smiling so widely I probably looked like my face would split in two.

"Well, I'll be." Chris grabbed my hand and shook it. Then he pulled me into a hug.

That night Cliff and I gathered around the dinner table with Sue and Chris, Levi and Keya, our precious goddaughter, Mom and Dad, and even Xander, who'd been invited to share the celebration.

After we finished eating, I got everyone's attention, reached over, and took Cliff's hand. "I want everyone here to know how much I love you all. You're my family, especially this one." I playfully elbowed my husband.

"I couldn't have written these books without the support of everyone here. Levi, you helped me graduate from college, Mom and Dad, for paying for college," I said, causing them to snicker. "Chris and Sue, for being a support for me all these years, and Xander, for being a true friend. And my amazing husband, who continues to inspire me every day and helped these novels find their personality and place in the world."

I grabbed my champagne glass and lifted it in the air. "Here's to the best family a man can have," I said, and everyone lifted their glass to drink.

"And to many more of those golden books too," Chris added, and everyone chuckled.

The future seemed so bright. Cliff and I knew we eventually wanted children of our own, and until then we had our goddaughter to spoil. Cliff's business was already getting off to a great start, and I'd managed to write a bestselling series that, thanks to all that was holy, paid enough that I didn't have to go back to teaching or find another job.

I knew my already amazing life would only get better, though I also knew hard times came to everyone. All Cliff had endured in getting to this place now, with me, was proof enough of that. But with the fantastic family we'd created, I knew no matter what came our way, we'd survive and thrive together.

If you're enjoying the world of *Bridging Hearts*, have a sneak peek at the next book in the series, *Mending Bridges*

Xander

MY HEART raced as I stepped up onto the porch of the little bungalow that sat haphazardly next to one of the county's covered bridges.

I hadn't even knocked before Ms. Healy opened the door. I couldn't quite read her expression, other than it seemed weary.

"Come on in," she said, and I followed her to her living room. She pointed to the stuffy furniture, indicating that's where she wanted me to sit, then went back to her kitchen, only to return a moment later with a huge mug in hand.

"I've made you coffee." She handed me the steaming mug. "Your mother said you like it dark and bitter, with a dash of cream, so that's what I've fixed."

I'd already had too much caffeine that morning, but I understood the ritual and the need to steady herself before I handed over the journal.

"Would you like me to leave this with you?" I asked as I set the coffee mug down. Then I drew my aunt's journal out of my jacket pocket and placed it on the table.

Ms. Healy stared at it for a long time and finally shook her head. "I loved her, you know. Your Aunt Greta. I've never loved a woman or man like I loved that woman."

She took a deep breath and let it out slowly. "She wanted to move to the city—Portland or Seattle. Had convinced herself that we'd be more accepted there. I just couldn't see it. The world didn't allow people like us to love one another back then. My nephew had just left for college, and she was convinced it was our time."

The woman glanced at me. "I should've gone. I knew it the night she left. I should've said yes, but I was afraid. Not one day of my life has passed that I've not regretted that."

She paused, took another deep breath to collect herself, and looked me in the eye. "Cid Stewart—Stewie—has been a good friend. I don't guess I have to tell you, if he finds out the reason I've never been willing to be with him is because I'm a lesbian, I imagine that'd hurt him real bad."

I nodded. She was asking for discretion, and her relationships were her own business. Certainly, it wasn't my or anyone's place to expose her sexuality.

I stood up. "I'm not going to pretend this won't be hard to read. Her words weren't directed at me, but even I felt their sting. But I'm happy it's worked out this way. I think and believe that she'd want you to know how she felt about you. How much she loved you, even if that love caused both of you a great deal of pain."

Ms. Healy gasped a bit, and I could tell emotions were getting the better of her. I paused, put my hand on her shoulder for a moment to show my support, and then left her sitting alone with the journal and the consequences of the life she'd been forced or had felt forced to choose.

I didn't expect to get the journal back. How could someone who'd loved another, only to lose them, ever give back their words, especially when that's all they had left?

I drove back to my mom's house and sat next to her on the porch swing. "How'd it go?" Mom asked.

"About as well as you'd expect," I said. She didn't respond. The journal had been heart-wrenching to read—so much love and life tossed away for reasons that didn't seem so important now.

"Back when they were young and in love," Mom finally said, "the world was a hateful place for women who loved one another like they did."

"You know, I told Aunt Greta I was gay before I told anyone else," I admitted, causing Mom to pause her swinging and look over at me.

"Really? She was in the home by then."

I nodded. "Yep, she was already in hospice, but she'd always been someone I could talk to. Of course I had no idea she was gay or bi herself."

Mom sighed and kicked her foot, setting the swing back in motion. "I guess that's appropriate, then. It's just so overwhelming to learn this after having grown up with her. Hell, the woman was instrumental in raising me, not to mention that even now I consider Helen to be a friend."

"Had things been more like they are today, they might've gotten married and Helen would be related to us."

Mom nodded, and we sat like that for a long time before she finally got up to go inside. I stayed out on the swing even though the nights were still cool and the chill was beginning to set in.

Society had changed so much over the years. I hoped that one day I'd find a man I could love enough to marry. Of course, all the mushy lovey-dovey stuff going on between Brandon and Cliff, not to mention Levi and Keya, put it in my face.

Still, even before they found love, I'd always wanted it, I think. Not the kind of relationship that Aunt Greta had with her horrible husband. That, if anything, turned me off to the idea of marriage. Mom and Dad's relationship wasn't that stellar either, and even after he passed away, Mom hadn't dated anyone, at least not to my knowledge.

Regardless of my not-so-great relationship role models, I did hold out hope that I'd beat the odds where love was concerned.

Of course, not right away. I loved men and enjoyed tasting the different fruits on the proverbial tree before I settled for just one.

I laughed at my stupid analogy and leaned back in the swing. I picked my feet up and let it go higher, like I used to when I was a kid.

After a while just swinging back and forth and pondering love and loss, I went inside and kissed Mom goodbye, then left for Portland. I had a late-morning meeting, and with all the talk of love, I had a craving for a decidedly less permanent relationship.

Maybe love was in the cards someday, maybe not, but I'd be damned if, like Aunt Greta, I'd ever spend my life pining away for a man who didn't have the nerve to take the plunge. Not when there were so many willing men on Grindr.

GREYSON MCCOY loves to travel. After years of being tied down to a life of kids, work, running a small farm, and all things domestic, he and his husband have taken full advantage of their empty nest to travel the world.

The joy of writing came to Greyson late in life. While completing his master's degree, he found himself fighting between desperately wanting to write fiction and finishing the homework and papers he'd been assigned.

After his master's was finished, Greyson decided to shirk his life of responsibility and pursue his dream of writing full time. His stories reflect many of the locations he and his husband have visited over the years.

Visit Greyson McCoy on his website at www.GreysonMcCoy.gay (his husband assures him that's a real domain extension) and sign up for his newsletter to stay informed of his journey in the world of romance and all things love.

BRIDGING HEARTS · BOOK ONE

Bridging Hope

Raising kids
and finding
love is
impossible,
isn't it?

GREYSON McCOY

Bridging Hearts: Book One

When workaholic Pierce Simms's sister passes, he suddenly finds himself unemployed, back in the hometown he fled, and raising his niece and nephew. Despite that, he's confident he has things under control—at least until his sister's high-school sweetheart shows up.

With his teaching grant ended, Dalton O'Dell is at loose ends and tight purse strings. Just as the world crashes down on him, he learns his ex-girlfriend has passed and named him guardian of her two young children. Chaos ensues when he and her brother, Pierce, are forced together to raise the toddlers in Pierce's family farmhouse.

Nestled in the enchanting beauty of the farm, Pierce and Dalton bond over the challenges of co-parenting and their shared grief as unexpected love blossoms. Love might not be enough, however, if they can't learn to bridge the gap between their different worlds and overcome the trauma of their pasts.

Scan the QR code below to order

www.ingramcontent.com/pod-product-compliance
Lightning Source LLC
Chambersburg PA
CBHW051648260626
47170CB00004B/1391